THE VOICE OF THE SEA

—·—

MARA LI

The Voice of the Sea

published by

Dutch Venture Publishing

Copyright © 2022 Dutch Venture Publishing

Author: Mara Li (pseudonym of Marieke Veringa)

Cover design: Marieke Veringa

Text editor: Jen Minkman

<h1 style="text-align:center">1</h1>

STORM

I was born in the sea.

On the night Mum gave birth, the waves rolled towards the beach like giants, and my mother cried like the gulls. She cried out for the sea, long enough for my father to give in and carry her labouring body outside. There, she lay in a white gown on her back in the mud, her legs open in the surf. The waves carried me forth. Before even my father could grab hold of me, I had made my first acquaintance with the salty waters.

In my dream it is such a night once again, because everything around me is crashing and thundering. I am underwater, deeper than anyone would dare swim. Like shadows, the dark shapes of seals float past me. From far away, the sound of tolling church bells reach me. It is muffled by the vast expanse of water and I ignore it. Unfamiliar voices pass by my ear: 'Swim down deeper...come to us...'

'Nim!'

I feel a sudden jolt. The voices instantly hush and the ringing grows louder.

'Nimue, get up!'

I awake with a shock. My brother Arthur is tugging at my arm. There is just enough light to see that he is fully dressed. The shutters of the window stand ajar and rattle in the wind. Again, I hear the toll of the bells. For a brief moment, I find myself disorientated, but then I remember what's going on: tonight is Sailors' Mass.

'It's midnight already?' I groan.

'Nearly. Grandma says we'll go without you if you don't get up soon.'

I sigh and throw the bed covers off me. I rummage around for my clothing: socks, boots, a worn-out pair of jeans and my anorak with long waterproof sleeves. I tie my tangled curls together and take a look outside. I gasp.

The tree in front of the house is lashing its branches like whips. Rain is pouring from the sky. 'I don't want to go out in that!'

'Do you want to stay here?' asks Arthur, his hands by his side.

For a brief moment I seriously consider it, but then I think of Grandma and her brittle bones and I shake my head, sighing. 'I'm coming. Just let me close the shutters.'

'Don't burn yourself.'

'Make sure Grandma doesn't get burnt,' I say. 'Give her the plastic anorak that we got from Flat Hannah.'

'Yeah, yeah. Grandma's ready; it's you we're waiting for.'

I look out at the pitch-black night and listen to the roar of the storm. The noise mixes with that of the chiming bells. The rain brings a strange, iron-like odour with it.

The wind blows a toxic gust of rain into the room. My hands immediately begin to sting, as if I've grabbed a thistle. 'Sack of crabs!' I curse, as I pull my sleeves over my stinging hands and bolt the shutters tight. 'I'm ready. Have you got everything? Is your hood secure?'

My brother walks around impatiently. 'Check and double check. Come on, Grandma is calling and so is the church.'

The house shakes under the force of a heavy gust as we make our way downstairs. Grandma stands by the door waiting for us, shrouded in a large plastic anorak that keeps out the rain.

As we walk out the door, a shiver runs through my body. The night is dark and wild. Even my sturdy anorak is unable to prevent drops from falling onto my face. I hiss from the pain. Grandma staggers through a gale that blows her hood clean off. I grab hold of her elbow just in time and hold her upright, Arthur taking her other arm.

We follow the track which leads to the church. I look behind me, only to see our house is nothing more than a dark shadow. Above the wailing of the storm

I think I can hear the wooden beams creaking. For a moment, I'm taken with fear: what if the walls don't hold up? What if the stable collapses? Our cow Yssi lives at the rear of the house, with only a few planks of wood to protect her from the storm.

I shake my head and turn my eyes again to the road before us. Tonight, we are preparing ourselves for the beginning of the storm season, the most dangerous time of year for a community of fishermen and sailors such as ours. It's the beginning of September and the autumn nights are quickly drawing in. Soon, the cliffs will be lashed by driving rains and churning seas. But to this day, our house has managed to withstand every harsh storm.

Further up the hill, the lanterns of the other villagers are flickering. Grandma, Arthur and I join the procession. Nobody speaks; it seems everyone is saving their breath to fight the wind. The church is only another kilometre further on, but tonight, the march seems endless. Grandma has to pause three times to catch her breath before we reach the top of the hill.

The doors of the church stand open, inviting us in. Behind them lurks nothing but darkness. I know it will change soon, but I can't shake a sinister feeling when we enter the gloomy building. Arthur loops his arms around Grandma and helps her to a pew in the round annexe, where she can lean against a raised stone altar.

Jost the Netter closes the gate. As the two large double doors crash shut, a sigh of relief passes through the gathered people. The storm doesn't seem so close now. I can still hear the rain rattling against the tall windows, and the howl of the wind over the roof, yet the walls stand steady and strong.

I pull the dripping, wet hood from my head and immediately feel that far too familiar burning sensation, creeping into my fingers as if I've been squeezing a stinging nettle. I sigh and look around. The church is the only building in the village that doesn't rely on walls of cob, having instead been raised from grey blocks of stone. As far as I know, it is the oldest building in Gwennec, older than the settlement itself. It must have weathered many a storm already.

At school I have seen pictures of churches with tall towers, but this church doesn't have one. It has a peaked roof, topped off with a stone cross, and a rounded chapel. The windows are small and vaulted and made of coloured glass.

MARA LI

It is named St Gwenhael's, after the man who gave his name to our town of Gwennec.

In the dim light, I can just about make out the carved icons in the alcoves in the walls. I wonder who these men are. Were they kings or saints? Some bear a crown, while others hold their hands in prayer and cast their gaze upwards, as if they can see the heavens through the roof.

The church stands forgotten atop the hill, surrounded by crumbling stone walls. Nobody has ever tried to pull it down to make way for a pasture, or uses the stones for building new houses. Except for the broken window in the roof, the building is completely unscathed.

I know the church well, as I have been going there since I was a child on Dad's shoulders. Every year, the whole village will climb up, light candles and sing old songs with melodies that ascend to the ceiling like birds on the wing. Before Dad's accident, I would sing the Sailors' Mass with full voice; now I find that the trusted words of those hymns are stuck in my throat. What forces can take pity on fishermen if the sea has free reign to do what it wants?

Without counting, I estimate there to be around eighty people present. Our village is too small to host a larger community. We don't even have a name, but we cling like a limpet to Gwennec, the small town that lies higher up in the hills. I bump into someone and see it is my best friend Yannick. We quietly greet each other. She lives with her family in a large, sturdy house outside the village, with a slate roof and a bunker below. Compared to our mud-walled house, with only a thatched roof on the open beach, her house seems a fortress.

Arthur drapes his jacket over Grandma's shoulders against the cold air. I look intently at her face, wrinkled like a gnarled tree. Her eyes are swollen and bloodshot from the rain. As she sees me looking, she smiles.

'This is not my first storm, Nimue.'

'I know.' I remind myself that she is tougher than she looks. Grandma has lived her whole life on the coast, and it will have to be quite the violent storm to crush her spirits. Yet as I look at her, all I can see is how small she is and how the hump on her back pushes her narrow shoulders forward. I take off my anorak and drape it over her shoulders, over Arthur's jacket.

Grandma exclaims: 'You'll both catch your deaths!'

I shrug.

The raised stone altar she is leaning against is also a carved image of a man lying down, wearing a long robe. He is lying on a kind of altar and, just like the saints in the alcoves, his hands are folded in prayer on his chest. This is Saint Gwenhael himself, who lies buried beneath the monument that is carved in his image, or so they say. Along the flat edges of the altar are chunks of melted candle wax. As I run my fingers over them, they almost feel as cold and hard as the stone itself.

'Will Yssi be alright?' asks Arthur, who sits down next to Grandma.

I slump down next to him, my back against the stone. The pew is hard and uncomfortable; to think I could have been back in my nice, warm bed! What idiot made it so the Sailors' Mass takes place at night?

'Yssi has her animal instinct, she'll be fine,' says Grandma.

'The storm will blow over,' I add.

Grandma wraps her arms around us. 'I have the feeling that the storms out there are just getting started.'

'Last storm season wasn't as bad,' I say. 'There hasn't been a hurricane since...' My voice falters. *Since Dad's accident.*

'At school they say that the storms are the aftershocks of the Impact,' Arthur says. 'And that they'll stop completely after a few more years.'

'Yes, after the Impact, the world seemed to have been torn open,' says Grandma. 'Can you smell the iron in the air?'

Arthur shakes his head, but I remember the strange smell that came in through the window, like thunder mixed with the smoke from the Oakfields.

'That smell was our warning,' says Grandma. 'You are too young to remember, but we were taught to barricade the doors. Aftershocks, don't kid me. No, these are omens.'

The wind whistles above our heads. I begin to imagine it trying to find a way inside. 'But the church existed long before the Impact, didn't it?'

Grandma says nothing, simply giving me a pinch on the shoulder.

We fall silent as the mass begins. Katell lights the first candle. She is a little younger than Arthur, her blonde hair framing her face like dandelion petals. She clasps the tall candle between her hands and approaches us, step by step, down the aisle towards the statue of Saint Gwenhael where we are sitting. There she halts, looking upwards, as if she's in silent communion with the motionless stone figure. Then she lights one of the candles at the foot of the statue. The flame flickers, wanes, gains some strength and keeps burning. Katell hands the candle to Arthur.

Someone starts a song, a few bright notes floating slowly upwards: 'Saint Gwenhael, lord of the sea...'

Arthur lights the next candle and passes it to me as the hymn begins to pick up around us. As always, I stand in silence. I light a new candle and pass it to the person sitting next to me.

Slowly, the gloomy church is filled with light. I shut my eyes, the words of the hymn beginning to ring forth.

Saint Gwenhael, lord of the sea
Tonight, a barque puts out to sea
Oh Gwenhael, lord of the sea
How frail the barque, how wild the sea
Tonight, a soul sets out to sea
Oh constant star, lord of the sea
Sail out with them, we ask of thee!

It's not the words of the hymn that are turning around and around in my head like the wind that's swirling around the church's roof. I think about what Grandma said and I hope she's wrong; I hope that I haven't smelled that same iron smell and that this will be an autumn storm like any other, reaching its peak either today or tomorrow.

I rest my head against the cool stone of the wall and feel sleep entering me once more. Grandma might say that Yssi has instinct enough to fend for herself, but I have never considered our cow the sharpest tool in the box. Besides, where will she hide when the roof of her rickety old shed gets blown down? What about the chickens? The nets? The boat? What if the storm destroys our boat so we can't go fishing? It has happened once before, years earlier, but that was back when Dad was still around to patch things up.

Gwenhael, lord of the endless sea

we ask of you our lives to keep
and aid us when the seas are deep
Lord of the churning sea
Constant star, our good shepherd be

I lift my knees up to my chest. By Gwenhael, it's cold! I begin to regret giving Grandma my anorak.

And yet, my face is burning. It must be from the rain. I carefully touch the first sores forming on my forehead and down my left cheek. This isn't the first time I've been blistered by the rain, but it's still far from a pretty sight. I should have brought some camomile balm with me, which I keep on my bedside table. I quietly curse my stupidity. All I can do now is massage my skin until the stinging turns into a dull throbbing.

I'm half asleep when Arthur hauls me to my feet. The mass is over. Like a somnambulant I stumble down the hill, grateful that we have the wind to our back this time. As slow as our outward journey has been, so quickly are we whisked home now.

I take off my clothes the moment I enter the bedroom, and roll into my bed without bothering to fold them. The sound of the storm is still ringing in my ears as I fall asleep.

2

REPAIRS

I jolt awake with butterflies in my stomach.

The house is quiet. Usually, I hear Grandma puttering about in the early hours, or else Arthur will lie snoring next to me. Now my brother is breathing softly and evenly. I move my head to try to listen to the storm, but behind the shutters all is still. I get out of bed, open the shutters and stick my head out the window.

The early morning air is clear and crisp. As I breathe in deeply, I can taste the salty air coming off the sea, while from the beach the whisper of the sea enters my ears. It's not the sound of rolling waves or the crashing surf, far from it. It is just as I'd hoped: the storm has died down to a strong breeze, which now blows into the room and over me.

Arthur flails his arms, as if to push the cold air away from him. I laugh and in one motion I pull the covers off him.

He yelps and shoots out of bed.

The threat of the storm is as far away as the forgotten continents beyond the ocean. I laugh again and stick my tongue out.

'It's freezing!' cries my brother.

'It's beautiful weather!'

'What time is it?' He looks around. Outside, dawn is beginning to break, but it is still dim in our small bedroom.

'Nearly sunrise.'

'Pfff.' Arthur collapses back onto the bed.

'Chin up, boy, you're still young and fit,' I say, imitating Grandma's voice.

Arthur tosses his pillow at me. I manage to duck away and the pillow hits the wall instead.

'Fail!' I say mockingly, then, switching back to my normal voice: 'The storm's ripped a load of branches from the trees. We should go see if the boat or the house has been damaged at all.'

Arthur is finally won over by this, getting out of bed and getting dressed. 'Your hair's sticking up on end,' he says, looking over at me.

Next to my bed is a shard of glass about the size of my hand. In the reflection I can just about see myself; a sun-kissed girl of seventeen, with a shock of red, curly hair and freckles dotting her face. I turn my nose up and braid my slightly wild hair into a plait falling onto my back as best as I can. 'Take a look at yourself.'

Arthur's face is swollen with sores and his hair is like a bale of hay; just as unruly as mine, but blond like a field of barley in the summer. I move over to him and begin to laugh. 'You look like you've been stung by a dozen wasps!'

Arthur runs his fingers over the sores on his face and winces in pain.

'A dab of balm will sort that out,' I say more gently. My rain-sore balm is my pride and joy: I make it from camomile, which grows from spring to late summer in the ditches along the edge of the road leading to Gwennec. Grandma taught me to use an infusion of flower heads when my monthly cramps first started; only later did I learn that a compress held against my bloated skin would have the same calming effect. Since then, I always have some supplies tucked away at home in order to survive the winter. I have a special cubby hole in Yssi's stall, where I dry out the flowers.

I notice Arthur staring at me. 'Is there something on my head?'

'You were covered in sores too; I saw them in the candlelight,' he replies.

'That's true....' I touch my head and notice that the skin is smooth and un-harmed. My palms are normal too, no red marks to be found. Speechless, I look from my hands to Arthur's red face and back again. I'd completely forgotten the pain – what's more, I'd forgotten to apply any balm before going to sleep. 'That's odd,' I say. 'I guess it wasn't as bad as I thought it was.'

I quickly get dressed and we make our way down the stairs. I put my finger to my lips as we creep past Grandma's box-bed. Last night's proceedings have worn her out.

Scattered across the ground lay the branches of the tree, the bare trunk looking like a kind of wooden column. We kick the branches aside and then turn to inspect the damage to our home.

The walls of the house have been spattered with mud and one of the shutters on the kitchen window has been broken. It hangs crookedly from its hinges, creaking as it stirs in the breeze.

Arthur jabs at my shoulder. 'Look at the roof.'

'Shark teeth!'

I can see that the thatch in the roof is broken in two places, ripped off by the wind, leaving visible the bare wooden beam skeleton below. 'I'll have to get up there and fix it then.' I'm not exactly thrilled about the idea; it's a pretty large drop down, should I fall.

The rest of the damage isn't so bad. The cowshed has survived the storm with only a bit of straw blown onto the floor. As soon as Yssi catches sight of us, she begins to low woefully, as if to express her displeasure with the current state of things. I can't blame her, really. Milk begins to drip from her huge swollen udders.

'Poor thing,' says Arthur. He grabs a bucket and kneels next to her. There is no need to tie Yssi up, for as soon as Arthur touches her teats, the milk comes spurting out without complaint from Yssi. Last month we lost our calf. The creature was weak and of poor health despite our efforts to care for it. In the weeks after we had killed it, Yssi was not quite her old self. Sometimes, she'd spend whole nights mournfully lowing, and she had so much milk that her udders were always bursting.

I leave my brother alone with the cow and head down to the quay. A few planks have been washed away, the water splashing onto the jetty. Unsurprising, given the flimsiness of the wooden planks.

Our boat is called *The Ragdoll*. The letters Dad painted on the prow had once been clear and bright, particularly high above the waves; now the paint is dull and the boat is low in the water. Too low.

I anxiously walk across the jetty. I run my hand over the battered keel. I'd left the sail tied up on the deck and was sure I had left it securely fastened. Now it's dangling partly under the waterline, with a large rip down the middle resembling a ragged lightning bolt. I stoop down and pull the sail from the water. What could have caused such a terrible tear?

I spot it almost immediately: a large piece of metal sticking out of the side of the boat. A fishhook bigger than my hand, which must have been picked up by the wind and ripped open the sail. There's a door on the deck that is the entrance to a small compartment where we store the nets and hooks. The bolt is loose and the door rattles as loudly as the kitchen shutters.

Angrily, I throw the hook back down into the hole. Once again I feel how *The Ragdoll* is a little lower than usual. As I move further on board, my fearful suspicion is confirmed: my boots splash in the water on deck.

'Arthur!' I call out at the top of my lungs. 'Come here!'

If *The Ragdoll* is broken, then the rest of the village's boats will be too. I curse the storm. There's only one shipwright nearby and the other, who lives in Gwennec, is far too expensive for us. Is *The Ragdoll* damaged so badly that Arthur and I won't be able to repair it ourselves? And if so, how are we ever going to scrape together the money to pay for such repairs? Our income relies solely on the fish we sell at the market in Gwennec. There'll be no fish without a boat. And without a boat, there'll be no fish.

Arthur shows up and casts his eye over the boat. 'What's the damage?'

'Three holes perhaps...I'm not sure.'

He clambers into the boat and looks down at the water reaching halfway up his boots. 'They can't be big holes, or else she would have sunk last night.'

'The sail's ruined as well.'

'Help me pull her ashore,' Arthur says.

That isn't easy. We're lucky the tide comes in, helpfully pushing the boat forward, while the two of us drag her onto the beach with two steel cables.

Arthur inspects the underside of the boat. After a while, he says: 'The worst holes are in the front part of the hull. If I we still have any sealant, we just need to clean up the aluminium and the rivets. Then we'll just apply as much sealant on the top as possible. I think that'll hold things together until we've saved enough money to actually get it repaired.'

I relax a little. 'Dad would be proud.'

Arthur grins. He can still remember Dad, unlike our mother, Rona. This is his boat, the one in which he always took us fishing. It was in this boat that he taught us how to cast and haul in a net, when was the best time to hoist the sail and how to safely make it back home through rough seas. Even if money were pouring out of our ears, I doubt we'd ever get rid of this old boat. It's the only thing we have left of Dad.

Urged on by Arthur's practical words, I take another look at the tattered sail. A large part of it has been torn to shreds and cannot be repaired, but the lowest part only had a few holes. 'Don't we still have a piece of old sail up in the attic somewhere'?

'I think so.'

'I can try to remove the top half and patch up the holes with the old pieces. It won't be as strong as a new canvas, but I think we can use it to sail the boat on calm days.'

'It's better than nothing.' He looks around hesitantly. 'Do you think it'll be alright?'

'It'll be a while before we can go fishing again, but I think it will.'

'How are we meant to survive in the meantime, then?'

'From the fish traps, and from our preserved fruit, or from seaweed. And Yssi's milk of course. I guess we can even sell some of it; she's got plenty.'

'The traps are ruined,' says Arthur. 'If that's all we have, we'd better start weaving some new ones.'

'Don't forget the holes in the roof. If it's stormy again, we're done for.'

'First we need new straw.'

'I'll ask Jost for some,' I reply. Jost the Netter usually has everything tucked away in his shed, and he doesn't ask much for it either.

'Wait a second.' Arthur kneels down on the ruined jetty and plunges his arm elbow-deep into the water. A few fish traps have also been washed ashore and are now no more than a pile of broken twigs. The others have simply disappeared into the sea. Arthur pulls something up, and to my surprise reveals a still-intact trap. In it are a few small, grey fish flapping about. We'll have something for dinner at least.

Most of the fish are already dead. The few that are still wriggling in the trap are quickly taken care of by slitting open their bellies with a sharp knife that we always carry with us. One by one, I toss them into a pile, the soft wet flesh smacking as each new fish is added.

'Ugh, this one is contaminated.' Arthur lifts it up and holds the fish between his thumb and finger. It is a plump, grey fish with plenty of meat, but its gills and fins are so black it looks as if they are scorched. It stinks.

'This one too.' The fish I have in my hand has sunken eyes, as if it were already half rotten. 'Put it back in the pot, then we'll put it on the fire.'

We check the rest of the catch, but find no other contaminations. Doing these checks is one of the many important lessons taught to us by Dad. First, he taught us how to swim, even in the roughest of seas. After that, he'd take us to sea and spent days teaching us how to look out for fish with sunken eyes, slimy bodies or off-coloured patches. He got us to identify the contaminated fish and showed us the correct way to dispose of them.

Many factories in Old Europe were destroyed by the Impact, when the meteorite struck the Earth. No one could count the exact number of dangerous substances that were released as a result, but I reckon there were enough to cut the population that hadn't found refuge in Arks yet in half within a few months. I personally believe that many of these harmful substances shouldn't have been stored in vulnerable buildings in the first place, but I suppose that wisdom serves no one anymore, and I've been told that mine is a typical Periphery attitude. The people of the large cities of Central Europe are proud of their flourishing industry. In any case, no one really knows what causes the contaminated fish, or the acid rain that still falls over the hills and cities. For a long time, no crops grew in the fields, and when they finally grew back, there was still a fair chance that someone would ingest so much poison they'd die. Nowadays, the toxins have weakened considerably. Still, there is always the risk of catching a fever or getting stomach cramps if you drink water straight from water tanks, or if you take it from a stream or pond. The very poorest among us run that risk simply because they cannot afford plastic bottles of purified water. I'm grateful that we've never had it quite that bad, and I am determined to never let it get to the stage where Arthur and Gran have to drink rainwater.

And then there are the sores that develop on a person's skin when exposed to the rain, yet no matter how painful or uncomfortable those sores may be, they are never fatal.

What happened with the sea was a little stranger. Dad could never really explain why some parts of the ocean remained completely unaffected while other areas would suddenly become blighted. The currents tend to move the toxin and swirl it around, and so it is the task of a good fisherman to know which are the best fishing spots and which spots are no-go areas. Of course, every fisherman will find a couple of contaminated fish in his catch from time to time. Unlike the plants, the fish never died from the poison. They changed, perhaps over the course of time or perhaps from birth. In any case, the end result is never pleasant.

Contaminated fish, burns and –if we're unlucky – a day or two of stomach aches. Arthur and I have never had it too bad, but Grandma would often spend the evening recounting tales from her youth. 'It's a miracle that my family survived the bloody thing,' she would say. She spent the entirety of her younger years in the worst and darkest period, where uncontaminated food was scarcer, water was too dangerous to drink, and purification facilities were still in their early stages. Industry across the whole country crashed to a halt. Painfully slowly, the old continent picked itself up again; Old Europe became Central Europe, ruled from the great city of Rome.

Here in Breizh, we have little to show in terms of this industrial progress. Only the large oil platforms, such as the Oakfield, remind us that there is another world out there, where machines have taken over the work of human hands and the fresh air is smothered by fumes. I wonder if the people there grow as hungry as we do after a storm.

Arthur has little patience for my meditations. For him, Rome is farther away than the bottom of the sea. I can't blame him: our life is here in Gwennec, and that already keeps us busy enough without dreaming away our days. We burn the contaminated fish in an old oil drum and leave the fire to burn itself out, until all that remains is a thick, stinking smoke creeping skywards. The same columns of smoke rise up all along the shoreline of the village, mingling with the air. Here on the coast we adhere to the law of the sea, and it dictates to us to go out and fish as long as we still can.

3

DREAMS AND TREASURES

G randma earns a few cents with Yssi's abundant milk, the money being
spent almost immediately on nails, string, wood and needles made of
fishbone. After three days, I have only managed to repair one hole in the roof.
Meanwhile, with the help of Jost the Netter, Arthur and I have managed to haul
the boat up to his slipway. Arthur is busy sealing the holes in the bow while I
try to repair the sail. If Arthur isn't busy with the boat, he is tying trap after trap
with his nimble fingers.

One day, Yannick comes by with her father and helps us to fix up the cowshed.
She leaves us with a basket of freshly baked bread. Each day grows darker and
colder than the one before. The weather is still calm, but I know from experience
that the next storm isn't far off.

For us, the summer months are when we leave for the sea for days on end.
When we aren't sailing, we're at the market in Gwennec selling our fish. Now
that the fishing season is over and the storm season has begun, it's too dangerous
to just sail out. A storm can brew without warning. A storm can tear sails and
break masts as if they are twigs. A storm can hurl towering waves at a boat and
drag the sailors overboard with the strength of a giant.

During these dark months, we know better than to go to sea. For Arthur and
me, this means going to lessons at the only school in the area, the village school
just outside Gwennec.

We go there two mornings a week, to learn how to read, write and count. The
top classes are also taught a bit of pre-Impact history. These classes fascinate

me immensely, even though I can barely imagine what that world must have looked like. What I enjoy the most are the stories of newly discovered continents, strange peoples living between the trees and the huge, brand new cities that were erected on virgin soil.

I sometimes imagine a day when Arthur and I will hop aboard the *Ragdoll* and just keep on sailing, until we, too, reach one of the great, extinct continents: Britannia, where the last inhabitable area was swallowed up by the rising oceans some ten years ago. People fled in droves to Central Europe; many remaining here in Breizh.

Perhaps we would even reach the far and distant America.

Or, perhaps, even that mysterious island that I cannot point out on a map, but which Mum would always sing about when she tucked me into bed. Always, I asked her where it was, and she'd always give me the same answer: 'In the mists of time, my little seal pup.' The island seemed to lie in the mists of her memories, or perhaps it was simply a fairy tale from long ago, when the world was still so very different. My childhood fantasies turned it into a far-off place, where mountains and cliffs were covered by a thick veil of mist, surrounded by the ocean. In my stories, the travellers who went ashore there never once returned.

Now that I am seventeen, I only have a few months of school left. After that, I'll have to commit all my time to our tiny fishery, just like Dad and Grandma, sailing out every day and selling our fish at the market in town.

As always while I'm at school, my gaze wanders over to the notice-board near the entrance, where a notice is pinned up. The long list had gone around the school during last storm season. On it are the apprenticeships in Gwennec that are offered to village children like me and Arthur. Tanner, tailor, shipwright...I could yawn.

I know exactly what I want to do. I also know how impossible it is. The training course to become a medical caretaker costs too much money, and besides, I'm the eldest child. Keeping the fishery running will soon be my responsibility.

With a pang of envy, I think of Yannick, who is exactly one year older than me and who now lives in the city because her family agreed to let her pursue her studies. She came home for the Sailors' Mass, but I suspect it won't be long before she leaves again. The course lasts three years, and during that time, you get taught by real doctors who show you how to mend broken bones, how to stop bleeding, how to combat fever and vomiting and how to make pills and balms. Every time I imagine myself in the blue uniform that Yannick proudly shows off to me, my heart begins to flutter like an excited sparrow.

I walk slowly to the classroom, sit down at one of the tables and begin to draw lines in my workbook, paying little attention to the lesson. The best thing about being a medical caretaker is that you receive a monthly grant from the hospital. I'd be able to save up and finally get a better house built for Arthur and Grandma. With stone walls, like the church, so when it is stormy we won't have to worry about the fish market or the boat...

A prod against my elbow makes me jolt. I look to the side and find myself looking into the grinning face of Mart, who is sitting next to me.

'What?' I hiss.

Before he can reply, I hear a stern cough and I realise that the whole class is staring at me. Our teacher, Miss Franseza Madec, looks over at me with raised eyebrows. Was I called on? I quickly look around the class for any sort of indication, only to be met with the grinning faces of the handful of students present.

'Sorry, I...I didn't hear you,' I mutter.

Franseza gives me a disapproving look. 'The builder of the Arks,' she repeats in her articulated, clipped voice.

'Umm... in 2017, Miss.'

The corner of her mouth twitches slightly towards a smile. 'Not when it was built, Nimue, but by whom.'

'Oh, by Noah Odivo. That's why he called the bunkers *Arks,*' I reply, in a last effort to save my dignity. 'After the story of Noah's Ark and the Great Flood.'

'Very good, Nimue,' says Franseza and I sigh in relief. 'Can you also tell us where the nearest Ark is?'

I shake my head. I have never seen an Ark, so it can't be anywhere near Gwennec. To me, they seem like stuffy, underground labyrinths. It must've been awful to have been shut away in there for years, with no windows onto the outside world. It occurs to me how very different St Gwenhael's is. There, the windows are built to draw your gaze to the sky, like the effigies in the alcoves do. I raise my hand and ask: 'Why are there icons in the church?'

My sudden question causes Franseza to lose her flow. She looks over at me with raised eyebrows and the class stops taking notes. 'In the church?'

'I mean the carvings in the walls of the chapel,' I explain. 'I was wondering who they represent, who those people were?'

Franseza is quiet for a moment, as if she's pondering whether or not to carry on about the Arks. Finally she says: 'Who do you think they were?'

'I think they were definitely saints. And kings and knights. But why are they in the church?'

'To remember them,' she replies.

'But no one knows their names.'

'Well,' Franseza says slowly, 'maybe they weren't built for us to give them names. Perhaps they were made to keep watch over us.'

I grin. 'Nice guards, these stones.'

'Still, these people once lived here in Breizh. Do you all know what it used to be called?'

Someone replies: 'Brittany, Miss.'

My attention wanes. Absent-mindedly, I doodle the altar of St Gwenhael's, wondering what the people thought and did back when the world was a different place.

As usual when class is over, I wait for Arthur by the school gate. Yannick is already waiting for me, not in her blue uniform this time, but in a plain brown skirt and a sailor's vest. I hug her briefly. Her clothes always smell of detergent and have never been patched up. My own jumper is a stark contrast to that, because the elbow patches have been repaired so often that I've lost count. We talk until Arthur and his friends come out.

'Are we going to the beach?' Yannick asks.

I hesitate. 'Our roof's still not done yet...'

'Ah, come on, Nim!' interrupts Arthur. 'We've been working hard enough. I want to fly the kite!'

The blue sky is dotted with clouds, like tufts of wool. There is a light breeze coming off the land, perfect weather for flying kites. I feel the excitement brew in my belly and I smirk. 'Okay, let's go kite-flying.'

Arthur tears off ahead of us with the other boys in order to be the first one to get to the beach. Yannick and I follow behind at a slower pace, walking next to each other without saying a word.

The coastal road runs slowly downwards, snaking around a couple of hills until it reaches the beach. Like the other roads in the area, it is nothing more than an uneven dirt track and I can clearly see the mule tracks that run along it. Brambles with the last berries of the season grow on both sides of the path. I remember I was planning to pick some leaves to make a new kind of tea. I explain my idea to Yannick.

'Perhaps I'll try that too,' she says. 'The doctors say that bramble leaves work well against flu.'

'Are you going back soon?'

Yannick shakes her head. 'I was planning to just help with the clear-up after the storm, but there are so many people with all kinds of ills. Broken bones and bruises everywhere. Dad's also caught a stinking cold from when he was herding the cattle back in. His nose is bright red.' She laughs. 'Snot everywhere and now Mum's starting to complain too, so the doctors from the course have said that it would be good practice for me to stay here.'

'I'd trade my boat for that,' I say under my breath. As we reach the end of the path, we remain there for a moment, staring out over the sea. The tide is going out and the beach is covered in razor clams. Pools of water have gathered in the deepest gullies. We kick off our shoes and shiver as we always do when we take our first steps onto the cold sand.

Only when we have jumped over the first gully, Yannick says: 'I could teach you some things, if you want.'

I grab her arm and pretend to push her into one of the deeper gullies. 'Teach me everything you know or I'll throw you in the sea!'

Yannick regains her balance. 'Not like this, you cow.' She giggles and then adds in a more serious tone: 'Why don't you come to my house tomorrow morning? You can accompany me on my rounds.'

'See how important you sound,' I say, smiling. 'You need to check on yourself, Dr. Yannick.'

'You know the course won't make me a doctor.'

'You could go to Central Europe.' I gulp and turn towards the sea. There's something more to my dream, something I'm scared to admit, even to myself. For our small family, even a course like Medical Caretaking is too expensive...I don't even dare to imagine how much more expensive a full medical degree would be. Certainly far more than we could scrape together between the three of us.

'You should tell your grandmother, you know,' says Yannick unexpectedly.

I don't reply.

'She'd let you study, Nim. Everyone knows that you have a talent for it.'

'Yeah, yeah, talent.' I wave my hand at her. 'But the storm has destroyed far too much and all the repairs are expensive enough. I can't ask them to spend all that money on me... I wouldn't know how they'd earn money while I was away! Arthur is still at school and Grandma can no longer fish.' I bow my head and draw lines in the wet sand with my toes. 'I should forget about it and just go to sea, like Dad.'

'You shouldn't say that, Nim. I know you...you deserve to take that course, storm or no storm. You know what my father always says? Never leave something behind that you might regret.'

'Well, your father's rich. We have almost nothing,' I say, doing little to shield the bitterness in my voice.

'That's not true.' Yannick looks a little hurt. 'You're more talented than me. You're smart...'

'And poor.'

She pulls a face that shows she has lost her patience. I cross my arms over my chest and say nothing, knowing deep down that I'm right. Yannick really doesn't know how privileged she is. Her house could withstand storms, her father has fifteen cows, her clothes are always immaculate and she doesn't wear plastic shoes that have already been worn by two other girls in the village.

After a moment of tense silence, in which we slowly start making our way to the boys, Yannick says: 'Well, you know what I think of it. What's Arthur's opinion about all this? '

'I haven't told him anything.'

Arthur is holding his homemade kite while Mart is spooling off the long string. He runs backwards, lifting his arms and throwing the kite into the air. It soars like a bright yellow bird, trying its best to break away from the string tethering it to the earth.

'But you two tell each other everything!'

'Not everything.'

'Well go tell him, then,' she says. 'And who knows? Arthur only has a few more years left of school and then he can take over the fishery. You don't need to leave right away.'

'Perhaps,' I says hesitantly. 'First, let's do some kiting.'

The wind picks up and blows the kite higher than I have ever seen before. We pass the string between us all: from Mart to Judikael, Judikael to Taran and then to Yannick, who gives it to me. I run over the vast expanse of sand before me, my eyes focused on the dancing yellow dot far up in the sky, until my arms begin to shake from the sheer pull of the kite, and I pass it back over to Arthur. He has to try his best to keep his feet on the ground. We run towards the small incline, where the ground suddenly stops and the rocks down below stick out like terrible needles. I cup my hands around my mouth and shout: 'Arthur, look out!'

Falling off the rocks here will mean certain death.

Arthur sees the danger and lets go just in time. The kite spirals off in a swirling flight over the sea. I stare at the yellow speck against the ever-greying sky until it is no longer visible. *Where are you going?* I muse inwardly. *Will somebody find you?*

I turn around and begin to climb the next cliff, steeper still than the first one. From here, I can see the whole village below: the clay houses with their moorings, the swaying fishing boats at the dock, and the sails of windmills turning around and around. Someone is lugging a couple of sacks on his back on his way to the mill. Two children and a dog are running towards a wooden barn and soon disappear from sight.

As I turn to the east, I can make out the shape of Gwennec in the distance. The only asphalt road in the whole area leads directly to the town. Once in a while, a car drives from one direction to the other, but mostly, there are just mule carts. I wonder what life in town is like. Only the very wealthy can afford to buy a home there, so most people rent cheap apartments in narrow, crowded housing blocks.

I sit down on a large, flat stone and draw up the collar of my anorak as high as I can, trying to shield myself a little against the vicious howling of the wind that whips around my head up here. The past few days have been calm and almost windless. Now I can see the waves lashing at the shore at high speed. Foaming and roaring, they crash against the razor-like rocks. The last streak of blue sky at the horizon has disappeared, smothered by a new layer of clouds that begin to take on an ominous, green hue.

Arthur sits down next to me. I point to the sky. 'What do you think?'

'Time to get the boat ashore.'

I sniff the air. Is that a hint of iron I smell? I can't quite tell, as the wind also carries the industrial odours of the Oakfield.

'Mart and the others are going home now.'

'We should too; it's getting dark.'

Still, we don't move. We sit in silence for a few minutes, the low grumble of the ocean surrounding us on all sides.

'Next time, we should attach a message to the kite,' says Arthur. 'In a bottle, like in your stories, and wait for someone to answer.'

'Who do you think would answer it?'

Arthur shrugs. 'Where do you think the kite might end up? America?'

'I think America might be stretching it a little.'

'Maybe the island, then. We should have attached a message, imagine Mum finding it... What's up with you?'

I shake my head. 'That kite's just going to fall back into the sea. There's no one beyond the ocean.' *And definitely not Mum.* I press my lips tight and stare straight ahead. I'm in no mood to talk about stories today.

'What did I do?'

'Nothing. I'm not angry with you, it's just…' I tear my gaze away from the ocean to look at Arthur. Yannick is right; it's not fair to snap at my brother without telling him anything. With a sigh, I move closer to him so he can hear me over the rising wind. 'Do you ever think about the future? I don't just mean short-term, in a month or a year, but what you want later on? What kind of person you want to be?'

He looks back at me with big, round eyes, and I involuntarily hold my breath. What does his silence mean?

'Well,' he replies after a brief pause. 'Well, I do think about it, but it's so far away. You'd find it stupid anyway…'

'It's not so far away,' I say as I wipe my suddenly sweaty hands on my trousers. 'I don't think it's stupid to think about your future, Arthur.'

He shrugs his shoulders, as if trying to shake off an unwanted thought. 'We have the fishery. You, Grandma and I. That's all we have.'

'But is that what you want to do? Fishing?'

He doesn't answer.

'Tell me,' I insist. 'I keep thinking about the list at school and…'

'I'd like to do an apprenticeship to work on the railways,' interrupts Arthur. He strings the words together hastily. I close my mouth, too stunned to react. Arthur looks down at his hands, his face blushing. 'I want to become a train driver or an engineer, so I can travel through all of Central Europe and see the great cities.'

'But that's incredibly expensive, Arthur,' I blurt out. Immediately, I hate myself as he cringes, looking like a dog caught doing something bad. Why did I have to bring up the costs? Especially when I've just half convinced myself that I should pursue my dreams, money or no money. Why am I trying to take that away from Arthur? 'So, how does that work? Would you have to move to town?'

Arthur shakes his head. 'A driver takes you on if he has a place. You learn on the job.' Finally, he looks back up at me. 'I'd hardly ever be home again, Nim.'

Now I am the one who is silent, as I don't know how to react to his news. He's never told me anything about these plans, and as far as I know he has never told Grandma either. I lean forward and bury my head in my hands. It's as if a storm is now raging in my head.

'Say something, please,' begs Arthur.

'I don't know what to say,' I answer honestly, looking down at my hands. 'It's...I had no idea.'

'You think it's stupid. You think I'm too selfish.'

'No! I don't think it's stupid, Arthur, believe me. It's just that...' I lick my lips and take a deep breath. 'My time at school is nearly over and I don't think I want to keep fishing. I... I want to go to the town. I'd like to study Medical Caretaking, just like Yannick. I want to learn about what causes illnesses and how to cure people, how to make salves and tinctures, and I...I want to make people better. Dad died because there was no doctor, and ever since then, I've wondered...if only someone had known how, could he have been saved? If I were a medical caretaker, I could help.'

'I get it,' says Arthur. 'But I'd make much more money as a train driver.'

'You'll also cost us more!'

'I would earn that back within two years! You and Grandma could live anywhere. In a stone house, in the town, with a cleaner for every room.'

I cross my arms, frowning. 'You've got it all figured out, then.'

'Yes, I've given it a lot of thought, and if you did the same, you'd realize what a good idea it is!'

I can think of a hundred reasons why it isn't a good idea: private courses cost twice as much as public courses. Arthur would be gone most of the time, leaving it up to me to both look after Grandma and to go fishing. I'll be finishing school well before him, and most of all, I am the oldest child... I shut my mouth and reflect. 'We can't both study. Even if I went first and you three years later, it'd still cost too much money. I don't think *The Ragdoll* will survive that long, and without a boat, well...' I shrug. We both know that as much as we would like to turn our backs on fishing, without a boat, nothing would be possible.

'How much does a medical caretaker earn?' asks Arthur. He seems a little calmer.

'Not enough to send you out into the big, wide world,' I mutter. 'But enough to buy a good, stone house. I mean, I'd have to save up for it, so nothing much will change during the first few years, unless *The Ragdoll* gets destroyed, or something. But we'd never be poor again.'

'With a driver's grant, we...'

'I know,' I interrupt him. 'So you want me to give up my dreams for you?'

He reaches for my hand and gives me a helpless look. 'It sounds terrible when you put it like that.'

'Well, that is how it sounds. Perhaps we should go home.'

He says nothing as we get up and leave the beach to walk home. Smoke is drifting up from the chimney stack, a sign that Grandma has lit the fire to ward off the chills of autumn. From a distance, the farmyard looks almost untouched by the storm, except for the hole in the roof that still needs to be fixed. I think about how much work I've put into this house, and into our fishery, and I feel my anger clench like a fist in my stomach. Since Mum left and Dad died, it was me who'd taken care of Arthur. And when Grandma grew weaker, I'd not just taken over most tasks of the fishery, but most of the household chores as well. If there is anyone who deserves an opportunity to study, it's me. At the very least, I know I have a talent that could take me places. Arthur is a terrific coxswain and a good fisherman – Dad made sure to teach us well – but who says that'll be enough for him to become a good train driver? He might be terrible at it; then we might as well just cast that money into the sea.

When we step over the threshold into the house, my mood plummets even more. I throw my boots into the corner and get to the stairs.

'Aren't you eating with us?' asks Arthur.

'I'm not hungry,' I say, without turning back. 'Tell Grandma I'm going to patch the roof.'

I expect him to object, but he doesn't. With a sigh, I go upstairs, up the ladder through the hatchway that gives way to the attic. This is a place of cobwebs and forgotten memories. I don't think anyone's been up here since Grandma's back has become so bad that she can't climb the ladder anymore.

In one of the corners is something I recognise as a figurehead: a seal's head made of wood, the rest of the body broken off and gone missing. Suddenly, I remember *The Ragdoll* as it used to be, back when Mum still lived with us. The figurehead, both head and body, once elegantly adorned the prow of the boat;

Dad always said that was why the seals would follow us. I smile. I can't believe I'd forgotten about that.

On the other side are piles of boxes, broken furniture, fishing rods and tangled fishing nets that have been thrown down carelessly and were never picked up again. Dad had obviously kept them for some reason – to repair or sell them, perhaps. The sight of all these unused things, these unfinished plans, saddens me. Poor Dad. When we finally found him and towed *The Ragdoll* back to the wharf, he'd already been entwined in a net in the icy waters for so long that nobody could help him. He'd still been breathing, but his lips had turned blue. We'd brought him home, wrapped him in blankets and placed him by the fireside. An hour later, he had stopped moving. There'd been no time to call a doctor, no car to take him to the town's hospital fast enough, and anyway, there'd have been no money to pay for any of it. That day, I cried so hard I thought I would be left hollow inside, like an empty shell.

It's tricky to find a place for my feet without treading on something. Carefully, I make my way to the hole in the roof, brush aside the cobwebs and lean out. It's just like an open window, looking out into the twilight. The sea is a vast, dark plain, and the cold wind has free access to the attic room. I shiver and step away. If I want to get anything done, I'd better fetch a lantern.

My foot catches on something on the floor. Before I know it, I'm on my behind in a cloud of dust. I cough, wave away the dust and glance at the floor. It seems I've stumbled over a rough-timbered wooden box, no larger than a breadbin, with a round lid and wrought-iron lock. Just as everything else around me, it's coated in a thick layer of dust. I blow the lid clean and then, for a moment, forget to breathe. Something's been written on the side: *For Nimue.*

My heart skips a beat before it starts to pound loudly in my throat. That's Dad's handwriting!

Was he planning on giving this to me? As I carefully shake the box, I hear a muffled clonk, as if there's something big inside. I dig into my memories – has he ever mentioned something about this? If he has, I don't remember it.

No matter how hard I pull, the lid won't open, and the wood is too tough to break. Besides, I'm worried that the mysterious contents of the box may get damaged if I try to open it forcefully. I glance at the lock. Was there a key when I knocked it over? Perhaps it's somewhere on the ground nearby. I grope around on the floor. Just behind me is Mum's old wardrobe. Over the years, I have worn all the clothing she's left behind and patched it up where necessary. I get down on my stomach and stick my hand beneath the wardrobe, in the gap between its feet and the floor. At first my fingers just find soft and sticky strands of spider web. Goosebumps slowly crawl up my back; I can deal with jellyfish, crabs and fish guts without blinking an eye, but the large spiders in the attic give me the creeps.

Finally, my fingers touch something that is solid and small, and I pull it towards me. That's it – that's the key. It fits the lock perfectly. I excitedly turn it, hear the click and lift the lid up with a slight tremor in my hands.

The chest contains only two items.

The first is a white pebble, strung on a leather cord. I hold it in my hand, letting the last rays of daylight fall on the stone. The precise outline of a small seal has been carved into the polished surface. I stare at it in wonder. Whoever made this must have been a real artist.

The second artefact is a leather-bound ledger, tied with a simple piece of string. There is nothing on the cover that reveals what might be inside. As I lift it up, a whiff of smoke and fire enters my nose. It's so feeble that it feels like the memory of a smell. I untie the cord and open the book. For the second time, I'm shocked enough to hold my breath. This time, I don't immediately recognise the handwriting, but I don't need to. It's clear who the leather tome belonged to.

Long, cursive letters that have slightly faded from the yellow pages – though not so much that I can't read them – spell out the words: *Rona's Diary*.

4

RONA

'Nimue!' calls Arthur through the hatch.

Arthur's cry startles me, the book lying open on my lap. I don't want to risk closing the book too quickly, scared the paper will be damaged somehow. Or perhaps I'm afraid I'll read something unexpected about Mum's disappearance – find out she didn't love us as much as we thought?

I stare once more at the first page, at Mum's looping handwriting, admiring how she has written her own name. Besides the burnt smell it mostly reeks of old paper, like those few books they have at school that were written before the Impact. How long ago must my mother have written these first words?

'Hello? Nim?' calls Arthur impatiently.

'What?'

'Gran says you have to come down and eat. Is the roof done?'

I close the leather tome and fasten the cord. 'It's too dark; I need a lantern.'

'Do it tomorrow then. Gran's worried about the weather and you falling through the roof because of it.'

'Who's going to fall through?' I call down, feeling offended. I stuff the pendant and the book underneath my jumper and get up. I don't know why, but for some reason I want to keep my find a secret for the time being. Besides, Dad has written *For Nimue* on the chest, so he clearly intended this treasure to be for me and not for Arthur.

By the time I come down from the attic, Arthur has gone down to the kitchen, so I dip into our room and hide the book under my pillow. I hold onto the unusual pendant, the stone hidden underneath my thick jumper, and then with an excited, tingling sensation running through me, I walk into the kitchen to join Gran and Arthur at the dinner table.

'It must be pitch black up there,' Gran says. She places a thick slice of bread on my plate and passes me the lard.

'Yes, it's rather dark,' I say as I spread the lard onto the bread. My heart is still in my mouth; I wonder if Arthur or Grandma can read my emotions from my face. 'It's got dark early tonight.'

Grandma doesn't seem to notice anything strange. She breaks off small pieces of bread and stuffs them into her mouth. She is missing half her teeth, which makes eating difficult for her. 'What were you doing up there if you weren't fixing the roof?'

'Just looking at stuff,' I say, nonchalantly shrugging my shoulders. 'You know, at Dad's old things. Arthur, do you still remember the old figurehead from *The Ragdoll*?'

He shakes his head, his mouth too full to answer.

'I'll show you tomorrow, I bet you'll remember it then.'

'Nimue, you could have broken your neck up there,' says Gran. 'I don't want to lose any more members of this family, you hear?'

'Yes, Gran.' Arthur and I exchange a look. If Gran ever found out that we spent our free time climbing steep cliffs and exploring the forbidden underground system of tunnels and caves by torchlight, she'd never let us set foot outside the house again. I put on my best smile and plant a kiss on her cheek. 'Don't worry, I'll be okay. Why don't you go sit down by the fire? I'll milk Yssi tonight and Arthur can do the washing-up.'

Arthur looks up and seems like he is about to say something, before I silence him with a single gesture of my hand. Gran abandons her stern look and lovingly takes hold of my hand. 'That would be lovely, dear. Ever since that bleeding walk to the church, my back's been playing up.'

'Tomorrow I'll make you a salve of lard and comfrey for your muscles,' I promise. 'That ought to ease the pain. Yannick showed me how.'

'You're just like your mother,' says Gran with a warm smile. 'You always have some sort of remedy at the ready. Don't forget to barricade the barn door when you've finished. There's something suspicious in the air.'

Am I like Mum? I know I haven't inherited her physical traits, because Rona had thick black hair, large dark eyes and pale skin that would never tan even in the brightest sunlight. I don't particularly look like Dad either; he was a thickset man with hands like coal shovels with which he would readily haul the heavy nets out of the water. But maybe Gran means to say something else; maybe she's hinting at the fact that like her, I had the gift of healing people.

The notion that I have been born to be something more than a fisherwoman makes me feel giddy. Was Mum a doctor or some sort of herbalist, perhaps? I'm ashamed to admit that I have no idea what Rona was like as a person, or what she may still be like. I remember her sudden departure eleven years ago. I was six years old and didn't really understand what was going on, but the seriousness in Mum's voice wasn't lost on me.

As I walk to Yssi's stall and begin milking her as usual, my mind takes me back to that day; my mother kneeling in front of me, her hands on my shoulders and her face pressed against mine as I breathed in her sweet smell. Eleven years later, I can still remember her exact words: '*You must be brave and strong, Nimue. Look after your brother. Never let him out of your sight, you hear me? You and Arthur must stick together.*'

She'd kissed me on the lips and had left after that. I watched her walk away until she disappeared out of sight. The smell of sweet herbs had stayed with me for a long time afterwards.

All these years and I never found out where she'd gone. Dad believed she was dead, but in a way that I couldn't quite put into words, I always had the feeling she was still alive, even though I didn't understand why she had to leave so suddenly. She hadn't even taken any of her clothes with her. Did she no longer love Dad? Were we no longer enough for her?

Over time, Arthur had begun to forget her. In the middle of the night he'd sometimes wake from a nightmare and call for me instead of Mum. I would take him in my arms and cradle him, rocking gently back and forth like Mum had done to me. I buried my head in his hair and hummed the only lullaby that I knew, the same one Mum had sang for me time after time until I heard it in my dreams: '*Will you, will you follow me, breaking the waves and braving the sea.*'

The wind rattles the door of the stall and a cold draught passes through me. I squeeze the last drops of milk out of Yssi's udders and lovingly pat her on the neck. She looks back at me with her soft eyes.

'Thank you for the milk,' I say. I give her an extra handful of hay and bolt the door of the stall. I head back indoors with a bucket full of fresh milk, where Gran is sitting in front of the fire with a woollen blanket. 'Make sure you don't catch fire,' I say jokingly as I make my way down to the cellar where the milk can keep fresh and cool until tomorrow morning. It's a good thing Yssi produces so much milk, because the milk churn is empty and Gran has sold most of the milk.

That night we all go to bed rather early. I wait for Arthur's breathing to slow down before taking the leather book out from beneath the pillows. I light the lantern next to my bed as quietly as possible, pull my coat over my shoulders and lean against the wall with bent legs, my pillows propped up under my back. As I take out the seal necklace, I run it back and forth between my fingers. It gives me the feeling my mother is somehow closer. As I finally open the book, I feel a lump in my throat. I move the lantern nearer and pour over it. On the first page there is a large burn mark. As I leaf through the rest of the book I find that most of the pages are damaged to a certain extent. It seems as if the book has fallen into a fire and was quickly plucked back out. I can only speculate what might have happened: was it an accident, or did someone mean to destroy it? In several places it's obvious that pages have been torn out, leaving only ragged edges. Fascinated, I turned back to the first page, where most of the words are still legible.

August 2117 A.D.

What happened before the revelation

Let me start at the beginning and write the events in order. With any luck my thoughts will spill out in order too, as right now my mind is all over the place.

When my mother gave me the name Rona, she named me after the shimmering seals that could be found outstretched along the sandbanks between Gull Island

and the cliffs. She told my father it was a word from the old language; a language that has long since disappeared from our island.

*

One week ago, I stood at the cliffs, looking down at the vast ocean stretching out before me. If I were to fall I would fly like a bird, carried by the wind before I splashed into the sea. The seals were nothing more than dark shapes, the beach on which they were laying a white blur. I was standing on the edge of the world. It would take less than a heartbeat to leave the island, my family and my life behind. I wanted to feel the waves over my body, to see the light disappear from under the murky waters. I wanted to glide down to the shadowy depths with the seals...

Of course I didn't jump. I saw my mother at the beach below, a black-and-white shape that could not be mistaken for a seal. The weary feeling of before seeped into my bones.. She was moving smoothly, as if she were gliding over the beach rather than walking. Her white dress hung over her spindly frame and her black hair was a mess. She spread her arms, twirling or dancing. For a moment she looked like a little whirlwind spinning into the surf; then she lost her balance and fell over. I ran down the steep path that led to the beach, where the sound of the wind was drowned out by the roar of the waves. Mother staggeringly pulled herself up and stared at the waves. She was shivering.

I remembered that before, she'd often come to the beach and let the waves wash over her feet. Even then I'd always had the feeling that she saw something beneath the waves that nobody else could; that she heard things that were hidden from the rest of us.'

I asked if she had hurt herself. If she was cold. As usual, she kept quiet.

*

It's strange. I remember how she used to sing for me when I was little, and at the same time I can't remember that my mother had ever been happy. And yet sometimes she suddenly sees and hears me again, as if a veil has been pulled away from her cloudy thoughts.

I had to pull her all the way back home.

The ashes in the fireplace were long cold.. I started a new fire and helped Mother into a clean dress.

Before, she used to wear beautiful dresses which made her look like a fairy from the Other World. At that moment, Benji burst into the house, complaining that he was starving.

Of course he was hungry, we were all hungry, but my brother never seems to have had enough, not even when our neighbour Tamsin feeds us a little extra. He was also clutching that dreadful jar of maimed insects and he got even angrier when I took it from him and shook it empty into the fire. They're just stupid bugs to him. Sometimes, I don't know what's wrong with him.

I couldn't soothe him when I said that Fergus could return at any moment, with a fresh catch of fish. It only seemed to enrage him more. Benji still thinks that Fergus will start to take care of us. He even calls him "Father" still, as if that could somehow persuade Fergus to take an interest in his own children. It makes me so angry when Benji says such things. Fergus is no father. He returns home each day, reeking of liquor, hitting Benji whenever he does something he doesn't like.

I watched Mother and Benji, noticing how skinny they were. I didn't need a mirror to know that I was getting thinner myself. I was very sure that we'd never survive the winter if we kept hoping that Fergus would feed us. Mother was already at death's door, and for months Benji has had a peculiar look in his eyes that makes me uncomfortable, even though I can't quite place why. Sometimes he looks so much like Fergus that it unsettles me.

I'm also unsettled by the state of our house. Long ago it had been beautiful with a concave roof and walls decorated in colourful stone and shell patterns. It has since become a sad place. The walls are dirty, the floor caked in mud and the cabinets and wardrobes are covered in a thick layer of dust. Everything and everyone feels broken. Mother, Benji, our house. And me. I have the feeling that a great tear is running through me and that I can fall apart at any moment.

When I wanted to take Mother to Tamsin, she stood there like a child who'd lost her doll. If I could have just run out of the door, I'd have found a cave to crawl up in. She didn't respond to any of my questions, so I left her with Benji.

It's risky to go into the hills at falling dusk, for it is too easy to slip and break something. But if Fergus wouldn't return with the fish, at least we would have brambles.

From the highest peak of Avalon, you can see all the villages. Their lanterns shine like stars in the darkness, save for the furthest village, where no one was living anyone. I'd often wondered whether we should just flee to one of the nearby villages but I had always discarded that plan again. Avalon is too small a place to hide, no matter where we would go.

*

When I returned with a bucket full of brambles, the barn was on fire. I don't know how the fire could have caught on so rapidly. My barn, where all summer long I'd stored sheepskins in the hope of washing, carding and spinning the wool over the winter. Tamsin would lend me the necessary materials and had promised to let me keep the profit for myself. It was the only way I could earn a little money without Fergus having any say in it.

My first thought was that I had to make sure that Mother was safe, but she stood at a small distance, watching the people quenching the flames

Fergus appeared next to her, and he was reeking of liquor again. When I kept asking him where Benji was, he yelled at me. He yelled that it was not his fault that Benji had fallen down. I screamed at him and he delivered a blow to my face. He called after me what a fool I was when I ran through the flames. Benji was unconscious in a corner. I think he had been trying to save my wool when he had gotten overwhelmed by the smoke. How I managed it I cannot quite remember, but I dragged him out. Somebody threw some water over me. It took a long time for me to cough the smoke from my lungs. Benji came to and Tamsin made him drink water. Ana had spotted the fire and had come down to our house. She stayed by my side the entire time, holding my hand. I could only watch Fergus, who was finally bringing pales of water like the others. I wagered that it had been his lantern that had been left too close to the dry wool! Had Fergus left Benji to his fate when the smoke had taken hold of him? My blood was boiling under my skin.

I've hit him. Right in his face, the way he had hit me. I have spat at his feet and I've raged at him. Fergus didn't do anything. I think he was too shocked to be mad.

After that, I yelled at Mother. I'm not proud of it, but I just couldn't contain it anymore. Benji could have died and she had just stood there, like a ragdoll! Only when my rage had petered out and all I could do was weep, she quietly stretched out her hand to me. Her icy cold fingers shocked me.

She hugged me so gently, as if we were made of glass and could break at any moment. I smelled her: it was the sea, the eternal scent of the sea that hung over her.

The embrace came too late. We were already broken.

*

I've taken Benji away to Tamsin. She was the one who eventually told me the saddest story I had ever heard. I refused to believe it at first but Tamsin calmly insisted it was true. She didn't force me to take her at her word: she simply asked me to go take a look in the cave myself. The next day I decided to go.

August 2117 A.D.

What I found in the cave

Ana insisted on coming with me when I rowed to Gull Island. Without her friendship, I think I might have lost my mind years ago.

The cave was like an open mouth in a protruding rock face. Tamsin had warned me that it was only accessible at low tide, as at other times the entrance would be covered with water. Whoever was stupid enough to go in there when the tide was rising would be unable to find a way out and would drown. The moment I looked up at the narrow opening with the sound of the retreating water behind me, I was afraid. Afraid of the long climb up, of the hard fall I'd suffer if I lost my grip on the rocks, of the water than could rise so quickly, but above all, I was afraid of what might be waiting for me inside.

Ana has a terrible fear of heights. I assured her that she could wait for me down on the beach, rolled up my sleeves and began to clamber up the rock face.

It was tougher than I'd thought. I could hear my heart beating in my ears, overpowering the sounds of the sea, the seagulls, and Ana's shouts of warning coming from the beach.

The opening of the cave was narrow. Inside, it was pitch black and it smelled of rotting fish. I really should have brought a candle. The small amount of daylight that shone from the entrance of the cave finally let me see the first part of the cavity: the ground was strewn with objects from the sea, as I had expected; the damp walls were covered with algae and the twisted stalagmites seemed to rise up out of the stone, like strange beings from the Other World. I could imagine any one of them suddenly coming to life and scaring me senseless.

The few sprigs of sage that I'd brought with me, I left on the floor. I hoped that it was enough and that the Other World would protect me rather than hamper me, now that I was trying to unravel its secrets I wasn't doing this for myself, after all, but for my mother...For Sela..

I left the lighter part of the cave behind me and it grew even darker around me. This seemed to be the only way inside, but if I wasn't quick enough, the sea would crush me.

I must admit it was in that moment that I almost decided to turn back. There was an eerie pounding in my chest and every heartbeat seemed to bring the rising tide nearer.

How long I walked, I still don't know today. The track was steadily going upwards. It got narrower and lower until I was forced to crawl along it on my knees, all the while wondering how Fergus had ever been able to get down here.

Just when I felt I couldn't go on any further, I sawdaylight.. I entered a hall The space was large and round, with a dome in the roof that let me see the sky.

I knew I had found Mother's secret when my eyes fell upon the dark bundle. Fergus had thrown seal's hide into the far corner, as if he hadn't cared about the state it would be in, so long asone would ever find it..

This was Sela's secret, which she'd kept quiet about all these years, which had kept her a prisoner, and which had made us all so unhappy. To see it here in a crumpled pile thrown carelessly on the floor made my heart sink.

The hide felt dry and brittle in my hands. I was worried I'd tear it.. It was also much smaller than I'd imagined. I might be able to wear it as a cloak, but itseemed impossible that Sela would fit into it. For a long while, all I did was examine the neglected, sealskin. Without a doubt the strangest treasure anyone had ever hidden or found ...

August 2117 A.D.

The first day after Sela's departure

She's gone. She stood on the beach, her dress cast off like torn rags, and let her body be lashed by the north wind and the flurries of sand carried with it. She said

*nothing to me, not even a goodbye. She took my head in her hands and kissed me..
I could taste the sea on her lips.*

*Without Sela, Fergus's anger seems to have doubled. The worst thing is that he
takes it all out on Benji. Last night he came back to Tamsin's house covered in
bruises and all I could do was treat him with comfrey, while his burns had barely
healed. Benji didn't cry – he never cries – but I saw something else in his eyes...And
to be honest, it terrified me. It's understandable that he's angry; he hates Fergus as
much as I do, but the look he gave me was the same look that Fergus would give us at
times: a look of disgust, a desire to destroy something. I'm scared for Benji, scared
of what Fergus is destroying within him. A few hours ago I caught him again with
that terrible jar of insects, which he seems to hold onto both day and night. Half
of the creatures were writhing at the bottom while Benji pulled off their legs and
wings one by one. I don't know what has gotten into him. Maybe it numbs his own
pain. I wish I could make him stop, but he insists that I'm being too dramatic about
it.*

*Without Sela I no longer seem to have any purpose. To avoid Fergus and Benji,
I spend every day wandering over the island. I stand again on the cliffs, close to the
edge, thinking of whether to jump or not. I want to dive down with the seals – if
they came to catch me. Would they come? Would she come?*

*Every day the same song runs through my head; it pursues me, I dream of it, I
wake up with it in the morning and go to sleep with it still ringing in my ears. The
song that Mother used to sing:*

Oh, isle of my dreams, full of heather and moor

Where the wind 'round the hilltops will whisper and roar

Where the waves and the sand like two lovers do meet

I must part now and leave you, my lone island sweet

So farewell and adieu, my well-beloved land

With your wild, foaming waves and your wide open strands

And adieu and farewell, my heart shall be there

On my lovely sweet island, wherever I fare.

*

*Sela has left, so why don't we? There is nothing for us here, only an empty house,
a burnt-out barn, and Fergus. I'd miss Ana, but I know her life here is good.And*

what does Benji have apart from his sweet Esoldi? Bruises and burns, that's all. I'd have to ask him what he thinks about my plan, but the more I think about it the surer I get. One last effort to free my family. At the first light of morning I shall …

A large burn mark has destroyed the rest of Mum's words. Disappointed, I turn the page. I can't make out what else Mum has written about Sela or about her preparations, but eventually I find words that are legible once again. Relieved, I dive straight back into the story.

I can't believe that we are on the eve of departure. I still can't quite come to terms with what we are about to do; this island is the only place I have ever known. No one knows exactly what lies beyond the sea … are there ports? Cities perhaps? Probably. They say the world has been a different place since the meteorite struck, but that holds no meaning for me. For me and Benji, the world will be a strange place no matter what. But also a new beginning, and that's the idea I cling to most dearly.

A little while ago, Esoldi visited us. She insisted that she wanted to go with us and Benji got it into his head that he wouldn't go if she couldn't come along. I didn't know what to say, for fear that this would put our flight in danger and Fergus would thwart our attempt. I told Esoldi that she could come with us, on the condition that she won't change her mind when we are already halfway. She and Benji went down to her house walking hand in hand to get things packed. I've warned them that we can't take much. The boat is too small for three people and their luggage. I've packed a dry dress. One of Mother's – the light blue dress she took off before she stood naked on the beach.

I'm also taking my pouch of herbs and plants, clean underwear, a lantern and this book. That's all I can think of, except for food, drink and a knife.

Spirits preserve me, my head is about to burst.

August 2117 A.D.
The seventh day after Sela's departure

Dawn has broken, but only just. We have to go. I haven't slept at all and I dare not close this book. Benji is calling me from downstairs. Come on, Rona, do what you have to do. If you're not strong, no one else will be.

On the next page my mother has drawn a sky above a stormy sea. Five pointy stars are arranged along the horizon like a garland. In the corner she has scribbled a few sentences in tiny lettering.

'So farewell and adieu, my well-beloved land'... Whenever I see these stars in the sky, I will be sure that they are twinkling in the sky above the hills of my homeland.

The day has finally come and the sun is getting stronger. We lifted the oars and Benji has hoisted the small sail. With the strong wind that was brewing, all he needed to do was sit down at the helm. I have no room to move and nothing to do other than to write in my diary. We're on our way, we really are. In the semi-darkness of the early morning, the island lingered behind us like a shadow for a while, but by now all trace of it is gone. Now there's only sea before us, behind us and as an immeasurable depth below us. The sea that I love so dearly. And yet, this immense mass of water is overwhelming, especially when I realise that all that separates us from it is a thin, wooden boat.

*

Was this the right decision? Benji looks quite relaxed, but his eyes betray his true feelings, the uncertainty he must feel within just like me. Esoldi has turned towards the horizon, as if she can summon the continent if she looks out long enough.

What if there's no more land? What if we won't fit in over there? What if a storm comes and we all perish?

No – I know that we've made the right decision. I just cannot say whether our escape was timely or not.. Benji hasn't spoken of the fire in quite some time. He no longer complains of the bruises that he carries as mementos of Fergus's fists... and he doesn't talk about Sela at all. Maybe he does talk to Esoldi. When she takes his hand or whispers something in his ear, I see his face light up.

Isn't it strange that, in spite of all my talk of never returning, all I can think of is home? That I sit here in the boat feeling terrified that over time, I'll forget my mist-shrouded island? It seems to me that should anyone else ever get their hands on this book, he or she will think that there's nothing pleasant or precious on that island. But that couldn't be further from the truth. My island home is beautiful all year round.

The best time of day is just after dawn, when the fresh, new sunlight falls onto the cliffs and causes the sea to shimmer like a large diamond. Further inland there are hills and valleys in hundreds of shades of green. When summer is at its height, this rolling landscape transforms into an endless sea of purple heather. The sea changes colours every day, together with the sky. In the gardens and valleys wild apple trees grow, so that in spring the island is covered in blossom like the veil of a young bride. If I close my eyes I can hear the eternal cries of the seagulls that live in huge colonies on Gull Island, and on the sandbanks just before the shore I can see the dark shapes of seals. All year round the morning mist clings to the edge of the island, as if it wants to protect the islanders from the outside world.

I had better stop writing now, before Benji and Esoldi see me crying.

August 2117 A.D.
The first night at sea

I was jolted awake and am now writing by the light of the lantern hanging on the mast next to me. The wind has picked up and is shaking the boat back and forth. The sail is holding strong and from what I can tell we are still on course. Despite the swell of the sea Benji and Esoldi are fast asleep. I had a strange dream: a pale man stood before and spoke to me, although his lips did not move. He said 'be brave and strong, Rona, daughter of Sela.' Right now I don't feel I could be either of those things. The darkness hangs over me like a suffocating blanket.

After that bleak comment, a page is missing from the book. On the page after that, my young mother seems to have regained some of her spirits. She describes her relief when they finally moor at a dock in a small town, and her amazement at the grey clothes of the residents, the square buildings, the straight roads and the cars that she had only seen as wrecks on the edge of her village. Still, her doubts re-emerge soon enough – where have they landed and where should they go next? I wonder if it was a harbour in Gwennec that she had found, but nothing in mum's descriptions can give me a clear answer to that question.

Money. Not one second have I considered money before. The few coins that I still have in my pocket turn out to be of no value here on the mainland. This means we have nothing: no room, no bed, and no chance to have a roof over our heads. We are homeless. I never thought I'd have to use that word. Any sense of relief about our escape has dried up completely, transformed into a burning sense of guilt. It feels like the demons in my head would rather choose home over the great unknown that awaits us here.

Benji said we should go; that we should start walking, if only to keep warm. A helpful man with a red hat has given us directions to a bigger town. Benji is more motivated than I am, so I've let him take the lead.

*

My diary is the only thing that I can cling to at the moment. This book reminds me of why we left. It reminds me of what I must not forget. Perhaps I will reread it one day, in the knowledge that this was the path we all had to take in order to emerge from the darkness.

August 2117 A.D.
The new world

Esoldi just accosted me. 'I thought you had a plan,' she said to me. No doubt she's beginning to think it would have been better not to have come with us.

Everyone's hungry. The last good meal we've had was at Tamsin's house…no, I have to stop thinking of home; that will lead us nowhere. I must look ahead, think and work out a strategy. The priority for now is money… I suppose we could work somewhere and start earning an income. The port would have been a good place if Benji would have been willing to do some fishing, but that is too far away now. If the city we are headed to is really as big as the man claimed, then surely we will find something there? I realise that we don't know this world or its norms, but all three of us have hands that we can put to work. I should allow myself to hold out some cautious hope.

*

A wagon just passed us by, drawn by two oxen. Benji jumped up and begged the driver if we could hitch a ride. On the seat of the cart was a woman. She didn't look terribly friendly, but she allowed us to climb up on the back. We are now crammed together, in between stinking sacks, which seem to contain some kind of root vegetable. I don't know if the people here eat these, but the smell isn't very inviting for sure.

*

The woman said something worrisome. I asked her if she had any work for us. She said she did not, and added there was no work to be found in the countryside these days.

Then the woman said we should avoid the city as if it were a dung pile. She told us about a sickness. The Black Influenza, they call it. A sickness that gives you black scabs all over your skin and makes you bleed in places where blood shouldn't come out, she said. In a matter of days your body stops working.

The tiny glimmer of hope that I was desperately clinging to immediately slipped away.

*

We are yet again at the side of the road. The city is waiting for us in the distance. All we have to do is walk down the road to get there.

Benji thinks we should risk it. I don't think he has quite taken the woman seriously, or else he doesn't betray his fear of this frightful disease. I want to convince him to stay far away from the city, but I can't come up with good enough reasons to do so. If we stay here sitting next to the barren fields, I'm afraid that we'll die of cold, hunger and exhaustion sooner rather than later. The countryside offers no jobs, if we are to believe the woman...

I have to be realistic: the prospects are far from encouraging, but at least in the city we'll have a chance of finding warmth, shelter and something hot to eat. The city is our only hope. If this disease comes our way, I will...

A low, unfamiliar rumbling distracts me from my reading. I look around me, not quite able to place where the sound is coming from. Is it the machines at work in the Oakfield? No, it can't be – not at this time of night. What's more, the sound is far too close to be coming from the oil platforms. I peer down at Arthur's bed to see if he is awake, but he's still fast asleep. The sound grows louder. My heart unwittingly begins to beat faster. With an ominous premonition, I move over to the window, open the shutters, and look outside.

5

THE HUNGRY SEA

For a few moments I stand staring without comprehension at the scene that is unfolding before me in the darkness. It must be an illusion; the night playing tricks on me…I grab a lantern. The light falls over the huge mass of water that is flowing past our house, as if we were a rock in the middle of a river. It dawns on me that the groaning is caused by the water: the sea is flowing with such force past our house that its walls are creaking around us.

I stagger back and hold onto the wardrobe to support myself. Suddenly the air seems to have vanished from the room.

Think, Nimue, do something! I open the wardrobe, grab a handful of clothes and chuck them on Arthur's bed, after which I shake him awake. Arthur lets out a cry.

I turn away from him, feverishly heaving on my trousers, jumper and anorak. Where's the lamp? What should I take?

'Nim!'

'Water!' I cry, while I feel around me in a state of panic for things I have to take with me. My hands grab the diary and I tuck it underneath my anorak, not really realising what I'm doing. 'Water everywhere! Look outside!'

Arthur turns to the window and makes a choking sound. 'What should we do?'

Get Grandma and go to the church. I'm too stunned to answer out loud and I have no idea if there still is a church or even if we can get that far without being swept away, or if…My head is spinning. Together we stumble out of the bedroom, the lantern in my hand. Gran is asleep downstairs. I start to blindly run down the stairs, but Arthur grabs my arm.

'Let me go! We have to...' Then I look downstairs. My whole body goes numb. There is no longer a downstairs; only cold, murky water that roars under the staircase like some sort of sea monster.

'No... No, we have to ...' I stammer out.

If the water has already reached so high, that means the living room, the kitchen and Gran's bed-box have already been flooded... As soon as the awful truth hits me it's as if something in my head bursts. I scream and scream until I feel a tug on my arm and I realise Arthur is trying to pull me away from the staircase. Bile bubbles in my throat and I struggle to breathe. On top of my sheer disbelief, another voice begins to scream in my head: *Get out! We'll both drown if we stay here!*

That thought clears my mind instantly and I rush to the other side.

'Nim, where should we go?'

We reach the ladder. 'Higher! We need to get to the hole in the roof.' I press the lantern into his hand and push him forward. He climbs up and I follow behind. The attic is darker than ever: if we didn't have the lantern, I wouldn't know where to go.

A loud thud reverberates through the house and throws us to the floor. I remain shocked on the floor while I try to gauge what's happened. Below us the sound of the water is swelling.

'Arthur!' My heart pounds in my head. The whole house seems to be leaning to one side. I creep across the attic to where I think the gap is and thrust the lantern out in front of me. I feel Arthur's hand gripping mine and trembling, we make it up there. 'Hurry. I think the house is going to collapse.'

'This way.' He leads me past the items I was looking at not a few hours earlier, past the wardrobe under which I found the key, to the hole in the roof. An ice-cold wind blows over us. 'I... I think we have to jump.'

'Jump...' I'm unable to form a whole sentence. I look around helplessly. My gaze is drawn to the disused chest on which Arthur has placed the lantern. I pull it towards us. 'Climb up. Crawl over the roof on your stomach and don't let go before I get there.'

He nods. In the dim light I see an anxious grimace on his face. His eyes dart back and forth nervously. 'Don't wait!' I insist. 'Go!'

He jumps on the chest, thrusts his hands out and pulls himself up. For a moment I think he won't make it, but then he bends his legs and disappears from sight. I scramble after him, but the second I want to pull myself through the hole, I turn around one last time.

The attic is dimly lit by the warm glow of the lantern. I catch a glimpse of the old seal figurehead and I know with sudden, painful certainty that I will never see this house again. All the treasures that are still waiting for us here will now disappear under the waves of the sea forever.

'Nim, come on!' Arthur stretches his arm out and I force myself back into reality, grab him and let him help me onto the sloping roof of our house. I stare down at the raging waters below us. The roof shudders, as if the house knows it is losing its battle against the water. The mud brick walls of the house could give way at any moment. If that happens, Arthur and I will inevitably be swept into the maelstrom of debris.

Somewhere above the roar of the wind, the chimes of Saint Gwenhael's begin to ring out. The sound penetrates like a lifeline through this nightmare. It is something to focus on, a guiding light in the stifling darkness. If the bell is chiming, there must be people inside the church. We have to go there.

I slowly stand up and look past my feet down below. I can hardly see anything but I know there's only one way out: diving into the icy cold lap of the water below. Arthur and I grasp each other's hand. *You have to be strong, Nimue. Look after your brother. Never let him out of your sight...*

Before I can think, before the house collapses, I close my eyes and jump down, my arms wrapped around Arthur. As we splash into the ice-cold water all the air in my body seems to escape. The water fills my nose, my ears and my mouth. In a flash I return to my dream, the first night of the storm before Arthur woke me up. Swimming underwater seemed so simple then.

The current pulls me down left and right. I try to swim upwards but I'm hindered by the rising pressure of the water. It's as if I can hear my name coming from down there: 'Nimue, Nimue!' A thousand moving shadows try to grab me like whirling seaweed wrapping itself around my wrists and ankles to pull me down. I try to free myself, trying to find some sort of strength. What is above and what is below? Have I already drowned? I can still feel a heavy pain in my chest, which gets worse and worse with every second until it feels like I'm going to burst. Air... I need air!

Unexpectedly something grabs me and pulls me up.

'Try to kick,' gasps Arthur in my ear.

I try to get my legs moving but it's a struggle. The cold is numbing. I hold on to Arthur and try to swim against the current. The sound of the bells chiming is temporarily drowned out by the water roaring around my ears.

'Look out!'

Arthur pulls me over to one side. A cart is coming towards us with terrific speed and pushes a rapid current of water before it. I have the presence of mind to grab hold of the seat, which juts out of the water. Arthur follows my example immediately. We're dragged on a little way, but then our weight keeps the cart from floating any further. We pull ourselves halfway out of the water. I gasp for breath and wipe the stinging seawater from my eyes.

'The church is behind us,' says Arthur hoarsely. I'm astonished he can still orientate himself, but he's always been the better navigator out of the two of us. I look around in hope of seeing some sort of landmark.

'It's so dark,' I moan, 'and there's too much water.'

'It's not far. We'll have to swim.'

Swim? Sweet Gwenhael! I don't know if I have the strength to keep holding on to the side of the cart, let alone battle against the power of the sea. 'Are you sure?'

'Listen!'

I hold my breath and focus as best as I can on something other than the sound of water or wind. And yes, I can hear it: the bells are still ringing out, determined to be heard by all those who are still fighting for their lives.

It dawns on me that I can no longer feel my hands on the cart. The cold is going to kill us quicker than any drowning might, something I know all too well after Dad's accident. I dig deep for my last modicum of strength. Together we let go of the cart and swim against the current. Arthur's hand slips out of mine.

I need all my limbs to keep above the water and can't afford to grab him again. I fervently pray that we don't lose each other.

The struggle is sucking all the energy from my body. I lose all sense of time. Suddenly my foot touches upon something hard.

The bottom of this flood. Land!

I haul myself out of the water onto the dry hilltop. It isn't the hill where St Gwenhael's is but from here there is a winding path which leads to the church. I think the waters won't rise any further. I collapse like a wrecked ship, spitting out sea water and taking the deepest breaths possible as I do so. My body feels beaten, but we're here, and we're still alive – that is the most important thing. I look aside to find Arthur.

My heart stops. Where is he?

'Arthur? Arthur!'

He was just next to me. I heard him shouting and splashing! How can he have disappeared so suddenly? I only let him out of my sight briefly, no more than a few seconds... panic begins to brew in my mind. God, what have I done?

'Arthur!' I get no answer.

My self-control gives way as I begin to sob hysterically. Somewhere in my mind I realise I'm soaking wet. It makes no difference. I stand up, my knees trembling. The sea is still calling my name. I can hear it clearly now, better than before: 'Nimue, Nimue!'

I tremble as I breathe and stagger towards the edge of the hill, one foot in the water, where I stare down below with nothing to see. What should I do? I've broken my promise to Mum; I let Arthur go. He is now drifting somewhere under the surface of the water, gone before I could even turn my head. That's life; fragile as sunlight dancing on the water, and just as easily broken. Perhaps I should just follow him?

I don't move. My heart is pounding painfully, my lungs sucking up air over and over again. My body refuses to give itself over to the hungry sea, even though I don't know whether the alternative, a life without Arthur, would be worth living for.

In the middle of that solemn thought a movement catches my eye. It floats up briefly, then it's gone. I wade into the stream, careful to not be swept away with it again myself, and frantically scour my surroundings.

'Arthur, is that you?'

For a moment I see nothing except for the debris from the houses and the broken tree branches, but then it bobs up again: a mop of blond hair and a white face. It's enough to fill me with hope.

'Over here!' I cry. 'The hill is here!' I stretch my arms out towards him. For a time he fights silently, struggling against the water and I try to catch him. Eventually our fingers intertwine and I'm able to drag him onto the dry slope.

As soon as he's safe I pull him towards me and hold him tight in my arms.

'I'll never let you go!' I promise him in between tears. 'I'll never let you out of my sight again.'

6

—·—

THE PROTECTION OF SAINT GWENHAEL

As soon as we enter the church I hear a shriek. Yannick runs towards me and gives me a spontaneous hug. 'You're safe! Oh sweet Gwenhael, I was so worried!'

After a long pause she lets me free and looks around. 'Where's your grandmother?'

I helplessly open my mouth, but the words get caught in my throat.

'Oh Nimue,' whispers Yannick and she wraps her arms around me once again, more tenderly this time. I lean into her and begin to sob against her shoulder. They are long, hard sobs. Yannick strokes my hair and mumbles something that I can't quite hear. After a while I feel another pair of arms around my midriff: it is Arthur. We stand in the middle of the church, bound to each other like a chain. Only when I have no more tears left do I take a look around me. There are so few people. Icy, cold fingers of horror seem to grip onto my heart.

With trembling knees I sink to the ground. Granny, Yssi, the house ... *Let this only be a nightmare*, I beg inwardly. *Let me wake up from this.*

Arthur crouches down next to me and wraps his arms around my shoulders. Yannick crawls over to my other side and squeezes my hand.

It takes a while before I have room for other thoughts. 'Yannick, are your parents okay?'

Yannick nods. 'They're over there. We brought some blankets. Not as many as we would have liked, but...'

I nod, too stunned to take in the rest of what she was saying.

50

'Have you been able to save anything?' she asks.

Arthur shakes his head. 'Only what we were wearing. I'm still wearing the same pyjamas,' he adds after a brief silence, as if surprised he hadn't noticed it earlier.

'It's icy cold here,' says Yannick. 'Wait a moment; I'll fetch a blanket for you.'

I look around the church again. I recognise the faces of Jost the Netter, Flat Hannah and her daughter, from whom I got my plimsolls. I see Franseza with her husband, Mr Madec, who has such a bad back that he has to be cared for at home by their daughter Rozenn. I try to see where she is, but the pair seem to have come alone. I quickly turn my head, as I can't bear the thought of their grief.

The doors of the church open and another family comes in, their faces turned pale, dripping wet and shivering from cold and shock. There is Mart, his father and his younger brother. Their mother Orla is nowhere to be seen.

A feeling of weakness spreads from my head to my feet. The night will go on for hours. Long unbearable hours in which people will come into the church without their child, their mother, their sister... and I know them all. The survivors. The dead. Every missing face feels like a knife in my stomach. But the idea that Grandma is no longer with us hurts the most.

When Yannick returns I'm violently trembling. She hands us a woollen blanket.

'H-how did you get a hold of these?' I ask, my teeth chattering. 'All those things ...' I make a vague gesture towards the chapel, where in addition to a pile of blankets there are first aid kits and flasks of water. Yannick's father stands watch over these valuable treasures.

'We heard the bells toll. Dad looked out of the window and saw the village below being flooded. Take those wet clothes off. You too, Arthur.'

I feel uneasy. The church is dark, dimly lit by the flickering candles dotted here and there, but nonetheless I feel my cheeks turn red as I remove my jumper, trousers and t-shirt. Yannick waits until we're standing shivering in our underwear, then wraps the blanket around us. Immediately I feel the cold melt away.

'He told us to bring all the blankets we had to the church because he knew people would have fled there. I wanted to go to your place.' Something in her restrained appearance begins to crack. Yannick sniffs. 'I wanted to run to your house as fast as I could, but the road was blocked. I couldn't...'

I clasp her cold hand. 'We only had a few minutes, you couldn't have saved us.'

'But your house! Your grandmother and Yssi and ...'

I bow my head. 'The water rose so quickly. I don't think anyone could have got there on time.'

Before Yannick can say anything, another group staggers into the church. I quickly turn and see that the children all look worn and ragged. I reckon they are no more than ten years old. Yannick looks hesitantly from me to them before I muster up a faint smile. 'Go. They need you.'

'But ...'

'Go, it's fine,' says Arthur. 'Nim and I have each other.'

Yannick nods, gives us a quick hug and hurries over to the young ones to take them into the chapel. For a while Arthur and I are silent, huddled against each other beneath the covers.

I spread my anorak across the floor in order to dry it out. The leather-bound book, Mum's hidden treasure, falls out of the pocket onto the ground. During the terrifying moments after the flood I didn't think about it. Even now, it feels like an age ago that I was sitting in bed reading it. The leather cover looks damp, but it seems the waterproof pocket on the inside of my anorak has protected it rather well.

Arthur picked up the book. 'What is this?'

'A diary.' I hesitate. The diary seems so unimportant right now, but Arthur has just as much right to read it as I do. I shouldn't have kept it hidden. Of course Dad would have wanted Arthur to read it too. I feel a fool.

I carefully open the first few pages so Arthur can see them, making sure to not damage the damp pages any more than the fire has done already. 'It was in a locked chest in the attic. Dad wanted me to have it. Here...' I pull the pendant from my neck and hand it to him. 'This was also in there. I think it was Mum's.'

He stares at the chain, then back down at the book in my hands. 'Mum's diary?'

'Yes.'

'Did she write anything about us?' He suddenly seems so very young; his sea-blue eyes wide open.

I slowly shake my head as I turn back to the beginning. 'I think she was still young when she started writing.'

'Doesn't it say why she left?'

'I don't know. The book is half gone. Some of the pages are completely missing.'

He feels the large burn mark on the first page. 'So what does she write about?'

'I'll read it to you.' I put my arms around him and Arthur nestles against me, just like he used to when Mum had just left and I tried to console him with tales of enchanted princes and the untrustworthy seal people. Fairy tales that Mum used to tell me when I was young. I wet my lips and quietly begin to read from the diary: 'Let me begin at the beginning ...'

Mum's story seems to envelop us like a second blanket. As I read, it's as if the words come to life before my eyes. I see her going down to the beach at day break and stepping into small boat with a boy and a girl. The boat disappears over the water. Mum leans over the book which I now hold in my hands and as they sail, she tries to find the words to describe what has turned their life upside-down. Again, I'm unable to figure out what was the matter with Sela, Mum's own mother, and where she had gone. *Disappeared* is what Mum calls it again and again, just like she did all these years later when she abandoned me with me making the promise to always look after Arthur for her. When I come to the part where the woman on the cart warns them of the fearsome Black Influenza, my voice wavers and I fall silent.

Arthur looks as if he has just awoken from a dream. 'Why did you stop?'

'This is the last page I read,' I mutter. 'It was here that I heard the water racing under our window and that's when I stopped reading.'

'Don't you want to carry on reading?' Arthur seems unsure of it himself.

'I don't know.' I lean my head against the cold wall. It's such a sad story, and to be honest I feel too full of my own misery to continue reading.

'Mum was scared when she wrote this,' says Arthur, as my silence continues. 'and homeless, just like we are.'

'Indeed.' The bitterness of my laugh surprises me. 'What a coincidence.'

'And we have some family, Nim. Benji is our uncle.'

I hadn't thought about that. I let the words sink in. Up until this moment, my family has consisted only of Arthur and Gran, as well as Mum and Dad when they were still here with us. We had always been a small family, especially when compared to other families nearby, who sometimes lived with grandparents and aunts and uncles all under the same roof. I have never given much attention to Mum's side of the family, but Arthur's right: thanks to the diary we're now aware of Benji's existence. An uncle! And Fergus and Sela, Mum's parents, are our grandparents.

'It's a shame that our new grandfather was such a brute,' I remark. 'He drove them from the island, it seems.'

'The island.' Arthur looks at me astounded. 'I always thought that it was made up, like those other stories you used to tell me.'

'The ones that Mum used to tell, you mean,' I correct him. 'I thought the same thing.'

I turn the pages to see if the water has damaged any more of the book and my eyes are caught by a short, hastily scribbled piece of text.

Every time someone raises their voice or makes a sudden gesture I see Benji flinch. I don't know how long it will be before the haunted look leaves his eyes ... perhaps Fergus had damaged him so much that he'll never completely recover. My heart bleeds for him.

'She made that whole trip just in order to protect him,' I say. But if she cared for her brother so much, why couldn't she stay with us, her own children? Didn't we need her too?

'Where do you think they got to?' asks Arthur. 'When they reached the mainland, I mean. Was that in Breizh?'

I shrug my shoulders. 'All she mentions is a harbour. I'm wondering where Benji is now.'

'Perhaps he's dead, seeing as Mum never mentioned him.'

'Mum didn't tell us a whole bunch of things.'

'Maybe she went to him?'

'Who knows?' Or maybe he knew where we could find her. He was her brother, after all. 'If we can find him, maybe he can help us.'

'How do we know where we need to look?' Arthur reasons. 'We don't know anything about him.'

He has a point. Before I discovered the book, we never even knew that Mum had a brother, let alone that she'd fled with him in a boat across the sea. I bite my lip and ponder it for a moment. We might be able to find the port that she wrote about, but it'd be a long and daunting quest. How many towns that fit Mum's description are there just on the coast of Breizh alone? Hundreds, I think, and our town is just one of them. Even if we do manage to find the port, what then? It seems unlikely that someone might still remember that ragged group of travellers from so long ago.

'Well, perhaps we can find a clue in the diary,' I finally say. 'We've only read the beginning. Who knows, maybe Mum wrote where she went and why.'

My hands tingle in excitement as I turn the pages to the section that I haven't yet read. I yearn to plunge myself back into Rona's strange tale, to finally get to know her at last, even if it's only from the pages of an old book. I then turn to look at Arthur, who is sitting next to me. Suddenly I see how pale he is, how small he looks at that very moment, with the woollen blanket wrapped around him and his hair wet with seawater. Dark bags are under his eyes and there's a bleeding cut across his cheek.

It dawns on me how late it is. I push the book to one side. 'Go to sleep. If you're asleep you don't have to think about...all this.'

'But I want to read what she's written.'

'Can I read on while you're asleep?'

'No. We have to do it together.'

'Okay. Together.' I close the book and fasten the string around it. Then, I wrap my arms around Arthur and pull him close in an effort to stay as warm as possible.

'Do you think she loved us?' asks Arthur quietly.

'Of course.' I give him a kiss on the crown of his head and I'm happy to be able to hold him tight. 'Who couldn't love us?'

He gives a weak smile, which soon fades.

I hope I'm right – that Mum still loves us even though she left. I lose myself once more in the few paltry memories I still have of her. Those images form a comforting cloak on a night in which our world has fallen apart; like a talisman against the darkness of things.

The grey morning light reveals the complete destruction of our village.

We stumble outside like lost sheep, hesitating at the threshold of the church, unsure if either of us has the heart to face the bitter reality. Arthur's fingers weave into mine and I clasp my other hand on Mum's seal pendant, which hangs from my neck. The diary is pressed against my stomach, safely stored inside my anorak. And then, in horror, I set my eyes upon the fate that has befallen our village.

The waters have receded and the ground is littered with unrecognisable debris. Here and there are things I can still place: roof tiles, wooden beams and broken furniture. Just in front of my feet is a tangled fishing line that has been thrown up by the sheer force of the water. Otherwise, the immediate vicinity of the church seems untouched by the disaster. The hilltop is strangely empty; only where the narrow path reaches even ground and turns into the road to the village does the rubble seem to pile up, forming a clear marker of how high the water has risen during the night.

The further we walk along the path, the more I see the traces left by the sea: dead fish, crabs and clumps of seaweed which hang from protruding objects like strange wreathes. Where the beach once was, only a huge expanse of brown mud stretches to the sea; where the houses once stood, now only foundations remain. They remind me of the stumps of felled trees.

And another feeling sneaks up on me, cold as the invisible fingers of a hill spirit; everything is so *quiet*. The almost constant, low drone of the oil platforms is missing and the wind has become an almost unnoticeable breeze, as if the whole world were holding its breath in the wake of the terrible wave. Even the sea seems quieter and more distant than ever.

'There should be seagulls,' says Arthur, as if he were reading my mind.

I suppress a shudder. I've never seen anything of such magnitude and desolation in my entire life. It makes me speechless and empty inside.

'Do you think the water would have reached the city?'

I look in the direction of Gwennec and tiredly shrug my shoulders. 'The hills will have protected it.'

We look for a way down, stepping over the wreckage, taking a diversion when a gully of leftover water blocks our path, holding onto each other as we try not to slip on the hideous sludge that seems to coat everything. When we are halfway to our house, Arthur pulls something out of the mud, which in my daze I have mistaken for a rock. I now see that the layer of grey slime hides an old, leather backpack. Arthur turns the rucksack upside down. Out of it falls a black torch which fits in my hand like a glove when I pick it up. With my thumb I press the switch but no light comes on. No wonder. With a sigh, I return the light to the rucksack.

'How many people are under there?' mutters Arthur to my horror. The idea that there are dead people here, people who we know, turns my stomach and I have to swallow to get rid of the sour taste.

'Nim?'

'I don't want to think about it.' I turn around facing the hill. 'Let's go back to the church. I... I don't think I want to see the house.'

'But our things ...'

'They're gone. There's nothing left, Arthur, only junk.'

I feel overwhelmed, and the rest of what I want to say is cut short by a large lump in my throat. I turn around and race back up the hill again like a startled hare. I ignore the small group of people mumbling to each other next to the church, rush through the open doors and end up in front of the statue of St Gwenhael, my heart racing and a new sour taste building in my mouth. His stone face is as peaceful as ever.

'Oh God,' I mumble, and sink to my knees, my head tucked between my arms. I imagine the glaring eyes of the saints boring into the back of my neck.

'Nimue?'

I don't want to look up. The darkness of my arms is an agreeable hiding place, much safer than the outside world, but the voice is nearby. A moment later, I hear the soft rustle of clothing, then the feeling of a hand on my arched back.

'Nimue, are you ill? Do you need to throw up?' I recognise it as Franseza's voice.

'You said they were watching over us,' I whisper. With stinging eyes I look up. Franseza is so pale it looks like all the blood has drained out of her. 'You said the saints would protect us, even though they're made of stone.'

For a moment she looks at me, stunned, then shifts her gaze from my face to the altar of St Gwenhael and slowly nods. 'Nimue, long ago people didn't just make statues of saints in the hope they would protect them.'

'I think that people in the past were idiots,' I snap. 'What's the point of spending hours carving into a piece of stone if none of these icons can protect you from storms and floods?'

'Perhaps so that we, in turn, can be inspired by their goodness and strength,' says Franseza quietly. 'That's what I believe.'

I rub my eyes and sit up. 'So, what do we do now?'

'We have to organise ourselves.' She looks around and I follow the path of her gaze. The people who were lucky enough to reach the safety of the church last night now sit or stand with each other in small groups. Not everyone is there. I imagine some have gone down the hill to try to salvage some of their belongings, but most seem to have decided that it is a fruitless task. Or perhaps, like myself, they have still not yet mustered enough courage to face their destroyed homes.

I now see the church through different eyes. These walls are still standing, and have sheltered us once again when our houses could not, yet walls and a roof alone are not enough if we want to survive this day and the days hereafter. We need blankets, more blankets than Yannick could muster, as well as water and food.

'There must still be wounded survivors under the rubble,' I say, ashamed that I haven't thought of it before. 'Someone needs to look for survivors, care for the injured, see if there are any livestock still wandering about...'

'You understand what I mean,' says Franseza, a look of relief on her face. 'I want everyone inside the church.'

'Let me do that.' Now that I have a plan, my head seems to clear at last. *Be brave and strong* ... 'Perhaps they'll make a statue of me someday,' I say, with a hysterical chuckle.

Franseza doesn't smile. She turns around and marches off to the middle of the church, where the roof reaches its highest point and the light shines through the stained glass windows like a rainbow. I find Arthur and tell him what needs to be done. Together we tell the rest, send them back inside, and once everyone is gathered in a semi-circle around my old teacher, Arthur and I quietly join them.

'We need a team that can go to the hospital in Gwennec to get them up to speed,' says Franseza plainly. 'As far as I know, all the carts and vehicles have been destroyed, so you'll have to walk. Those who don't mind going on foot, raise your hands.'

A few people raise their hands, including Arthur.

'What are you doing?' I hiss at him. 'We have to stay together!'

'I want to help.'

A sense of panic comes over me, just as it had done when I'd let go of his hand and thought the sea had swallowed him up. 'We can't lose each other, Arthur! What if –'

'I'll be back sooner than you think, Nim. Don't be scared.'

'Okay.' I take a deep breath and force my body not to tremble. There's no reason to panic. 'We can go together.'

'My daughter will make preparations to care for the injured,' says Yannick's father. He sounds hoarse. His eyes have dark rings around them, yet he is unscathed. 'I myself will go out and search for survivors...and for the dead.'

'Thank you,' says Franseza quietly. 'And who will volunteer to search the rubble for remaining supplies? Mart?'

Mart, the boy who once sat next to me at school, nods.

Arthur jabs me in my side. 'You're a healer, Nim. You should stay here and help Yannick.'

'Splendid.' Franseza puts her hands together, as if she's unsure whether to clap like she did when she stood at the front of the class. 'As we all now know what teams we've been assigned to, let's get going. I'll help look for survivors.'

Arthur gives me a quick hug before joining the group that is leaving for Gwennec. I watch nervously after him until the path curves round and he disappears beyond the hill. Then, I slowly breathe out and focus my attention on the task ahead.

Together with Yannick, I collect the blankets from the night before. We make an inventory of the first aid kits and put some bottles of clean water from Mart's team aside. The water in the sacks that Yannick brought we'll use for drinking, the rest for cleaning wounds.

When the first injured arrive, we begin laying them out in rows next to one another in the chapel, gently pulling off the flakes of caked-on dirt from their wounds and getting them to drink something. By the end of the morning there are about ten men and four women on the floor. As the afternoon progresses, a further ten are added, and by nightfall there are no other new patients.

The dead are not brought to the church. I don't know where Yannick's father is taking the bodies and honestly, I don't want to think about it either. He takes me aside for a moment and puts a heavy, dirty hand on my shoulder.

'We can't find her,' he tells me. There is so much sympathy in his eyes I have to look away. I don't want to collapse and start whimpering like a dog, not now that all my strength is already going into keeping me upright.

'Nimue, you don't have to be alone. Yannick will gladly share a room with you, as long as you need it. You know that, right?'

I nod silently.

'I really am sorry. She was a tough woman. That her life should be ended like this is just...'

'Please don't.' I let out a sob before I can fight it. I know he means well, but I just can't think about it anymore. It hurts so much I can hardly breathe.

Perhaps he finally sees what his words are doing to me, because he squeezes my shoulder as an afterthought and looks down at me awkwardly. 'Oh my dear girl, I'm so sorry.'

I squeeze a few words of gratitude from my lips and turn away from him. Dear, dear Gran... I can't quite imagine what my life will be like without her. I find a quiet corner in between two recesses in the chapel and crouch down into it.

My first sobs are dry and restrained. After that, something seems to shatter within me and I cry long and hard into the crook of my arm. I rock back and forth from the pain in my chest.

I eventually wear myself out and sit there trembling. What would Grandma have wanted me to do? The dead are gone, she'd have told me. It is as if I can hear her voice. Let the dead rest and get on with living.

Dazed, I wipe my eyes dry. I've stayed behind to help Yannick, after all, and it's about time I get to it.

Yannick is dashing back and forth with reels of bandages, until our supply runs out and we are forced to use pieces of torn cloth. Never before have I felt more admiration for her, now that she's busy moving and setting bones, halting blood loss and sewing up wounds. She is a veritable angel amongst the saints of St Gwenhael. There's no time to teach me the tricks of a Medical Caretaker, so I just do what my instincts tell me.

I kneel down next to a young girl who is lying quietly in the far corner of the chapel, almost hidden behind the altar and the large statue. She looks as if she's made of twigs and spider webs, as if the slightest of touches might break her. With a shock I realise it's Katell, the flame bearer at the Sailors' Mass. Somewhere she must have a brother and sister, but she's lying here alone like an abandoned doll.

As I gently stroke her hair her eyelids flutter. I can hear her raspy breathing. Her arms are covered in bruises and there's a bloody scab on her forehead, which I examine in what little light I have in the shadows. I conclude it isn't a deep cut and she's probably hit it on a protruding object in the water during her escape. I use a little of the precious salve Yannick has in her supplies, but pull my hand back as she begins to moan and cough.

'Ssh, you're okay,' I mumble, not knowing if she has heard me or not. Katell rolls onto her side and curls up into a tense ball. Her fragile body shakes as she coughs. I've seen that posture before; not in a human, but in a dying cat. It's like she's suffocating. What should I do?

'Yannick!' I call out in panic. 'Yannick, help!'

When she doesn't answer I run to the other side of the church, where Yannick is knelt by the side of an unconscious man. She is up to her arms in blood. I look on in disgust until I shake myself out of my stupor. 'You have to help me with this girl.'

'Not right now,' Yannick says, barely looking at me. She is bent over the man and holds her hand pressed against his chest, just above his heart. 'Pass me a clean cloth.'

'But she's suffocating.'

'Cloth, now!'

I look around me, grab a more or less clean cloth that is lying on the ground and pass it to Yannick, who promptly presses it against the man's chest in a wad.

'I can't stop the bleeding,' she says with panic in her voice. 'If I let go, he'll bleed to death. I can't...'

'Katell is just a child,' I whisper. The man before me must be about fifty years old: younger than some of the injured in the church, but also a lot older than Katell. Her desperate gasps can be heard through the whole church.

Yannick closes her eyes, tired and dirty from her work. 'Take over for me here,' she then says. 'Keep the pressure on his wound. Press down firmly! Do not let go until I get back, do you understand?'

I nod, relieved but anxious at the same time, and I kneel down on the other side of the man, pushing my hands down on the wad of cloth on his chest, which is already soaked and red with the blood that has come spurting out.

'How long before he bleeds to death?' Yannick doesn't hear me; she has already gone off to tend to Katell. I can hear her making soothing sounds and saying something that I can't quite hear. I need all my concentration to keep my hands constantly pressing down on the wound, without actually knowing how hard I have to press. What if I accidentally do something that might bring him closer to death? Maybe I shouldn't have forced Yannick to leave him to me. Perhaps she was his only chance of survival.

'I'm sorry,' I whisper, the man giving no indication that he heard me.

Very soon the piece of material is soaked through. I try to ignore it and concentrate on my breathing.

In, out, in out... what kind of healer has to try her best not to faint at the sight of a patient that needs her help? I swallow a few times, trying to stop the dizziness. A healer should be able to cope with blood, even though there is now so much that my hands become dirty and sticky. On the floor is a large, dirty fishhook, almost as big as my hand. That must be the cause of this bleeding. I try to imagine the wound underneath the soiled cloths, how skin and muscle and bone have been pierced by that viciously sharp hook.

'Stay alive,' I urge him. 'So many people have already died tonight. Were you spared by the water just to die now?' I let out a shaky sigh.

On the other side of the church Katell's coughing starts to loosen up. 'See, everything's going to be okay,' I mutter to the unconscious man. 'Your body can heal itself, if you just stay alive. *Come from Camlann, lift anchor, set sail…*' I hum a few notes of a lullaby I remember from my childhood. Was it Mum or Dad who had sung it to me?

My hands begin to grow cold, very cold. That's from the fatigue, I tell myself. Now that evening has fallen, Arthur and his team must have reached Gwennec and hopefully they're mobilising the hospital crew right away. I hope they'll come soon.

Someone has lit a few candles in the church so we have a bit more light to work with. I gently pull a few millimetres of cloth away and look at the wound underneath. It may just be my imagination but the bleeding seems to have lessened, and on the wound a thin scab has formed. I take the risk of letting go and fetching a cleaner cloth, which I neatly fold before carefully placing it onto the man's chest, throwing the dirty one into the corner.

When Yannick comes back, I can hardly bend my fingers and a feeling of cold runs from my hands all the way up my arm.

'You're white as a sheet. Have you eaten anything? Mart and the others were able to save a few tins of beans.'

'It's fine,' I say as I vainly rub my hands together in an effort to warm them up. 'How is Katell?'

'She's alive. At the moment her breathing is normal.'

'What was it?'

Yannick shrugs her shoulder. 'She swallowed too much water, the cold, maybe some bronchitis. She really needs to see a doctor.'

'They'll be here soon,' I say, more to reassure myself than her.

Yannick fetches a candle and leans over to inspect the man's wound. 'Has he come to at any point?'

'No, he has…What's up?'

Yannick opens her eyes wide and holds the candle dangerously close to the makeshift bandage. I quickly move my hand to prevent the cloth from catching fire. Yannick seems to realise what she's doing and pulls the candle away, but the curious look doesn't disappear from her eyes. 'He was bleeding like a stuck pig. What did you do?'

I look at her, not understanding her question. 'I only did what you told me; keep the pressure on the wound. Then I got a clean cloth, because the other one was so dirty that I figured it wasn't good to keep using it, so I...'

Yannick looks in disbelief at my bloodied hands. 'Is that his?'

'Yes, but I think he's improving because this cloth isn't as dirty.'

'You can say that again,' mumbles Yannick. 'Take a look.' She lifts up the folded piece of fabric slightly from his torso to reveal the wound. What had been a newly formed scab when last I looked is now soft, new skin. Other than some dried-up remnants there's no blood anywhere. The hole in his chest has healed.

'But that fishhook had pierced right into him,' I stammer.

Yannick picks a loose string up from the bare skin. 'I tried stitches but they just wouldn't hold. Are you sure you didn't try to sew him back up or...'

'You were holding the thread yourself,' I say, pointing to her hand. 'I swear I didn't do anything apart from holding down that piece of cloth! At first he was bleeding terribly, but after a while I took it off and replaced that cloth with this one.' *And that's when my hands went so terribly cold.* I look down at my bloodstained fingers... No matter how much I bend or stretch them, they just won't get warm.

'Nim? Have you ever seen such a thing before?'

I keep quiet.

'Wounds don't just cure themselves,' mumbles Yannick, more to herself than to me. 'Not so quickly.'

But maybe they do, I ponder in confusion. I slowly lift my hands up to my face, which two weeks ago still had the blisters caused by the rain. They too disappeared in the course of one night, I remember, without me having done anything except... except for rubbing my cheeks with my hands.

'Nimue? Are you feeling okay?' Yannick looks at me, frowning.

'Me? Yes, it's just a headache, that's all. I should really eat something, I think.' I don't wait for her to answer, and in a daze I walk from the chapel to the entrance of the church. There are a couple of boxes and bottles that have been pulled out of the rubble by the survivors. Franseza is sat next to it, wearing an exhausted expression on her face. She gives me a little water, perhaps no more than a cupped handful, which I use to wash my hands and wipe them on my anorak. The blood won't come off completely, sticking under my nails even when I scrub them with a brush. I give up in the end, as my stomach begins to rumble with hunger, which I hadn't really noticed before but now I can't ignore it. Franseza has clearly taken responsibility for rationing out the food, and all I get is a bowl of beans and a piece of still soggy bread.

With this scant meal in hand I find a quiet place to sit: a small alcove where a stone king looks down at me. Exhausted, I lean my head against the stone. The food doesn't actually have any taste, but still I slowly try to force it down, as it could well be the last thing I'll eat before help arrives from Gwennec. In the meantime I try to think; a task made difficult by the pounding in my head. How is it possible that a simple touch could heal my blisters and even a fatal wound? I think of my salves, all lost now that the house is destroyed, and the herbs that I could easily find as relief for one disease or the other ... but that's nothing unusual. I shake my head. There are other people in the vicinity of Gwennec who have knowledge of herbs and plants. Whoever lives this far into the Periphery should be able to look after themselves, after all. Didn't Grandma say that Mum also had a talent for healing? She's even written in her diary that she brought herbs with her from the island ... I feel around for the book, which I am still carrying in my anorak. It's unlikely I'll find something in the pages of the diary about sudden healings, but I have to be sure. If Mum has written something that could explain the coldness in my hands, I have to know what it is.

As soon as I open the book on the page where I stopped reading, I hesitate. Arthur made me promise not to read any further without him; a promise I should really stick to. However, I'm burning with desire to find an answer and the book is right there in my lap, inviting me to leaf through it. I decide to give in to temptation and I let my eyes wander over the open pages.

7

·

SELA'S GIFT

September 2117 A.D.

The third day in the new world

This world is strange, so very strange... it is forbidden to drink the water from the many streams outside the city – even the water in the water-butts isn't safe, as the rain that falls from the sky is toxic and burns the skin like fire. The only safe thing to drink is the purified water sold in clear bottles, made of a material which feels unnatural in my hands.

As long as it doesn't rain we're able to take shelter between the houses. Yesterday we slept in an abandoned barn, nothing more than a coal shed at the back of an uninhabited house. We could have slept in the house itself but Esoldi said that the supports were so decayed that they could collapse at any moment. I could see the fear in Benji's eyes. After the fire in the barn, he prefers to sleep under the stars to sleeping in a house that might fall down on him – and who could really blame him?

Before I know it, I'm once again engrossed in Rona's voyage. I read how the impoverished bunch managed to scrape together money and shelter in villages, along deserted country roads and finally in more inhabited areas. Nowhere were they very welcome, except with farmers here and there who let them work in exchange for a place to sleep in the barn. At one point they came across a wealthy couple that let Rona and Esoldi clean their monumental house for a short while; a castle the likes of which Rona had never seen. I still can't discover any of the names of the places they went to, but I get the impression that my young mother was leading the party deeper into Central Europe. The industrial towns, which rub shoulders with big, densely populated cities under a perpetual haze of oily smoke, are nowhere to be found in Breizh. Even Brevalaer, the largest city on the edge of the Periphery, doesn't have dozens of factories where workers toil both day and night, causing them to never fall silent nor give respite to those who lived nearby from the constant thumping, clanking, and hissing that Mum said came from the chimneys.

I discover my mother prayed daily to the spirits of the Other World – not so different from how we seek the protection of St Gwenhael at the Sailors' Mass. But just like my own faith in the patron saint of our village, my mother's faith seemed to have weakened a little every day. Yet she still built a small cairn altar wherever she could, where she'd leave a handful of berries, a tuft of hair, a flower, or a piece of bread as an offering.

She was determined to look after Benji. Increasingly she writes about his changing mood and about how he'd sometimes wake up in the middle of the night screaming from a nightmare he didn't want to talk about. I begin to suspect that it was mostly the love of Esoldi and Rona that was keeping him from descending into complete and constant fear.

The thing that chills me more than the penetrating cold of the church stones, however, is Rona's description of the Black Influenza, which cast a shadow over them as their journey progressed. I read with clammy hands about an encounter with a victim, having to remind myself that this took place before Arthur and I were born.

June 2118 A.D.

On the sickness that reigns here

The hair on one side of his head has fallen out. What remains are loose clumps scattered across his scalp. His gums have receded, causing his teeth to look like crooked gravestones and they've started to rot from the base up. He's told me they'll soon all fall out of his mouth. Even more repulsive is his skin, grey and flaky as if he were made of ash. His face, arms and hands are covered with large black swelling; pieces of puffy, dead flesh which give him a monstrous, deformed shape.

People tell us that those who are unlucky enough to catch this disease already have their fates sealed. Almost everyone who is infected lives no more than a week – a month at best. In different areas it seems that people have alternating names for it: the fleshkiller, the grey death – I assume because of the grey skin the victims suffer from in the early stages – and the Black Influenza. I've seen flu before and Tamsin's mother had spoken of a sickness that reigned on Avalon long ago ... but this is no Influenza; it's a plague. Teeth and hair like these, which seem to fall out so quickly as if the body wants to be rid of them, are not a part of any normal disease I've witnessed, and those black lumps look like subcutaneous bleeding.

My eyes dart over the following pages, pages in which they move from town to town without daring to stay for long. The Black Influenza was always near: just a few houses, one street, or a day trip away from the three of them. Somewhere Mum writes:

I'm beginning to believe that various strains of this disease exist. All strains seem to be accompanied by – or at least begin with – the large black buboes all over the body, some as big as an apple. In most cases the skin turns grey and the victim suffers terrible blood poisoning. In some places the buboes burst.

But I've also witnessed the disease taking root in the lungs, hence my initial thoughts of it being a lung condition.

And later on:

In the same city a young girl was unable to utter a few sentences before she began coughing up bile and dark, red blood. To my horror it splashed onto my hand. I quickly wiped it off and ordered Benji and Esoldi to stay away from her. Benji didn't understand that I feel the need to attend to every victim we encounter, that I have to try and do something for them. He was afraid for himself, for Esoldi and for me, and I'm afraid for them too. I've tried to tell him I'm not scared of getting sick and that I've inherited something from Sela...something that he hasn't. At least, I've never seen anything to indicate that the same gift lies dormant in Benji.

An inheritance? A gift? I read those words again and flick through the remaining pages of the diary. My mother has inherited a gift from her mother, but very little is being revealed about Sela herself. How did she come to have this power and why did she disappear?

Questions whirl round and round in my head, but no answers come.

Frustrated, I turn back to the most recent page and ball my hands into fists. Why can't Rona stop being cryptic just for once? Perhaps it's so obvious for her that she didn't feel the need to entrust these facts to the page. I haven't yet finished reading the diary, though. It seems the next few pages are a few days, even a few weeks older than the ones I've just been reading.

December 2118 A.D.
About our red house

We've finally left the bustle of Central Europe behind us and we've reached a town where the grip of the sickness isn't so strong. And at last we can find enough work here to earn a decent wage. Esoldi and I have found a job as delivery girls for a grocery shop, which means I spend the whole day surrounded by the wonderful smells of cinnamon, thyme, camomile, apricots and all the other things that are sold here. I can't describe how relieved I am to be here after the industrial stench of the big cities and their grubby, cobbled streets. Benji has become a cleaner at the station, but lately he's been going on the trains themselves, now that the drivers have noticed that he's rather handy with technology and engineering. Who'd have thought it? Until a few months ago he'd never even seen an engine, let alone repaired one!

Somewhere in a narrow street far from the centre we discovered an abandoned house. The front wall is painted dark red and while the windows and window frames leave much to be desired, it is warm and dry inside. Benji spent an afternoon crawling over the roof on his belly just to see if there were any leaks. He's patched up the holes where possible. According to Benji there's surprisingly little damage.

Since nobody seems to want the house, we've taken up residence here. Our own little house! It gives me such a pleasant feeling. For now it's still a rather bare home without chairs, tables or beds, but who cares? Come spring, I'll decorate the kitchen and living room with garlands of flowers. As soon as we can afford to buy the material, Esoldi and I will sew curtains and tapestries. Outside, on the red façade of the house, Benji has hung a wooden sign which proudly proclaims the new name for our house: 'Avalon', in honour of our lost island. It was Esoldi's idea. She also thought up the idea of planting an apple tree next to the front door. Within a few years we'll have the first fruits of autumn right on our doorstep.

On the top floor is one large bedroom, enough to give two young lovers the space they need. Next to the living room is a smaller room with a box-bed, where I'll make a home. I wish Benji and Esoldi luck and hope that this house will give Benji the peace he so badly needs.

April 2119 A.D.
One winter after our arrival

The apple tree has bloomed for the first time. The sweet smell flows through the house and reminds us of days gone by.

In the beginning it was Benji who brought us news of the Black Influenza as he returned from his travels, but for a few months now Esoldi and I have been the ones who brought home news ... Yes, it was always inevitable: the disease has surfaced in our town – the only place in the world where I felt truly safe. Not long after the first reports, Benji brought the first victim to me, in spite of all my warnings... I should actually be grateful that he's accepted Sela's gift to me as a privilege, or so he calls it. I'm not sure if this gift is a privilege, per se. It's true that the touch of my hands can do more for the sick and ill than all the medicine in Central Europe has achieved until now. The more healing I do, the stronger the healing powers that are active within me seem to get. I thank the spirits every day for the powers they've granted me, because there's no doubt that this is a mystery from the Other World, woven into me with Sela's blood. Yet the deeper I penetrate into the heart of this hideous disease, the weaker I begin to feel. I have the suspicion that this is more than just a germ...I can't explain it, but the shadows I feel inside me when I lay my hands on a victim writhe in me like snakes, making me dizzy and ill. It's now got to the point where, after I touch a victim, I have to stay in bed for a day, with the feeling that nothing in the world could warm my frozen limbs. Sometimes even opening my eyes seems to be too much effort ...

With my heart pounding, I look up from the diary and stare into the darkness of the church. All around me I can hear the breathing of sleeping people. Here and there, someone groans or mumbles something, due to pain or a troubling dream.

Rona has described the unearthly cold that I felt in my arms when I healed that bleeding man without knowing it. 'A mysterious power from the Other World' she calls it, woven into her through Sela's blood...

A thousand questions float around my mind: what was my grandmother like as a person? Why did she leave the island so suddenly? What was this shadowy past shared by Rona and Sela that Rona was so desperate to shake off? Was it so terrible that Mum couldn't bring herself to write about it, even in her diary?

I put the candle on the floor and hold my hands up to the light. There's nothing special to look at, except for the dried blood that I can't scrub off. There are a couple of freckles on the back of my hand and my fingers are long, straight and rough from a life spent fishing. I know I'm not living a nightmare, but I now wonder once again whether I'm dreaming or not, because it's just too crazy and too absurd to think that I have even the smallest hint of magic flowing in my blood! Sure, Mum's fairy tales about talking trees and living hills have certainly given me a good dose of superstition over the years: just like most people in Breizh, I'm careful about venturing out in the middle of the night and I sew trinkets and amulets onto the inside of my anorak in order to protect me from the dangers of the sea. Everyone knows a cousin of a friend who once got lost in the hills and never returned, or someone who heard singing in a sudden patch of mist rising from the sea and couldn't turn their boat around fast enough.

But me? I am Nimue Pesketaer, Nimue the Fisher, Nimue of the sea in a nameless village near a town of no importance or consequence. Earlier this week I wouldn't have bet on a thousand sea pearls that I have a real reason to be superstitious.

My mouth is as dry as sand. I take a swig of precious water from the jug that I have with me in case Katell wakes up. In addition to the feverish excitement about my discovery I also have a feeling of oppressive anxiety, which makes me feel like I'm being choked. Mum may have been a powerful healer, the only one who could tackle the Black Influenza, but the price she paid for her powers was far more than just cold hands. Her description terrifies me. What if I, too, lose my energy and can no longer get back up? Who would look after Arthur? This church is no place to stay in the long term, even though it protects us from the wind and rain. The village needs to be cleaned up, the houses rebuilt, the sick attended to and the dead given a proper burial. I have to be strong – strong and brave.

And yet, Mum hadn't succumbed to the exhaustive effects of her gift, I remind myself. She'd moved to Breizh, had children...could it be she'd found a way to overcome this weakness?

As I turn the page I notice some of the following pages are missing. How many pages have been torn out of the book is hard to say, but as I begin to read, it soon becomes apparent that a few years must have passed. Esoldi has given birth to a son, Finn. This means we don't just have an uncle somewhere in Central Europe – we also have an older cousin. I'm so curious to find out where they live and what has become of them. Do they know that Arthur and I exist? Benji has taken a job with the Phoenix Group, an organisation that I've never heard of. Rona writes he always talks a lot about the reconstruction of Central Europe to facilitate flourishing of the industry – to wipe the last hundred years from our memories. Together with Esoldi he bought a large house near Rome, so his job must have been going well. The red house that had been their salvation stood empty once more. Rona writes that she went back to the heart of Central Europe with her brother, living close to the factories, the smoke and the eternal noise.

Benji has set up a small clinic for me behind the house, away from the living rooms, kitchen and bedrooms of him and Esoldi. It seems as if the patients are doubling every day...My work never ends.

Fortunately not everyone visits me because of the Black Influenza. I'm grateful every time someone comes in who I can help with a simple herbal concoction, a salve, or by setting a broken arm. Benji, however, insists I should devote my gift solely to this terrible disease, which simply will not go away...I should cure it completely, if possible. He says I'm the only hope for hundreds of people who flock in droves to our house, like pilgrims to a holy city. I think he's right that it is my task and my duty to devote all my energy to this mission, but why do I increasingly get the feeling that it is his mission – Benji's obsession, not mine?

I'm worried about the effects that the healing is having on my body, which have increased in recent years. Last week I noticed I'd suffered a nosebleed, and yesterday a small trickle of blood came out of my mouth. This morning I woke up with bruises on my arm. If didn't know better, I'd think that Fergus had come out of a nightmare to pinch me, like he used to do. I'm now wearing a dress with long sleeves, even though it's scorching hot outside. Why am I ashamed of this? Why can't I bear the thought of Benji finding out what's happening to me? Come on, Rona, let's be honest. You know why: Benji will blame me for not trying to be stronger. He'll tell me he's given me a home, a bed, and a comfortable life – and the only thing he asks of me is to cure people of this terrible disease. But I... I'm simply not strong enough. Every day, my body loses strength, while at the same time I save the lives of dozens of people each day.

May 2121 A.D.
News

Bertram has asked me to go with him to Camlann, the port where Benji, Esoldi and I first landed. I've said yes. Benji knows nothing about it yet.

Bertram, my father. He suddenly pops up in this narrative without earlier mention! Tears begin to well in my eyes. Mum must have met him sometime after that last troubling comment. I suddenly miss him more than I have done in years.

August 2123 A.D.
Even better news

The greatest of miracles! I'm still glowing from excitement and delight and I now feel freer and stronger than ever before. Yet at the same time, I'm aware of the gravity of this moment, of the dangers, of all the obstacles, all my fears... I'm carrying a child inside of me. Bertram is so proud. He's beaming like a lighthouse in the night. My beacon, my guiding star, my beloved and I have created a new life. I know it's early days and it will still be months before our child is born, but when that day comes I shall hold him or her in my arms and never cease to thank the spirits... I'm now sure that this is the time to shut down the clinic. Now that

I have a new life growing inside me, I can't afford to exhaust myself or to make myself bleed. I cannot and will not take that risk.

The child that Mum wrote about with such love must be me. I feel a lump in my throat. Who knew that I was conceived in such circumstances, that my existence was a sigh of relief for my mother, as it gave her a chance to escape from Sela's gift, and from her own brother?

There's something else I notice: the name of the port from which Mum first set foot on the continent. *Come from Camlann, lift anchor, set sail, if death won't withhold you, then nothing else will...* The lullaby I hummed for the wounded man was about the very same harbour.

Someone puts their hand on my shoulder. I startle, shove the diary under my clothes and turn around. Yannick looks at me apologetically. 'I thought you'd heard me coming.'

'I was away with the fairies,' I mutter. 'Is everything okay?'

'I'm just making a last round before I go to sleep. Do you want to help?'

'Sure.' I was so fixated on the diary that I almost forgot about the church and the patients lying on the ground around me. Embarrassed, I get up and we walk down the rows of injured people. Most are now asleep.

I tuck in a blanket here, move someone into a more comfortable position there, change a bandage and check wounds that were bleeding earlier that afternoon. We give those who are thirsty some sips of water, since we have very little potable water left. The plastic bottles that Mart found are all empty. Yannick's canteens only contain a few more drops.

'If help doesn't come soon, the sick will dehydrate and wounds will start getting infected,' whispers Yannick, the shadows of the church dancing over her face.

'I'm sure they'll be here soon,' I answer just as quietly. 'The roads will be difficult to navigate after the storm, even with cars.'

'Well, they should try a little harder. I have nothing left, not even a rag to be used for bandages.'

'I know.' I picture the road between the village and Gwennec. Even on a clear day it is a morning's ride by donkey cart to the city, and when the fog clings to the hills it's more dangerous. I wonder whether even the headlights of a car can pierce through the thick darkness of that night. Still, I manage to smile reassuringly. 'You've saved dozens of lives today, Yannick. Everyone's so proud and thankful.'

'You too,' she says. 'You've performed a miracle today.'

For now this simply confuses me. Mum's words swirl around in my head. 'How's Katell? I haven't heard her coughing.'

Yannick looks over her shoulder to where the girl is sleeping. 'To be honest, I'm not sure. A while ago I went to check on her and she was burning like coals. I don't like how she's breathing either, but I can't do anything for her.' Yannick makes a helpless gesture. 'All I can do is wait until the doctors come. I'll stay here to monitor her tonight, just in case something goes wrong.'

'But you look awful,' I say as I see the dark bags beneath her eyes and her sagging mouth. 'Promise me you'll get some sleep, Yannick. I'll stay here with Katell.'

She looks at me with eyes darkened by the shadows. 'You look like you need a rest too.'

'I'll be okay,' I say, with more bravado than I feel. The truth is that my eyes are heavy and stinging from exhaustion, but I have a good reason to stay awake. Now that Mum has mentioned her pregnancy in the diary, I want to keep reading and find out everything about my birth. What's more, I want to find out more about Sela's gift. Did Mum know I have this gift as well?

'Very well.' Yannick sounds relieved that she'll finally be getting some rest. 'But promise me you'll wake me up if something happens.'

'Promise.' I give her a gentle pat on the back and Yannick turns around to join her family in the chapel. I look over at her with a slight pang of jealousy. They're sitting there, the whole family with their arms wrapped around each other – something I'll never have again. I know that if I were to go over there and beg her family for help, they'd take me and Arthur in at the drop of a hat... I turn around and blow out the candles around me, all except for the round candle I have with me for reading. Yannick's family will never be ours, no matter how much empathy they might have for me and my brother. The truth is that Dad and Gran are dead. And Rona...Rona could be anywhere.

I sit down on the floor next to Katell, not fazed by the cold stone beneath me. She's pushed her blanket off, whether in her sleep or due to the fever. Carefully, so as not to wake her, I pull the blanket back over her bird-like body and very lightly run my fingers over her cheek. She truly is burning up. Even her breath is hot as little wisps of it are blown against my skin. Should I try to cure her? I put my hand across her forehead and try to concentrate on her whole body, trying to create an image of the illness that is inside of her. When I look up, nothing seems to have happened. My hand doesn't feel cold either; if anything, it feels warmer because of her fever. With a sigh I go back to my spot on the floor and pick the diary back up. Rona knew how to activate her gift at any time, but I personally have no idea how to use or control this raw power. When the doctors from Gwennec get here, they really need to see to Katell.

I set the candle down in one of the recesses and read on.

January 2124 A.D.
After a snowy night

My greatest fear has come true. Oh God...oh great spirits of the land and sea....not Esoldi and Finn.

Despite being pregnant I travelled to Rome as quickly as possible. The journey seemed to take twice as long, what with my large belly and painful back.

Benji was destroyed. What else could I have expected? He couldn't even stand up straight, as if the impending loss has literally broken his body. I've never seen my brother cry, not even back on the island when time after time Fergus would beat him so badly that he couldn't walk for days. He hadn't cried when Fergus left him in a burning barn and he escaped death by the skin of his teeth. He hadn't cried about Sela's miserable fate or her disappearance. But today he was completely destroyed. I held him, rocking him back and forth and singing gentle songs from the island to him. The spirits know that I cried with him...but I couldn't do what he asked of me. I couldn't rid his wife or his young son Finn of the Black Influenza, even though my desire to save them made me physically hurt. The child I'm carrying is almost ready to come out into the world; how can I put it in danger? I simply no longer possess the power to cure a disease that roots itself so deeply in the body.

I tried to explain that I couldn't help him – I tried with kind words and arguments, but Benji wouldn't listen. After the crying subsided he began to yell at me. It was a terrible sound ... Fergus's sound. I recognised our father in his burning eyes, in his face twisted with rage and in the broad fists he raised to me.

Benji, my brother, what has become of you?

He eventually sent me away. I wanted nothing more than to stay, to keep watch with him until Esoldi's time came and bury her and Finn together. But the rage didn't disappear from his eyes, which were so cold, colder than ice. He told me that I could not stay and to never show my face there again.

'You've stolen my life and torn it to pieces,' he bellowed after me. 'From the very moment that you took me and Esoldi away from that island you put our future at risk. You just let our mother leave and you never spoke out against our father!'

Right then he could have punched me in the face and it wouldn't have hurt me as much.

'I have always tried to protect you,' I whispered.

He turned around and slammed the door in my face. My fatigue and pregnancy forced me to travel back to Bertram, but even now I'm making efforts to reconcile with Benji. Up till now all my attempts have been fruitless. My letters go unanswered. He didn't receive Bertram, even though Bertram has made two journeys to Rome in order to make contact with him. Meanwhile the due date is approaching fast, and I fear I'm putting our child at risk by worrying so much. Shouldn't this be a time of joy?

Oh, but I am happy! Let no one ever think that I'm not wholeheartedly looking forward to the moment when I can hold my child in my arms for the first time! But industry from the cities has spread across the whole land as if it were a sickness itself, and it pursues me. Camlann too, that small harbour town, has over the years fallen prey to the greed of industry. Where once boathouses stood when we first landed are now stacks of oil containers. Where once there were streets leading down to the quaysides, there are now canals allowing the passage of large, flat ships. And where the air was once filled with the silt and iodine of the sea I see now only flames and the smoke of the refineries.

I miss the distant views, the beaches, the eternal sound of the ebb and flow of the tides, rather than the rattle of carts and the roar of cars across the ever-expanding network of roads. Bertram told me he wants to take me to his mother, far away in the Periphery. There, we will find sea and sand, he promises, and the madness of Central Europe and my embittered brother will be far away.

April 2124 A.D.
On Nimue

In a flash of pain and amidst the waves of the salty sea our daughter Nimue was born. For a moment she disappeared completely under the water, until Bertram lifted her up with his broad hands, wiped her off and wrapped her in a towel. Tears were rolling down my cheeks. I was completely out of breath, but the light that shone from her face made even the sun seem pale in comparison. How fitting that my child, daughter of a fisherman and granddaughter of Sela, should have swum beneath the waves before her parents could hold her in their arms!

I must confess that I shuddered when I first held my bundle of joy in my arms. Her round face, the freckles on her nose, even the mess of red hair that looked like a crown of chick feathers covering her head... in those first few moments it was as if I recognised Fergus in her. But her beautifully bright eyes were from Bertram. I wonder if she'll look like Ana later on in life. Ana, who'd also looked a lot like Fergus and yet had been so warm and gentle. I sometimes miss my little sister terribly! If only I could see her once more...I could show Ana her young niece. She'd have been as delighted with Nimue as we are.

July 2124 A.D.
Benji's letter

Avalon, Benji's own company within Phoenix Group, exists no more.

In the margin Rona had made a strange drawing: of a snake, its tongue outstretched and it body wrapped around a staff.

Bertram brought me the letter. I'd never have believed that it had come from Benji if his name hadn't been on it and had I not recognized his signature. He wants to ... sweet spirits, I can't believe what he's asking of me – I can hardly write it down. He's asking me – demanding in fact – that I leave Bertram and return to him in Rome.

'Bring your child too,' he writes. 'It is your duty as daughter of Sela and as my sister to continue your work at the clinic. I have the money and resources to build a hospital that will be unequalled, with branches in every corner of Central Europe. A centre of healing and research, and a centre for the fight against the Black Influenza. As soon as your daughter is old enough I expect she'll show the same talent as you do. Then she'll make herself subservient to the land that received her kin when they were driven off the island. This is the time for reconciliation.'

Not a word about Esoldi, nothing about poor Finn, who died far too young. I threw the letter into the fire, where I watched it burn into ashes. I don't believe Benji is truly interested in reconciliation, only in an all-consuming war against the disease that took his wife and child from him. As for me... I am the face of death to him. I'm the traitor who allowed the very worst of things to befall him.

I clap the book shut, not wanting to read more, disillusioned at the bitter turn the story has taken. How could Mum have kept all this from me? Dad too! All this time he'd known about this, but he had always kept us in the dark. Could it be that even Grandma knew what was going on without ever telling us?

My thoughts become even more glum. How can Benji have said such things to his sister, after all they'd been through together? In my mind I'd begun to compare him and Rona to me and Arthur, but I can't imagine Arthur ever sending me away with such terrible words, or him accusing me of the things Benji accused Mum of.

I put the diary away in my anorak and lean over Katell. She lies motionless under her blanket, only her difficult breathing betraying that she is still alive. Her forehead seems to have cooled down, although it could just as well be the cold draught I feel rising from the floor.

I decide to rest my head a little and close my eyes. Only a short nap...as long as Katell is asleep it won't do any harm. I pull my blanket up to my chest and pull down the hood of my anorak, wrapping myself up like I'm in a cocoon.

But sleep does not willingly come to me. Questions are spinning around in my head. Shouldn't Mum have tried harder to help Benji? Did Benji really think he had the right to claim me? Had he been convinced otherwise by Rona, or did he still want me?

As I finally drift off, I have restless dreams of an overwhelming amount of cold water from which no one can escape.

When I wake up, the morning light is shining into my eyes. I've unwittingly slept all night long, and as I get up I see most people are already up and moving around. Their faces show a glimmer of hope. I get the feeling I've missed something.

Yannick appears next to me out of nowhere, her hair fixed into a new braid. She looks fresh, despite the gruelling past few nights. I feel my own head, where my curls are inelegantly sticking up like dandelion fluff, and sigh.

'Well, you look lovely, sleepyhead,' smiles Yannick. 'Didn't you say you'd watch Katell?'

'I'm sorry,' I groan as I try to straighten my clothing, which after two days in the church is a rather hopeless case. 'Is she okay?'

'She's doing alright, given the circumstances.'

I look around me. 'Why is everyone so excited?'

'Help from Gwennec has arrived. The hospital has sent five trucks with food, clean water, new dressing, medicine... and a whole team of doctors has been taken off duty in town to come help here.' Yannick smiles, but I can't bring myself to smile in response. I feel as hollow as a shell.

'Arthur has also returned. He's outside helping with the soup.'

I go outside to greet Arthur and find him near one of the jeeps. Around him are row upon row of water bottles and towers of plastic spoons wrapped in small bundles, and a group of people from the church is in front of him, waiting to be served first. I push through the crowd as fast as I can to get to the front. Arthur looks tired, with dark rings under his eyes and a pale face. Has he actually slept, or have they been on the road all night? The pot from which he's serving steaming soup is enormous; a child could easily take a bath in it.

'Alms for the poor?' I ask as I stand before him, holding my hands like a beggar. A muted smile appears on his face and he hands me a bowl, which I have to immediately put down on the ground before it scalds my fingers. 'I'm glad you're back,' I then say. 'It didn't feel right without you.'

'At first they didn't want to send more than two doctors, but we all resisted,' Arthur replies. 'Eventually we got them to send the whole emergency response team. They're just in the chapel now, setting up a clinic.'

'You look exhausted.'

Arthur stops serving soup for a moment in order to rub his face. 'I haven't slept since the first night in the church. At the hospital they wanted to know exactly what supplies we needed, how badly hurt the injured were, how many survivors we'd found...'

'Arthur ...'

'Then we had to supervise the packing and loading of the emergency kits, because the hospital couldn't provide any more staff. Patients from Brevalaer have been transferred to Gwennec, did you know? The hospital in Brevalaer must be bursting at the seams. Something about an epidemic going round. We all had to wear facemasks. Look.' He holds up a grubby paper mask. 'But the storm has destroyed things everywhere. I saw houses with tiles missing in the city, and there were a lot of things just lying in the roads. It was so bad we had to get out and clear the road before the jeeps could make their way through.'

I listen in silence. Arthur talks about everything he's seen and I dare not interrupt him again. I know the despair gleaming feverishly in his eyes all too well.

By the time his flood of words runs out, I've finished my soup. 'Come with me. Let someone else take over.'

'But I ...'

'Jost, could you take over a minute? My brother is about to collapse.'

Jost the Netter doesn't listen to Arthur's half-hearted objections and easily grabs the spoon from his hands. I take Arthur by his arm and lead him to the back of the church. We sit down against one of its well-weathered walls. For a moment I hear nothing except the voices of the survivors, who have now discovered the food trucks, and the wind that whistles around the ancient foundations of the church.

'They haven't found Gran.' I wish I had something else to break the silence with.

Arthur bows his head. 'Do you think there's still a chance that she's...alive?'

I look to one side and say the hardest thing I have ever had to say. 'The water rushed into the house within a few seconds. Grandma never even realised she was drowning. Besides...she never could have climbed up the ladder. She never would have been able to jump down safely from the roof and she never would have survived the swim. It was freezing cold and dark and the current was too strong. And even if she had survived all of that, Arthur, she'd now be hypothermic, exhausted and probably injured. There is no scenario in which she would have survived.' I shake my head and my heart aches as I say it: 'I think that quick drowning was the most merciful death she could have had.'

He doesn't respond. He doesn't even make a noise, and I think I understand why: crying feels pointless if you look at it from this perspective, and we're too tired to muster up a rage. I look out over the slope of the hill. The crumbled walls still jut out from the grass, but the long blades of grass on this side of the hill indicate that sheep haven't grazed it for at least one season. Someone should fix the walls before bringing in a new herd. I wonder if anyone will take the trouble, now that the village has been almost wiped off the face of the earth.

With heavy legs I eventually get up from where we're sitting. I take Arthur's hand in mine. 'Are you coming?'

'Where to?'

'Home,' I say.

8

REMAINS OF A LIFE

The place where our home once stood is barely recognisable now. Only the bases of the walls are still visible above the mud. The collapsed roof has become a huge pile of rubble, covering part of Yssi's stall. The whole interior of the house has been swept away: the table, chairs, cupboards and chests. Nothing remains to show that this was once a house that was lived in. The half-broken figurehead, which spent so much time up in the attic, now lies in the middle of the debris, the head of the seal poking up as if it were a living creature gasping for air. The jetty is gone and *The Ragdoll,* which Arthur and I have so painstakingly restored, lies broken in two on the slope of the hill. We'll never be able to repair it now, I think woefully. Even the best shipwright in the world couldn't fix a boat that's this broken.

We slowly walk through the remains of our house. I step over one of the foundations, feeling jittery from how crazy this whole situation is. Here, where I now stand in slippery mud, used to be the living room. To my left is our only couch, an old thing with holes in the upholstery that we'd hidden by covering it with a throw made from undyed wool. To my right is the door to the kitchen and there... there was Gran's bedroom, which was not much more than a walk-in closet containing a box-bed.

That's where she drowned.

Arthur groans. I look behind me. He's sitting on the floor with his head in his hands. I rush over to him, just in time to throw my arms around him and press

83

him firmly against him. He begins to shiver. A moment later his sobs swell into hysterical crying. His body is trembling against me – or is the trembling mine?

We sway back and forth like a boat on the waves. I don't tell him to be quiet or that all will be well. How can I, amid the remnants of our old life where everything we've ever owned now lies in ruins around us or has simply disappeared? We can't do anything except sit here and let the grief wash over us.

After a while, Arthur's cries turn into dry sobs, until he has no more energy even for that. I let go of him to wipe my own eyes. Perhaps we should go back to the church, where things are still standing at least.

'Nim, sing that song for me,' Arthur says unexpectedly. He straightens his back and pulls his legs under him.

'Which song?' I ask.

'That song you used to sing.'

With a dry tongue I lick my cracked lips. 'Are you sure you want to stay here?'

'A little longer. Just to accept it.'

I don't know if this is something you can learn to accept. I'm not sure I *want* to learn, but if Arthur can, then I might fit into this new life too, at least for a while. With a hoarse voice I begin to sing:

'Will you, will you follow me
Breaking the waves and braving the sea
Come from Camlann, lift anchor, set sail
If death won't withhold you, then nothing else will
Hold fast the helm through the mist all those miles
Sail past the cliffs to that sweet, secret isle
Will you, will you follow me
Breaking the waves and braving the sea
The wind turns west, then turns nevermore
The broken boat has run fast ashore
Hold fast the helm through the mist all those miles
I'll stay 'neath the cliffs of that sweet, secret isle

He nestles against me and together we look out towards the sea, which is now a wide, grey strip that reflects the sun back to us. It's difficult to believe that this same sea covered the land and destroyed everything in its path such a short while ago.

'I could smell it,' I suddenly remember. 'Iron in the air, the smell of thunder and factories mixed together... Grandma said that these storms were omens, Arthur. I thought she was mistaken, that it couldn't possibly be true. But now...'

Arthur looks at me, the track of his tears still visible on his cheeks, his eyes swollen and bloodshot. 'You think it's true?'

'Perhaps,' I mutter. 'In all the years that Gran and Dad lived here, there's never been a storm that caused this much damage. Grandma said the storms tore up the world after the Impact. That's exactly what has happened here.' I fall silent and look around me in horror, the hairs on my arms standing up through a sudden cold that doesn't come from the wind. Further along comes the noise of engines from the jeeps that are driving back and forth over the muddy terrain. I wonder if they'll still find more survivors. They'll certainly try, spurred on by Yannick's father and Franseza and helped by the doctors from Gwennec, but I think we all know that the chances of finding survivors under the rubble are getting slimmer with every hour.

'Do you know what I thought about during the journey to the city?' asks Arthur.

I turn to look at him. 'What?'

'Mum. I thought about everything she'd written and I tried to imagine what she looked like while she was writing it. When she was younger, I mean.' He is silent for a moment. 'I can't remember what she looks like, Nim. I've tried and I've tried but when I close my eyes, I can't see her at all.' He closes his eyes to show me.

'Oh, Arthur, you were so young when she left. It's understandable that you can't remember.'

'Do you?'

'Fragments of her,' I answer. 'I remember what she's like as if I were trying to remember a good dream. Sometimes I seem to remember something, but then I realise these are things that Dad or Gran told me.'

'I wish we knew more about her.'

'Well, thanks to this diary we know more about Mum than we ever knew before.'

'Can you describe her?'

'I can try.' I delve into all the things that I can still remember about her after eleven years of absence. Ever since reading the very first words in her diary, images of her have appeared in my mind's eye. 'Mum had raven-black hair and dark eyes like a seal.'

I tell him about her laugh, how she got dimples in her right cheek but not in her left, and how she always seemed to smell of rosemary and sage. As I talk about the last time I saw her, I pause. 'I don't think she wanted to go, nor did she want to leave us on our own, Arthur. She told me that I always had to take care of you, that...that we should never abandon each other.' After what I've read about Benji, I understand why.

'That doesn't sound like she was planning on coming back,' mumbles Arthur.

'You're right. But part of me has always been waiting for her.'

'All that time? Even now?'

'Yes, all that time.' But perhaps the time has come to stop waiting. I take out the seal pendant from beneath my jumper and gaze at the old, white stone in my hand. 'Arthur, I have to tell you something. When you were gone I discovered something, and later I read about it in Mum's diary...'

'What?'

'Something strange happened with my hands when I helped Yannick –'

'You said you wouldn't read on without me!'

'This is different! Just listen, I think...'

'You promised me,' he says, interrupting me again as he crosses his arms over his chest.

I lose my patience. 'I'm trying to tell you that there's something more impor-tant going on here!'

'Are you saying Mum's diary isn't important? Or perhaps only important enough for you to read it?'

I can feel my cheeks turn red. 'That's not true. Arthur, wait!'

Arthur gets up and stalks off. I stay put in the mud, surrounded by the ruins of our home.

When I finally find him he is sitting in the same position as before, his legs tucked against his chest and his chin on his knees. I kneel next to him and open the diary onto my lap. 'You're right. I shouldn't have read on without you. I know it's important, Arthur. The most important thing. I'm sorry.'

He mutters something indistinct and doesn't look at me.

'It won't happen again,' I say. 'I promised before, and this time I promise for real.' I scoot closer to him. 'I'll read you everything that you've missed, but first I must tell you what happened.'

He doesn't interrupt me once as I tell him about the man with the wound in his chest, how my hands had become icy cold as I had miraculously saved his life, and my discovery of Rona's healing gift. During my explanation I dare not look at Arthur's face, afraid to see some sign of ridicule or disbelief. Only when I finally fall silent do I look up at him nervously.

'Well? Say something.'

'I ...' He looks bewildered, his anger forgotten. 'Are you sure it wasn't a coincidence?'

I spread my hands and hold them up. 'Something happened. Yannick didn't know how it happened...I didn't know how it happened, but I can't deny that that man cheated death thanks to Sela's gift. Whatever that is.'

'So Mum could do it too?'

'I think Mum was much better at it than me.'

'And Sela too?'

I shrug my shoulders. 'Sela is a mystery.'

'What else is there in the diary?'

The memory of Benji's bitter words seems to creep over my skin. 'It's not good, Arthur. Mum wrote that Benji was somehow broken, either because their father used to beat him, or because of Sela, or maybe something else. In any case, something went wrong between them and I don't think things were ever resolved.' I place the leather book into his lap. 'Here, read it.'

Arthur is silent for a long time as he turns page after page. When he arrives at the point where I stopped he clears his throat and reads the following sections aloud.

March 2127 A.D.

My brother returns

Benji suddenly appeared on my doorstep this morning. Behind him was a car, a large jeep with that hideous snake painted on the door. The paint glinted in the sun and hurt my eyes. Benji looked different from the last time we were together, which was years ago now. I don't know whether it was because of the loss of Esoldi or because he's just so grown up now, but his features were longer and greyer than I remembered, and his eyes were darker. Only his hair remained as tangled as it ever was, when the sea breeze would mess it up, and the freckles on his cheeks were more visible than ever. Perhaps that was why, for a moment, I was filled with an old sense of affection, as if I saw the Benji from my youth once more.

In that moment of nostalgia I let him inside the house.

I already knew what he was going to ask me and I was sure he'd already known my answer before I had actually refused him. And yet, at that moment a shadow seemed to cross his face. The young boy from my vision disappeared at once and before me I only saw the tall, pale man that he had become...the empty man he'd become after he had lost Esoldi.

And yet, despite all my anxious feelings, in what I can only describe as a fit of madness, I lifted Arthur from his cradle. I placed him in Benji's arms, so he could see for himself that life carries on. I wanted him to know my son, his nephew, and would see him grow up together with Nimue. He asked if he could see Nimue. There was something in his eyes ... I should have known from the beginning, of course, that he had no interest in strengthening family ties, despite the hope that I'd nurtured all these years. He told me about his terrible plan, or rather, his commandment: if it was true that I'd worn myself out and was no longer capable of healing victims of the Black Influenza, and if it was true that Sela's gift could only be passed on from daughter to daughter, then he was prepared to only take Nimue with him. Even as I write these words I'm still seething with anger! My child, my daughter!

I told him not to think about laying a single finger on her, not even to look at her, if all he wants to do is use her for his own endless war.

He then said that I need not worry as Nimue would not be his only means to an end, and then…sweet spirits, he began to tell me about the other children and the cure he was trying to find. So far none of his patients survived his experiments, but that seemed to bother him less than the failure of his research. In fact he was hopeful that he'd soon develop a method that would allow sufferers of the Black Influenza to survive his cruel healing process. Healing, he calls it! Torture is what it is. An insult to the spirits, to the Other World that is intertwined with ours. A son of Sela should know better. I think it was then that it really dawned on me that this man was no longer my own brother. What is it that has been twisted inside him? How can he have forgotten what it feels like to be scared and hurt every day while others stand idly by and do nothing to help you? Or is it because he knows these feelings only too well that he's managed to switch them off? Has my Benji become so numb that he has done what I so desperately tried to protect him from? I thought my heart was going to stop and never beat again.

Benji grabbed my wrist, his fingers as cold as his eyes. And again I thought: sweet spirits, at what point did I lose him like this? At the same time, I also understood that I'd never get him back – that the boy with the windswept hair and the freckles on his face was gone forever. Benji is no longer capable of compassion; of feeling what other people feel, and I fear that I'm partly to blame. By his demeanour I could see he was consumed by a desire to avenge Esoldi and Finn. Was I not the person that had allowed them to die? He always loved her more than me, perhaps because I'm too much like Sela.

I can't recall now where I found the strength to kick him out the door, but one way or another I managed. I closed all the locks and waited for him to leave, trembling with fear. It took a while, but finally I heard the engine of his car start. I don't think he'll go very far. I have to…

The rest of the page is too burnt to be legible. Only at the very bottom, where the fire from long ago hasn't completely scorched the page, Arthur manages to decipher one last line with great difficulty:

As soon as Bertram gets home we must get everything ready, although I don't know how. Nimue is no longer safe here.

Our eyes meet. There's only one page left of the diary – one last chance to see a hopeful ending to this sad tale. I see Arthur swallow before he turns the page, and then we pour over the book together and silently take in the last words written by our mother.

March 2130 A.D.
To those whom I love

His vehicles are all over Gwennec. A whole fleet of cars with large doors and armoured windows, as if he needs all of this to abduct one small child. I have sent Nimue and Arthur out to sea with Bertram, even though there are storm clouds on the horizon. I pray that the spirits will protect her out there. I have left a trail for Benji to follow in the hope that he'll go after me instead but even if he doesn't, I promised myself I'd... No. I can't say it – I can't even write it down. The task that lies before me covers me like the darkest of shadows.

With all my heart I wish that it'd never come this far – and yet, what else is left to me at this juncture? Will the spirits ever forgive me? What about Sela – if she's watching over me somehow, will she be able to understand that a mother's love is always greater than any other in the world?

Finally, to my children, in case this book should ever fall into their hands: my thoughts forever more will only be of you. Know that my devotion has never wavered, and that the love I have for you is as true as the North Star and as constant as the tides of the sea. Never in my life have I loved something as deeply as you, and I cling to the knowledge that nothing, no storm and no darkness, can ever take that away from me.

God willing, we shall find each other again someday.

Rona

We keep quiet. Tears are running down my cheeks.

She loved us, it echoes in my head. She loved us so much that she...she did what, exactly? Nothing in Rona's diary reveals her destination or her plan even

now, just as the book is silent about Sela's fate. No more answers are left for us, only the blank back of the last page.

The ruins of our old house seem gloomier to me than ever before, now that the sudden realisation runs through me that Mum has unwillingly missed all the major events in our lives: Dad's accident, the storms, and now this terrible wave, which has flattened the house that she loved so much. *No storm and no darkness ...* Even this storm?

Arthur's voice brings me back to the present. 'She was in danger when she left. What if he found her, Nim? What if her own brother has taken her prisoner?'

'That's...' I gulp. 'I can hardly imagine that.' Yet what Arthur says must be true. Despite the missing pages and damaged paper, Rona's story is very clear about this point at least: Benji had become obsessed with finding a cure for this terrible Black Influenza and relentlessly pressured Mum to give up her life for that purpose. 'He even wanted me to train me in that institute of his,' I mutter. 'As if he had the right.'

'So she fled, and hoped Benji would track her down instead and leave us in peace,' adds Arthur slowly.

'If that's true then it worked.' I rub the seal pendant between my fingers. 'She had to have told Dad the whole story, just before she left, otherwise he never would have left me the diary in that box. He wanted me to find out eventually. Mum wanted us to know her story, because she wrote those last lines just for us.' I look at Arthur. 'But where did she go after that?'

'Maybe she went to Benji herself,' Arthur gingerly suggests. 'Voluntarily.'

'No...she couldn't have.' I don't want her to have done that, because it would mean he'd never let her go again. Or something a lot worse... a thought that I quickly dismiss. 'Didn't she write that she would leave a trail for him to follow? That must have worked, as he went after her and then left us alone. Perhaps she escaped from him but didn't want to risk coming back, fearing that he'd find her again and he'd come back to take me. To really take me this time.'

'But Nim, what if he did find her? I mean, he had all those vehicles and Mum had nothing.'

'I know.' I'm haunted by the thought that Mum might be trapped in Benji's hospital, sad and lonely, forced to work herself to death in an effort to conquer a disease that had its tentacles spread out across all corners of Central Europe. If Benji still blames her for the deaths of Esoldi and Finn, I also believe that what Rona wrote in her diary is true: that her brother hated her weakness and he pushed her to the limits of what was physically possible because he couldn't settle for less. Perhaps his grief has made him this blind; or else he's seeking to take some kind of morbid revenge on Rona because she couldn't save Esoldi. All the time we'd been living with Grandma, Mum had been a prisoner, kept away from her family and children, even after Dad died?

And what good is it all for, really? I had never heard of the Black Influenza before. There are dozens of ways to die in Breizh, but I've never seen black lumps under the skin. Does this mean Mum succeeded after all? Or did the disease just disappear by itself? Perhaps Gwennec is simply too far away to be affected by it.

'Do you want to keep the fishery?' Arthur has a strange look in his eyes, and when I look at him I believe it might be a reflection of the same horror that I myself am feeling. 'Because we could rebuild it, you know? We'd have to get a much smaller boat, and I don't think we'd be very rich, but...'

'We were never very rich anyway,' I point out.

'Even poorer, then. But it's still a life, Nim. Do you want to?'

'What about your plans to be a train driver?'

He shrugs. 'Forget it. That was before all this happened. Now all we have is each other.'

'I don't want the fishery,' I assure him. Rona's pendant sits comfortably in the palm of my hand. I curl my fingers around it. *God willing, we shall find each other again someday...* 'I've never wanted it and I never will. But I know what I do want.'

It's as clear in my head as a path lit up by a ray of sunlight. 'This is what we have to do, Arthur. We have to find Mum.'

9

JODOC

Yannick insists that we sleep at her house that night. St Gwenhael's has been transformed from an unorganised refugee camp into a fully functioning, albeit slightly improvised, clinic. The people who can go elsewhere have gone to make room for the injured, as well as for the doctors who tirelessly keep pacing from the chapel to the nave of the church.

That night we're crammed into Yannick's bedroom, which is bigger than mine and Arthur's had been, but is still rather small for the three of us.

I lie awake for a long time on my straw pallet, a candle flickering next to me. Arthur has his eyes closed but I'm not sure whether he is actually sleeping or not. I breathe slowly and in my mind go through all the memories that I have of my mother and father: the happy moments together during those short years, their love I was always sure of. I imagine Mum's long, tangled strands of hair blowing in the wind during those times we were on the beach, looking for shells and mysterious objects from far-off places that would occasionally wash up on the shore.

Before dawn begins to break, I blow out the candle. In the darkness, my mind brimming with memories, I stroke the white pendant between my fingers, clinging onto it as if this finely crafted, little talisman might bring me closer to my mother. 'God willing,' I whisper.

Yannick moves. She'll be getting up at first light in order to go help the doctors at the church. I'm sure they'll receive her with open arms. Her voice comes to me through the gloom. 'Are you sad, Nim?'

'I don't know.' It's hard to say what I feel, exactly. There are so many thoughts going around in my head, but there's one image that stands out like a candle burning in the dark, set apart from all the whirling turmoil: that of Rona, Arthur, and me locked in a warm embrace.

'Now, are you both sure that this is what you want to do?' asks Yannick, frowning. She does little to hide her concern and stands with her arms folded opposite me and Arthur in the warm kitchen of her family's house. Outside, the morning light is still battling against the darkness of night. I look out of the window and can see the chickens scuttling around in their coop, looking for any stray grains on the ground. I've put five fresh eggs into the leather bag on my back, carefully wrapped up in cloth. It's the bag that Arthur found in the mud. In addition to eggs, we have a full water flask made of sealskin, that we can refill once we're on the road, a few slices of bread and a chunk of cheese, a folded-up map of Breizh – which I suspect has been washed away from the ruined school building – and a box of matches; a rarity that we have to be rather frugal with, as they'll make lighting a fire in the cold night air much easier.

'Positive,' I tell Yannick, despite the lump in my throat. 'We need her, and I think Mum needs us too.'

Yannick pulls a small pouch from underneath her jumper and places it in my hand. 'Take this. I'd love to give you more, but we need it for the clinic.'

'Yannick, we can't accept this!'

She smiles. 'You won't get very far without money. There should be enough in there to get you to Brevalaer. Go on, take it!' she adds, her hands clasped around mine so I can't give it back. 'I can't let you go away empty-handed, I'd be sick with worry.'

'One day you'll sprout angel wings and fly away,' I reply before wrapping my arms around her. 'I'll miss you so much.'

'I'll miss you too.' She kisses me on the forehead, lets me go and wraps her arms around Arthur. My brother is wearing a new anorak with a lined hood that Yannick's father gave to him. They've always been so good to us, I realise. They wouldn't hesitate to make room in their house for us.

As Arthur frees himself from the hug, I turn around so Yannick can't see the tears in my eyes.

'Come back safe,' she whispers behind me. Both of us know it'll be a long time before we'll see each other again.

Not without Rona, I reply in my mind. Arthur and I wave our hands as we step out of the door and start down the road that will take us to the city. Yannick doesn't walk us outside. I know she doesn't want to watch us go. She'll wait in the kitchen until we've disappeared from view; gone beyond the hills. Afterwards, she'll head to the church to start another tough day.

When we reach the first hilltop, we stop as though we agreed to pause momentarily, and we look back at the sea. After a few moments, I close my eyes so the blue-green strip of water disappears into darkness.

I can still feel her. The push and pull of the tide pumps through my body like a second heartbeat. The wind blows in from the sea and for the last time, it brings with it the sounds that I've fallen asleep to all my life. The waves sound exactly the same as they did yesterday and the days before, a sound that we can hear from all sides.

'Farewell,' I whisper to the sea, the beach, the village and the people in the church. 'I promise we'll find her. We'll bring her home.'

Arthur grabs my arm to pull me along. I open my eyes and smile, in spite of the tears in my eyes, and take him by the hand. Gwennec is half a day's walk and the road is quiet now that no more carts ride from town to our village.

I find the walking is doing me good – the fast pace of our steps makes my head clear and keeps the dark thoughts away. It feels good to be moving and knowing we're headed towards our goal, no matter how far away Rona still is, in what distant part the world she may be hiding, and what state we will find her in. In any case, Arthur and I are finally on our way to find her after far too many years.

Above our heads, the sun climbs higher and higher in the sky; by the time we stop to rest, the clouds have gone and the autumn sunlight warms our pale faces. We eat a piece of bread and cheese, making sure we don't go through our supplies too fast, after which we resume our journey.

When we finally pass the first houses in town, the chill of the afternoon air begins to penetrate our clothing and the wind feels like an icy breath on my neck. We huddle down deep in our anoraks, the hoods pulled tightly over our heads.

The houses here are ramshackle, leaning against each other like tired old men. It's the poorest neighbourhood – poorer even than our village. Here live people with no trade, who built their existence from the waste of fishmongers, netters, shipwrights, tanners, tailors, masons, doctors and their students; in short, from the merchants and tradesmen who make up Gwennec's main population.

The stench that drifts towards us from the narrow streets is unbearable. I can smell a foul mixture of urine and faeces, alongside the unmistakable odour of rotting fish. My stomach turns and I pull my anorak over my nose before I start gagging. We pass through the area as quickly as possible, following a ditch filled with stagnant water that is probably one of the sources of drinking water for the local population. It's strongly advised to not drink ground water, just as it's not a good idea to drink the water from the outdated taps that are still present in many of the buildings. It isn't safe even for cattle to drink, because it may still contain poison, just like the rain and certain parts of the sea.

As the city finally emerges before us I let out a sigh of relief. It was once an old fortified town, as old as St Gwenhael himself, with its own church and a fortified citadel that had already fell into ruin in times past until it was knocked down completely seventeen years ago. The stones were reused in new houses which quickly shot up all across the city. This development didn't last long and Gwennec soon once more became the small, insignificant town that it has been during my entire childhood.

Arthur and I know the way through the narrow streets, corners and alleys where carts can't pass through. We begin to automatically zigzag past the buildings, which seem to hold people like warehouses. They're made of brown stone, with stately facades and large dormer windows. They must have looked very impressive once; now most of the windows are dirty and the walls covered in dark stains.

The weekly market where we sold our fish is on a wide, open square, and even though it's not a market day, we pass a handful of vendors peddling their wares. Gwennec's district officials have a tendency to overlook such violations; perhaps because they want Rome to stick its long nose into our business just as little as we do.

To the right of the market is the old train station. It is now a museum – a small tourist attraction for people who come to the city from the surrounding areas, as no train has gone through the station for decades and the rails are broken, with grass and weeds growing between the tracks. The last train to ever arrive here stands abandoned just outside the station. For as long as I can remember, its doors have remained half-opened, unable to be closed shut. The train consists of several old coaches and the words "*Rail Finistère*" are still legible on its side.

A mysterious name: *Finistère* is the old name for Gwennec. Franseza once said that it means "the End of the Earth". It sounds about right to me; beyond Gwennec there's nothing but wide, open sea.

At the market we manage to find what we're looking for: a farmer who's come to town on his cart and wants to ride back before evening. For a few extra coins he's willing to take us with him.

'I don't mind leaving early,' he tells us, glancing up at the sun as he bridles his mules and Arthur and I jump on the back of the cart. 'There's no market today, nothing to sell. I've been standing here freezing since dawn and I've hardly sold a thing.'

'Didn't you hear about the flood?' asks Arthur.

'I heard the news when I arrived this morning.' He puts up the cover so it suddenly looks like we're in a tent. Although it does little to shield us from the biting wind, we're at least protected from the rain, should the weather decide to turn. 'They said it was pretty bad, so no wonder there were no shoppers today in the city. Have you come from there?'

'Our village was destroyed.'

'I'm sorry to hear that.' The man shakes his head, takes his seat on the cart, and makes a clicking noise with his tongue which gets the mules to obediently start moving off. The cart is rattling along behind in suit. 'The sea is a cruel mistress to rely on. It seems you never know when she might save you or when she'll swallow you up.'

'That's true,' I mutter, more to myself than to him. I thought I knew the sea: her ebbing and flowing tides, her whispering waves and roaring surf, her dangerous undercurrents... but maybe I'd been wrong. I know that I'll never be able to look at her again without being reminded of that terrible night.

The paved streets of Gwennec quickly turn into well-trodden dirt roads as soon as we leave the city, the noise of the wheels and the hooves of the mules being muted. I surrender myself to the juddering rhythm of the cart, letting the conversation between Arthur and the famer wash over me without really paying attention.

As I sit back, leaning against a sack of carrots and my legs stretched out before me, I can see Gwennec disappearing into the distance. I've never really been very fond of the city, being too drawn to open spaces, and yet I feel a strange, empty feeling, as if I'm leaving bits and pieces of myself behind as we follow the road. *There goes my home and everything I ever knew.*

I keep looking until there's nothing left of the old buildings to see. I then focus my attention on the landscape around us, which even in the shadows of the approaching night seems more kind than threatening. The rolling hills quickly follow on one after the other. They remind me of waves, while the herds of shaggy-haired sheep that pop up every now and again look like small specks of foam. Here and there we pass villages. To us they appear like stars in the twilight, and disappear from sight just as quickly behind a hill. They're not fishing villages, because the sea is far behind us now, and instead of boats they are surrounded by vast fields.

When it gets too dark to carry on, the farmer stops the cart by the side of the road. Arthur helps him to unbridle the mules, while I grab a couple of pieces of firewood from the cart and start a fire with one of our precious matches as a way of thanking our driver for his hospitality, whose name turns out to be Jodoc. We share our last piece of bread with him and he gives us a piece of dried meat and a handful of carrots and apples from his supplies, since no one wanted to buy them anyway. I enjoy the feeling of having a full stomach; the memories of the hunger pangs at St Gwenhael's are still fresh in my mind.

'There's not much between here and Kersaoz, unless you like sheep,' says Jodoc between a bite of bread and a swig of milk from his own flask. 'The two of you don't seem to carry a whole lot of luggage for such a long trip. May I ask where you're headed?'

'We lost most of our belongings in the storm,' I say. 'There's someone we must find. Family.'

'Do you know where they are?'

Arthur shakes his head.

'Then I'm guessing you're planning to go further than Breizh,' says the man. 'Perhaps take the train from Saint-Thonan to Brevalaer?'

'That's our plan.' I pick the last portion of cheese from its hard rind and put it in my mouth. 'To be honest, we have no idea where she might be. I guess we'll just have to keep searching and searching until we find some sort of clue.'

Jodoc looks at me thoughtfully, his forehead wrinkled in a frown that makes his narrow eyes look even smaller. 'You've chosen the wrong time of year. First come the rains and the floods; after that, winter strikes inland like an eagle attacking its prey.'

His words give me a feeling of discomfort and I move closer to the fire. What he says is true: even on the coast, where it rarely gets cold enough for the sea to freeze over, the winters are mercilessly hard. Perhaps it would be better to remain in the village until spring, help Yannick to care for the sick and start to rebuild our house.

And yet there's been a deep feeling of unrest in my stomach ever since I read Rona's diary. Despite rain showers and harsh winters, there's nothing more that I want in the world than to find Mum as soon as possible. As I exchange a look with Arthur I can see in his eyes that he feels the same.

'It's not winter yet,' he replies, 'and we can find shelter in the towns and villages.'

'Hmm...' The man sounds unconvinced after Arthur's answer, but after a while he shrugs his shoulders. 'Well, it's none of my business, is it? But if I can give you one piece of advice: don't try to go too deep into Central Europe if you don't need to. There are rumours that it's not safe there.'

When it gets too dark to stay outside, we clamber into the cart and Jodoc pulls the front and back of the cover shut, thus closing the small tent around us.

'Here,' he says. 'It's not as warm as inside by the fire, but these keep out the wind and the rain, and the wagon keeps us off the cold ground. Take these.'

He passes us a couple of woollen blankets, which we partly stuff underneath our bodies like mattresses and partly drape over ourselves. I pull over one of the empty carrot sacks to use as a makeshift pillow. Jodoc is lying as far from us as possible in his own blanket, his back turned to us. In a short while I can tell by his breathing that he's fallen asleep, and Arthur follows soon after.

I listen to the sounds that come to me from outside our makeshift shelter. Every now and then, the canopy creaks in the wind, and the branches of the oak trees rustle above. The mules wander a little before they too fall silent. In the distance I hear the occasional bleating of sheep. As for the hills, they remain as silent as the dead.

I turn onto my back and stare into the darkness. It makes no difference if my eyes are open or closed. I realise how strange it is to not hear the sea nearby. In a wind like this, there'd be huge waves crashing against the cliffs, seagulls uttering their shrill cries above our home...

But we aren't home. There is no home to speak of.

I pull the blanket over my head so I won't have to listen to the empty sound of the wind and turn back onto my side. My hands seem to move to the pendant under my clothes almost of their own accord. I wrap my fingers around it in a motion that's beginning to grow familiar. I finally let the darkness wash over me like water from the sea, falling asleep without remembering my dreams.

'I have a farm where the apples in the orchard still need to be harvested,' says Jodoc as soon as we're back on the road and I sit yawning inside the wagon. 'We don't earn enough ourselves to pay you a decent wage, but you'd have somewhere warm and dry to spend the winter. I have a daughter around your age,' he adds, looking towards me. 'She'd love to have a friend her age to spend time with.'

Arthur glances over at me as I try to tame my hair – which has come undone during the night – into a braid. I look up at the sky and consider the offer. 'Can we still make Saint-Thonan before dark?'

'No, unless you can find another cart that's going that direction and is willing to take you the rest of the way.' He, too, casts his gaze up at the lead-grey sky overhead. 'I wouldn't count on it.'

'In that case, we'll gladly accept, but no more than one night,' I say.

'You're welcome. My house is in Daouloc, which we'll reach before morning is over. That is, if the spirits find it in the goodness of their hearts to keep the road clear.'

'The spirits?' asks Arthur, grinning. 'It seems more reasonable to hope it keeps dry.'

'The Hill Folk were already known to us before the Impact, and I'll be damned if a piece of rock from the sky is going to change that,' says Jodoc. 'Are you telling me your people don't know any tales of the sea?'

'Hundreds,' my brother responds. 'There are sea sprites, *korrigans* and *selkies* ... sea sprites are fish that have been disfigured by contaminated water. They lure fishermen from their usual routes by imitating the light of lighthouses. Once they have them in their grasp, they turn the boat over and drown the whole crew. Korrigans are found in the caves by the beach, and if you want to go into the caves you should take a bell with you, as they're afraid of the sound. But I've never seen one,' he adds, sounding almost disappointed. 'Then there are the seal people.'

'Selkies,' I supply. 'Rarer than all spirits, fairies or korrigans combined. They say that a selkie can shed her sealskin and walk on the land like a person. Every man who sees her is overwhelmed by her unearthly beauty, but a selkie must always return to the sea. Our grandmother told me that's why seals look like they have such sad eyes... They're forever doomed to a semi-existence, not completely on land and not completely in the sea.'

'Nim.' Arthur pokes me suddenly. 'Look, there.'

We pass by a shallow valley, where brambles are growing on the sides of the hills. In the middle of the open field stands a group of stones, some leaning crookedly on each other, a few others cracked and crumbled, but none so destroyed that it's unclear they are deliberately positioned into a circle.

'A *menhir*,' I say with awe in my voice. I recognise the image from a poster at school, but I've never seen a stone circle before in real life. Franseza says they're older than written history, almost as old as the land itself. I'd give anything to be able to get off the wagon and run my hands over the weathered rocks, but Jodoc keeps his mules rolling on. He must have passed this landmark hundreds of times on his way to and from Gwennec.

That isn't the only thing Arthur is thrilled about. He rummages around in the backpack and, to my surprise, pulls out Mum's diary. 'I knew I'd seen it somewhere before,' he says. 'Look!'

I look down at the page he is pointing at and suck in my breath excitedly. 'You're right!' In the margin of the page I recognise a hastily-drawn sketch of a small stone circle, with stones leaning over one another and crumbling like the menhir we've just passed. I look up from the book towards the still-visible valley. 'It looks exactly the same, even the stone that looks like a face, you see?'

'Mum was here.'

The tingling feeling that I now associate with Rona's diary comes over me once more. We must be on the same route that Mum took with Dad when they went to live with Grandma on the coast, carrying me with her inside her belly. The cart makes a sudden creaking noise as we narrowly get out of a muddy pothole. The same road that Mum once travelled down. We're following in her footsteps, but in the opposite direction. I excitedly put my arm around Arthur. 'This is it; we've found it, her trail!'

'Straight ahead is Daouloc,' says Jodoc, as we reach a fork in the dirt road and before us rise the barns and farms of a village in between the hills. 'Saint-Thonan is about four hours on foot up that way.'

'We'd like to stay with you and your family for one night, Jodoc,' I say. 'Arthur and I can work hard.'

Jodoc turns his cart towards the hamlet. 'There'll be rain before night falls. I can smell it in the air.'

With a clatter of hooves and the grinding of wheels on gravel we ride onto the yard of Jodoc's farm. The farmhouse is a tall, rectangular building with ivy growing up the side. At the back there is a low barn with small windows and a red-tiled roof, as green as the walls of the main house because of the moss. Next to the house is a large chicken coop; as Jodoc pulls his mules to a stop and jumps off the cart, a startled rooster shoots off with much protest in the opposite direction.

I slip off the cart and, together with Arthur, push the wagon cover forward, tying it up with a piece of string.

Behind the barn I see the orchard that Jodoc mentioned. The apple trees are growing in straight lines; the tops of the trees are carefully pruned so that none of the branches grows above the pergola, which is clearly built to protect the trees like an open roof. As I take a closer look, I can see a girl of about sixteen clambering up one of the ladders that leads up to the pergola as she pushes a lubricated tarpaulin out in front of her.

'Is that how you keep out the rain?' I ask, pointing at her.

Jodoc nods. 'Not very different from the idea of a canopy or tent. Apples affected by the rain rot faster.'

'How do you protect the field then?' asks Arthur.

Jodoc smiles as he loosens the straps and bridles of the mules. 'Glass greenhouses. The sunlight comes in, but the rain's kept out.'

In amazement, I try to imagine huge glass houses over the whole landscape. As Jodoc leads his mules away and Arthur runs after him to help in the stable, I walk towards the orchard. The girl is still busy with the tarpaulin. She's only covered three rows so far, and there are still four support columns left unprotected as the sky begins to take on a threatening, dark slate colour. I pull my hood up and clamber up one of the wooden ladders to the top, where the wind begins to tug at my anorak. For a moment I hesitate, unsure of where I have to put my hands on the small beams to the left and right of me, these being my only support. In between, a series of wooden slats have been laid down at regular intervals, so it looks like an elongated ladder built above the trees. A bundle of waterproofed sheets are tied to the top of the ladder. I gently untie the strings and begin to roll out the tarpaulin, mirroring what Jodoc's daughter is doing.

When I'm halfway done with the pergola, the girl sees me. She stops what she's doing and calls over to me, one hand waving in the air. 'Who are you?' It's obvious she has to yell loudly in order to make herself heard above the wind.

'My name is Nimue,' I call back. 'I thought I'd help you with these!'

'I'm Katarin! Did my father find you?'

I laugh, out of breath. 'Something like that, yes.'

The tall construction is no place to hold a longer conversation, so we continue to work in silence until all the trees in the orchard are under cover, where the rain can't touch their leaves and fruit. With sore limbs, I carefully lower myself down the ladder, where Katarin is waiting for me with curious eyes.

'Thank you,' she says. 'It would have taken me twice as long if you hadn't helped me, and to be honest, I can't stand it.'

'Your father's given us a lift and a place to stay for the night, so it's the least we can do,' I reply. 'That's quite a big job! I had no idea that crawling over all those bars would be so tiring ... my hands are bright red – here, take a look.' I hold my palms out towards her.

She chuckles. 'That'll wear off after a while but it'll still hurt. Better than having rotten apples, though. Did you say you were with someone else?'

'My younger brother, Arthur. He ran off to the stable as soon as he saw the orchard.'

'Well, that's a smart move.' Katarin takes me to the farmhouse and shows me where I can hang up my anorak. The smell of food floats through the hallway and suddenly my stomach rumbles with hunger.

'Thank God for the warmth,' I mutter. 'It was cold on the road.'

Katarin's big blue eyes take me in. 'You look dirty,' she comments drily. 'I'll wager you haven't washed yourself in a while.'

I feel my face and hair and find that the mud clinging to my hands is also on my jumper. 'Well,' I say, slightly embarrassed. 'So much has happened that I hadn't thought to wash myself. I'm sorry, it's not very becoming of a guest.'

She dismisses my words and takes me to the kitchen, in the middle of which is a large table covered in bowls and cutlery. It strikes me that there are already fives places set at the table, so someone must have been told that me and Arthur were joining them for dinner. 'No one expects travellers from the road to dress as if they were the president of Rome,' says Katarin behind me. 'We don't expect it of ourselves, even.'

A door opens and a woman comes through into the kitchen. She must be Jodoc's wife. She is a tall, wiry woman with her grey hair tied up in a bun. She has a wide mouth and round eyes, like her daughter, that stare at me inquisitively. 'I heard that my husband picked up two stray children along the side of the road,' she states as a greeting. 'My name is Maella. Welcome to our house. I hope you like carrots, as we don't have much else at the moment.'

'We're not strays, exactly,' I say, in defence of me and Arthur. 'My brother and I paid your husband to give us a lift out of Gwennec. We're on our way to Saint-Thonan.'

'And may God bless you,' says the woman, before putting a steaming pan fresh from the oven onto the table. 'You've come from that village that was destroyed by the storm.'

I nod, not knowing quite what else to say. For these people the flood is just a news item, with no real idea of the fear, the cold, or the people we've lost.

I'm saved by Arthur and Jodoc's entry. Maella announces that the meal is ready and we all sit around the table together. Maella isn't lying when she says all they have are carrots, as the large pan is filled with nothing but mashed carrots, with a few pieces of potato here and there, as if they fell into the pan by accident. Whether you live on the coast or further inland, it's hard work to make ends meet the whole year round, I think to myself.

Meanwhile Katarin and Maella want to know everything about the terrible storm, most of all about how Arthur and I managed to survive that night. I give the most detailed account I can, before I begin to falter and discover a lump in my throat that I'm unable to swallow.

'Enough,' says Jodoc gently, glancing at my face. 'You're making Nimue upset, Katarin. It's not a night that she or Arthur will want to think about.'

'No, it's okay,' I mutter. I take a sip of water and clear my throat. 'I don't think anyone can quite describe what it's like to look at your own house and know you'll never be able to live in it ever again, all your memories, and all your possessions... just washed away by the flood.' I can't bring myself to talk about Gran.

After dinner, Jodoc takes us to the loft above the barn to prepare us a place to sleep. It reminds me immediately of our own attic: it's full of broken chairs, hidden boxes and rolled-up lengths of cloth, likely belonging to Maella. We move a few boxes to one side, pull two old mattresses onto the floor and beat the dust out of a couple of old woollen blankets. Jodoc even manages to find two pillows.

As I place a lit candle on a chest next to the mattress, my eyes are caught by a large, brass compass that has fallen onto the ground. I pick it up. 'Jodoc, this is beautiful. In our village this would be deemed a treasure. Don't you use it?'

The farmer gives it a rather disinterested look. 'As long as my field doesn't start turning on its axis I know how to distinguish north from south. It's been in my family for years; I believe my grandmother came into it.' He shrugs his shoulders. 'I don't think they cared much for it. To be honest, I haven't thought about it in years.'

With my eyes I follow the path of the needle for a while, which always shoots back to north, no matter how fast I turn the compass.

10

THE CHURCH OF ST CORENTIN

We wake up early the next morning, but it becomes evident that Maella and her family have gotten up even earlier. Our breakfast is all ready for us in the kitchen: fresh bread with slices of cheese and a jug of milk, which – according to Katarin – came from a farmer nearby as they themselves have no cows. With a pang of grief I think of Yssi.

Once we finish eating and finally get all our things packed up, Maella approaches us with some things wrapped in cloth; a still-warm chunk of bread with cheese and an extra bottle of purified water. Thankfully we tuck it into our bag, next to the map and our own supplies.

'It's a pity you can't stay around,' says Maella as she firmly shakes our hands. 'A couple of extra hands this winter would be a godsend.'

'I'm very sorry,' I reply as I heave the rucksack onto my back. 'We're incredibly grateful for your hospitality. I hope the harvest will be plentiful for you.'

Katarin and her father accompany us to the end of the village where the road to Daouloc splits and the left fork goes towards Saint-Thonan. Katarin looks out towards the hills, her hand shielding her eyes. 'I've never been on a train. I wonder if it's like travelling by cart.'

'Some train carriages are like carts,' I reply. 'I'll think of you when we're on it, okay?'

The girl gives me a crooked smile.

Jodoc's gaze wanders over us. I have the feeling he's wondering whether it's safe to let us go off further on our own. 'Keep on the road and don't wander off into the hills,' he finally urges. 'God knows there are enough people who have met their maker in those hills. The valleys look safe, but they're full of bogs and marshes that you only notice when you're standing in one up to your waist.'

'Keep on the road and don't veer off into the hills,' I repeat aloud. 'I promise.'

The man takes his daughter by the arm and he raises his hand to wave us off as he turns right. Arthur and I linger near the crossroads for a while, watching them go. I feel the wind blowing against my back, as if it's pushing us forward further along on our journey. I obediently turn down the road we're meant to take, a path that seems to meander over the hillsides like a river without a visible end.

We walk at a solid pace, intending to reach the town before dusk falls and the path between the hills gets more dangerous. With the whole day ahead of us, it seems an easy task.

The sun moves westwards with us. By the time we take a short break, it has already passed its highest point.

My feet ache the whole time. I plop myself down on a flat rock by the edge of the road and kick off my plastic plimsolls. They have been too small for me since the previous summer, to be honest, after a sudden growth spurt. There are two red blisters on my heel that torture me with every step I take. If we are supposed to do a lot of walking on this trip, it won't hurt to spend some money on a pair of decent boots.

Arthur takes out our last two apples and hands me one.

'Apples?' I ask, sniffling. 'I can't bear to see any more apples. We should eat that bread while it's still fresh and there's also the cheese that needs to be...hang on, this must be a mistake.'

As I speak I pull out Maella's parcels, but when I open the piece of cloth expecting to see a small round of cheese, I fall silent. In my hand is the old compass that I admired the night before.

'Enjoy that,' says Arthur with raised eyebrows.

'They can't have given this to us,' I say. 'Maella must have packed it by accident, that's the only explanation.'

'By accident? Only if she's suddenly turned blind.' Arthur tears off a piece of bread and stuffs it into his mouth along with a piece of cheese.

I shake my head. 'We have to go back and return it, Arthur.'

'I'm not going back,' he says indignantly, although his piqued tone of voice has less of an impact because of his bulging cheeks. He gulps a few times and then says: 'Don't grumble, Nim. You saw it, you liked it, the family had no more use for it, and Jodoc decided to give it to you. Don't make such a big deal of it.'

I turn the compass in my hands and watch how the needle keeps endlessly turning. 'It's certainly beautiful...and heavy,' I say.

'Long as you don't eat it.'

'Ha ha, very funny.' I stuff the compass into a hidden pocket on the inside of the rucksack where it can't be damaged and get to my feet again. 'I'll be back in a sec.'

'Where are you going?' asks Arthur. 'We can't stray from the path, remember? The hills will gobble you up.'

'I need a wee. Don't tell me you want me to do that right in front of you.'

Arthur mutters something and pours over the map we've brought with us. I put my plimsolls back on and step off the road onto the verge that runs alongside, where the tall, wet grass reaches my knees, making it difficult to walk to the top and then down the other side.

Just as I undo my belt buckle it's as if a voice brushes past my ear. 'Nimue,' it whispers. My head snaps to one side, my eyes darting around looking for the source of that unexpected sound. When I turn around further, I nearly jump out of my skin with fright.

It is a tall figure, pale and wispy like a patch of fog. Just as my eyes begin to focus on it, it disappears. The hairs across my whole body stand on end and it isn't just the perpetual wind that's suddenly making me shudder. Overhead flies a blue heron, a silver fish as large as my hand glistening in its beak. Apart from that, I'm alone.

I nervously laugh. 'Scaredy-cat!' I scold myself. Jodoc's superstitions have got under my skin. I look back over my shoulder. There – see? Nothing strange around. Still, I run the last part of the way back and leap back up onto the road.

Arthur looks at my red face and asks: 'What's happened to you? Did you sit on a thistle or something?'

'Don't be silly. Come on, let's go.' I snatch the map from his hand and stuff it into my rucksack without folding it.

'Hey, don't put it away like that! We still need that.'

'Why? The city's that way.' I walk forward with long strides, intending to leave the barren hill with its strange stones behind us as quickly as possible.

It's your imagination, I keep telling myself, as I try to calm my nervous breathing by inhaling and exhaling at the same pace as my footsteps. Along the roadside, a thin mist begins to rise up from the ground, a sign that the earth is quickly cooling off. Nightfall won't be far off.

The apparition that I think I saw was nothing more than a foggy tendril, an airy cloud that flitted past me and made my ear cold. I put the incident out of my mind.

During the day we discover to our delight regular small signs that tell us we're still following Rona's trail. We find her sketches as footnotes in the margins of pages of the diary, and Arthur in particular remembers every drawing, no matter how quickly or vaguely each one has been scribbled down: an ancient gnarled tree here, a strikingly-shaped hilltop there, a sharp turn in the road and a ragged scarecrow in one of the barren fields that may have seen many travellers passing this way. Moreover, there's an entire page dedicated to a drawing of a huge building, the towers of which rise up in perfectly symmetrical peaks. *Saint Corentin* is written underneath. There's been no such building to be found near the road so far, but I keep wondering about it.

We reach Saint-Thonan quicker than I expect. This city, with its suburbs and monumental city centre, could comfortably fit Gwennec two times over within its boundaries.

I'm impressed by the large houses which stand close by each other. Unlike in Gwennec, the streets are wide and open so carts and people can easily pass by one another.

Arthur and I look for the way to the train station. Not a remnant of times past this time, but a real transport hub, with four platforms and tracks going off in all directions, and large signs on the platform displaying the times for arrivals and departures. Everywhere are vendors with large trays around their necks, selling hot soup and drinks to the passengers.

I pull a handful of money out of the rucksack and count out the coins, again thankful for Yannick's providence in this matter. The tickets to Brevalaer are so expensive we're left with only a few copper coins. For this amount of money we could have bought two weeks' worth of catch on the fish market in Gwennec, I realise somewhat shocked. Yannick had known this, of course. I, on the other hand, never having gone beyond the borders of our small town, had completely misjudged things.

'We have a bit of time before our train arrives,' says Arthur. 'What shall we do?'

'Look!' I delightedly cry out. 'Do you see those towers there?'

From the place where we are, they're clearly visible above the other buildings. Although the station denies us an unobstructed view, I recognise their shape immediately. 'That must be the Church of St Corentin's. Mum was there!'

We head into the city centre, through the broad streets and through the crowds.

Somewhat unexpectedly, the building appears in front of us. The whole town seems to gravitate towards the St Corentin's, like lodestones to the north. My mouth drops open.

The church is built from the same light-grey stone as St Gwenhael's and like the old sanctuary of our village, it has vaulted windows, but any similarity ends there. Whereas St Gwenhael's is square and squat, the twin towers of St Corentin's seem to rise out of the ground like dancers trying to reach heaven with outstretched arms. I'm overwhelmed by the beauty of the many arches, which frame the towering main entrance, and by the sheer brightness and space that the building seems to possess, despite its magnitude.

'What is it?' whispers Arthur beside me, clearly as overwhelmed as I am.

Somewhere in my memory I find the words that belong to the building. 'A cathedral. The king of churches.'

'Can we go inside?'

I nod silently and step out in front of him to open the doors, which are so tall that Arthur could have stood on my shoulders and still wouldn't have been able to touch the top. Inside I immediately pause to gaze at the curves of the roof and the many rows of arched pillars, which act as open gates to the chapels hidden along the left and right sides of the church. I have the feeling that I've entered the hold of a giant, brightly-lit ship.

'Saint Anselm, Saint Winwaloe, Saint Ronan,' mutters Arthur as we pass by the chapels. 'All saints.'

'Arthur, look at the windows. It's as if they're telling stories.'

'How did a building like this survive the Impact?'

'I don't know.' The same question is running through my mind. 'The people who built this must have really made sure that their cathedral would last for centuries.'

I take out Mum's drawing again. The sketch is nothing compared to the real thing. Rona's simple lines simply aren't able to catch the light and colours that shine through the tall windows, or the sound of footsteps on the gravestones covering the floor, worn flat by centuries of visitors.

Even so, I find myself drawn to the idea of sitting on one of the staircases leading to a chapel, taking out a pencil and paper and trying to draw the stained-glass windows, or just sitting and taking in the stories of these unknown saints. In the absence of drawing material, I let my eyes do the job. I stare at the elegant pillars that seem to rise ever upwards and then suddenly stop, curving towards each other in order to draw attention to the roof, where swallows fly between the beams without caring about the people on the ground staring up at them.

We wander around for a long time. I try to picture Mum as she walked around here for the first time. She must have had the same dazzled look in her eyes as Arthur now does.

Eventually, time catches up with us. It won't be long before the train to Brevalaer pulls into the station and we can't afford to miss that. I sigh before pulling myself away from the cathedral. I strangely feel more complete than before; it's as if the hole that the storm had ripped inside of me is now beginning to heal as I pass by all these monuments of Rona's journey. We're now finally following in her footsteps, and they're leading step-by-step back to the beginning.

11

·—

THE CELL IN THE WOODS

I wake up suddenly from an uneasy sleep as the train grinds to a halt. My head bounces off the wall and I nearly slide off the end of the narrow wooden bench and onto the floor. Arthur grabs me by the shoulder to keep me up. I rub my eyes.

It takes me a while before I remember where we are. Looking out of the window, I can see we are no longer in Brevalaer, but next to a small platform that seems to have no reason to exist in this isolated part of the country. All around, the landscape spreads out before us, with neither hide nor hair of a town or village to be seen. The rolling hills of the first half of the journey have gradually turned into large mountains with jagged peaks. Moreover, the rather barren landscape has been replaced by dense forests of spruce and pine. It's an inhospitable sight – not the kind of place where someone would want to alight from the train to go exploring.

'What's happening?' I ask Arthur. 'Why have we stopped?'

'They said there was something wrong with the engine. They need to repair it first.' He presses his face against the window to look outside.

I see two men in red and blue uniforms walking across the platform, followed by a boy dragging a large metal chest behind him. That's the apprentice driver, I reckon. Arthur watches him jealously.

'Hey, what's that?' He nudges me and points.

Through the open door of the train appear two more men, not in the colourful uniform of the train staff but in an inconspicuous green uniform, which

113

gives them enough camouflage to vanish into the treeline without being noticed if they wanted. They are dragging a girl with black curly hair along, who I estimate to be a few years older than me.

Her head is moving wildly back and forth, like that of a trapped animal. I'm shocked by the bitter expression on her face and her wide-open eyes. She's screaming something that I can't quite make out through the glass of the window, but one of the men reacts to this by giving her a resounding slap in her face.

I gasp for breath. 'What's he doing? Who is that girl?'

'A stowaway maybe?' Arthur turns paler. Stowaway or not, the way in which the girl is clearly being removed from the platform against her will is a frightening sight.

'Where do they think they're going?' In the area surrounding the station there is nothing but woods and mountains. An uneasy feeling comes over me, as if something is afoot that's not intended for my eyes.

I suddenly spring up. 'Did you see that?'

'See what?'

'Look!' I press my face against the glass next to Arthur's and point to the uniform of the man on the girl's left hand side. He has to turn towards her to keep her under control. 'Look at the symbol on his chest, under the collar. Don't you recognise it?'

I rummage around in the rucksack for Rona's diary, flicking through it until I find the page with the drawing of a snake, wrapped around a staff with its forked tongue outstretched.

Avalon, Benji's own company within Phoenix Group, exists no more, was written next to it.

'It's the same logo. Exactly the same! Look, here Mama's writes about them again...' I turn a few more pages and stop just before the end: *Benji suddenly appeared at the door this morning. Behind him was a car, a large jeep with that hideous snake painted on the door.*

'What does that snake mean?' I wonder out loud.

Arthur looks out the window again. 'They're almost gone.'

I try to think quickly, which is difficult now that my head is brimming with new questions. Who are those men, and why are they taking that girl into the woods? The platform is suddenly empty. Does this mean the repairs are done and the train is about to leave?

I put the diary back into the rucksack and make an impulsive decision. 'Arthur, come with me.'

'Nim?'

'Quickly, before the train leaves!' I get up, shrug into my anorak, and heave the rucksack onto my back. 'That symbol has something to do with Benji. I don't know what exactly, but if we find Benji, perhaps we can find Mum. Don't you see? This is far better than menhirs or cathedrals!'

With great effort, I force apart the metal doors of the train and leap onto the platform. Arthur jumps out behind me just in time, because at that moment a deep hum rises from the belly of the train, as if some great beast is just waking up.

Breathless with excitement and with my heart racing, I look around me. Where has that strange group gone? Which direction did they take when they dragged that girl away?

That way, I think to myself, looking towards the five steps leading off the platform where a barely visible track leads into the woods.

Arthur grabs my arm the moment I want to dash off. 'Just think for a moment! They've just dragged that girl off against her will. Don't you think we should be careful before they get us too?'

'Why would they want to get us?'

'How do I know? But what do we know about *them* exactly? Benji wasn't exactly a role model uncle, or have you forgotten?'

'Of course not,' I answer, annoyed, as I free my arm. 'Don't worry. We'll track them down and find out where they're taking her. There are plenty of places where we can hide if we want to go unnoticed.'

Arthur looks as if he wants to say something, but I'm no longer listening and begin to follow the trail down the hillside. Here the trees envelop me, making it seem as if we're in a different world all of a sudden. There's no longer a visible path, only ferns trampled down by animals that have made narrow crisscrossing tracks across the forest floor.

'Excellent,' says Arthur, slightly exasperated. 'Now what?'

I look around me until I see some footprints in the shadows, cutting across a muddy puddle and having scattered some branches, possibly caused by kicking feet.

'That way,' I point. 'Good grief, where do they expect to get to before nightfall?'

'Where do *we* expect to get to before nightfall?'

I pull out the compass and let the needle do its job. 'It looks like they're taking the girl westwards and the train was heading towards the east. As long as we head in that direction on our way towards Brevalaer, we should be alright.'

Arthur lets out a deep sigh, but it seems he's decided it's too late to kick up a fuss. He looks around. I follow his gaze, finally calm enough to fully take in our surroundings.

The tree branches form a natural canopy over our heads, the trunks of the spruces like huge, thick columns that remind me of the pillars in St Corentin's. The air is filled with strange smells. Above my head, the branches crash together in the wind, causing the ancient trees to creak and moan. Unseen birds make noises from all sides.

We follow the trail of disturbed leaves as quietly as possible, my heart beating louder than ever. There could be all kinds of wild animals in the forest... boars, wolves, even bears who have yet to begin their winter hibernation. If we come across a hungry predator, we don't even have a knife to defend ourselves. Shark blood! I should have thought of that earlier! I'm just beginning to wonder whether we'd still be able to reach Brevalaer before nightfall if we turned back now, when Arthur suddenly grabs my shoulder and puts a finger to his lips.

Just in front of us, the thicket is completely cleared away. The prospect of bears makes my hair stand on end, and for a moment I look on motionless as Arthur warily pushes on. I then pull myself together and follow on behind him. The trail could have just as easily been made by a deer...or by the flailing feet of a frightened girl.

A human footprint has been left behind in the mud. Too large to be a girl's, but just the right size for one of the men in uniform. My heart immediately begins to beat loudly, and as soon as I point the footprint out to Arthur, some deep voices emerge from the bushes nearby.

'They're close by,' I whisper in his ear. 'What do we do now?'

'Wow, some sleuth you turn out to be!' He moves down onto his stomach and crawls forward, his head hidden low between the ferns. I take off the rucksack and follow him as quietly as I can, though to me it feels as if my racing heartbeat can be heard from a mile away.

Behind the bushes, the ground slopes down into a deep ditch. Behind it is a meadow, where the densely-growing trees withdraw a few metres. In the clearing formed by the receding treeline is a small building.

It seems to have been carved out of a single block of stone. The door is completely hidden behind a long cascade of ivy, so I can't tell exactly if it's open or closed. There are no windows, except for a small hole at the top of the door where the ivy grows to one side so iron bars are visible. Arthur and I exchange a confused look. Is this a prison?

The girl with the dark hair is nowhere to be seen.

'I think she's locked inside,' I whisper into Arthur's ear as I point towards the building. If the gap above the door is the only opening in those four walls, she has no chance of escaping.

The three men look relaxed and are sitting with their backs to the door, so I have a good opportunity to take a closer look at them. One of them has a wide mouth. As I watch him, he begins to laugh at something his friend has said and he reveals a row of blunt teeth that remind me of gravestones in a way. He's got a sagging left eyelid, which hangs low. The second man is bald, with a pointed skull, and the third is so tall his head towers above the others. In my head I give them all nicknames: Droopy, Baldy and Lanky.

Droopy and Baldy are smoking cigarettes. Lanky unfolds a deckchair – a strange sight in the middle of the forest – and begins flipping through a folder of papers, which to my knowledge they didn't have with them at the station. None of them seem to be bothered by the fact they're so far away from any town or village.

It strikes me again how easily their uniforms blend into the background, making them almost invisible. Are they hunters, perhaps? But what would hunters want with a young girl? Unless… a cold feeling suddenly comes over me and I abruptly take a step back.

'We have to get her out of there,' I mutter to Arthur, who is still hidden among the ferns.

'How?' he asks quietly. 'There are three of them and they're huge!'

'If one of us distracts those men, the other can quickly open the door and…'

'What if it's locked?' hisses Arthur. 'They could take us too! Who's going to free us, then?'

I can't give him a satisfactory answer, so I fall silent and begin to anxiously chew on the inside of my cheek. There's nothing in the direct vicinity: no vehicles, no barns, no houses, nothing to indicate that any other humans live nearby. Only the bare building, which is clearly only designed to detain people, and even then by my reckoning only has room for about one or two people inside. Surely there has to be a way for us to break the girl out and quickly hide in the forest before the three men can get hold of us?

They may be thickset and wide like bulls, but Arthur and I are swift. We can also easily fit into small holes and other places where grown men can't, and from what I've observed, that girl wasn't exactly a pushover either.

Finally, Lanky closes his folder. He says something which I can't quite make out, takes out a bunch of keys from his pocket, and walks towards the door. I spring up, jab Arthur in the side and slide as close as possible to the ditch without revealing myself.

The man disappears into the building. For a long time nothing happens, while Droopy and Baldy continue to hang around the locked door as if they don't know what to do with themselves. Before I can consider whether this is our chance to move in, Baldy suddenly sets off in our direction. Terrified, I breathe in quickly and press my lips tightly together. Arthur is frozen beside me. There's no time to jump up and run away without immediately revealing ourselves.

I tense all my muscles, ready to defend myself if necessary.

Baldy comes to a stop. His eyes wander over the vegetation without a trace of surprise on his face. I breathe out very carefully and quietly. He undoes his trousers and for a moment I'm confused, until I hear a trickling sound running over the vegetation. Disgusted, I move back slightly. My hand touches a round pebble near me, big enough to fit into my palm. I pick it up and stare at it for a moment before I make a decision on impulse. I throw the stone as hard as I can at Baldy's head.

His gaze swerves up to me and for a brief moment I know he has seen me. Then, he drops to the ground like a felled tree. Arthur lets out a brief, startled cry, but to my relief he instantly puts his hand over his mouth.

My hands clammy with sweat, I look up to see whether the men near the stone cell are at all alarmed by the commotion. Lanky still hasn't emerged from the building and Droopy is leaning against the wall smoking a cigarette, his eyes fixed in the other direction.

I hook my arms under the armpits of the collapsed man and yank him roughly into the bushes. Arthur gestures wildly at me with an expression of deep shock on his face, but I pay no attention. I quickly examine the man's pockets for weapons or anything else that may help us if it comes down to confronting the other two. For a man who is clearly involved in shady business out here in the woods, he's got surprisingly little on him. Only when I pull his shirt up do I find something useful. I grin, and with a quick jerk I pull the keys from his belt, triumphantly holding them up for Arthur to see.

'You're insane,' he whispers to me with a hint of awe in his voice.

'That may be, but one of these keys has to be for that door, and as long he stays knocked out we only have to worry about two others.' I look with mild disgust at the pale face of the unconscious man. My eyes are drawn to the logo under the collar of his uniform ... *that hideous snake,* as Mum called it.

'You forget that those two are even bigger than this one,' Arthur whispers back. His eyes begin to dart nervously back and forth between our hiding place and the stone building. 'What do you suggest we do with *them*? Tackle them and tie them to a tree?'

'Just shut up if you don't have any better ideas.' I pull the rucksack towards me and feel around until I find what I'm looking for. 'Here, take this,' I say as

I toss Arthur the box of matches. 'Walk a little way into the woods and start a fire, but make sure it's not so far away that they can't see the smoke. Throw some damp wood on it; that'll get you a good amount of smoke. They'll see it and head towards it. In the meantime I can use the keys to free the girl from that cell.'

'A fire in the woods?' Arthur hisses. 'Are you crazy?'

'It won't spread; the ground is far too wet. Come on, before it's too late.' This might be the only chance we'd get today.

Arthur seems to make a decision and nods. 'Promise that you'll be careful, Nim?'

'Of course.' I throw my arm around him and hug him briefly before pushing him away from me. 'Go quickly. Let it burn!'

'You know I will.' Despite his reservations, my brother shows his crooked grin.

I look after him as he silently disappears into the trees before I turn my attention back to the problem in front of me. Baldy is still lying motionless on the ground before me. His chest moves up and down evenly, his eyelids flickering every once in a while, but otherwise it appears he won't be returning to consciousness any time soon. I must have hit him harder than I thought.

As I can do nothing other than wait, I try to determine which key is most likely to fit in the lock on the door. It would be best if I could get it right on the first try, because it's impossible to say how much time I'll have once Arthur lights the fire and Lanky and Droopy trot off to investigate. I sincerely hope that the men will be so confident about that girl not being able to open the door of her cell from the inside herself that they won't feel the need to leave one man behind to keep guard.

Even though I expected it, a sudden trail of smoke floats up from the other side of the clearing. All my senses are immediately on edge. I crawl into the ditch as quickly as I can, where I crouch behind the earthen wall and stare at Droopy with bated breath. *Look up*, I urge him in my mind. *Look up, see the smoke! Smell the fire, you ugly ogre!*

Almost as if he's heard me, the stocky man suddenly turns his head towards the end of the clearing. I see him squint his narrow eyes and hear him curse.

Go on, go get your friend.

To the right of the first column of smoke, a second plume appears among the trees, then a third on the left. Droopy swears again, more loudly this time, and pounds loudly on the door of the cell.

I grin to myself. Arthur was smart enough to light not just one fire, but three different ones. That'll certainly keep them busy.

Lanky sticks his head out the door, exchanges a few words with Droopy, then bounds out of the building. For a moment I think he's accidentally forgotten to lock the door in the commotion, but no – to my disappointment, he still turns the key in its lock before searchingly looking around him.

They're wondering where Baldy is, I realise. They exchange a few brief words; it looks like Lanky is giving a command to Droopy before they each go off in different directions, loudly crashing through the undergrowth.

My heart does a somersault in excitement. Without further hesitation, I jump out of the ditch and run to the door of the building, pushing a key into the lock and haphazardly twisting it to the left.

Nothing.

I have the next key ready to go. Then the next…it clicks in the lock and turns smoothly.

Success! The door swings open and almost immediately something hits me, causing me to fall over onto my back with a crash. I'm briefly blinded in a tangle of arms and legs.

'Stop!' I pant. 'I'm not one of those men!'

The girl hovers over me, breathing heavily, her eyes wide open as she takes in my face suspiciously. With one hand she pushes her ruffled hair out of her eyes, and with the other she presses me down in the mud, but her grip is already weakening. 'Who are you?'

'Nimue.' I roll onto my side and feel a stabbing pain in my ribs where she hit me. 'We've come to save you.'

'How?'

'My brother and I saw you being pulled from the train. Whew.' As I sit up, the air rushes out of my lungs. 'He's out in the woods, lighting fires to distract those two, but he'll be back any second.'

'There were three of them,' says the girl sharply.

Still out of breath, I point in the direction of the bushes. 'Baldy's over there, if you don't believe me.'

She opens her mouth at the very moment Arthur comes running into the clearing. He skids to a standstill, his cheeks flushed with excitement. 'They were so angry, you should have seen it,' he proclaims, grinning from ear to ear. 'One blamed the other and vice versa – they were like a cat chasing its own tail. But we really have to go now, before they figure out they've been duped. I'm Arthur, by the way.'

The girl glances between me and Arthur. 'I'm Mirna,' she says after a brief silence. 'I don't understand, why did you....?'

'It looked very suspicious, the way they were dragging you from that platform,' I say.

'But you got off that train and wandered through this cursed forest, all just to...' Mirna clasps her mouth shut and pricks up her ears. 'They're coming! Quick, over here, I know the way.'

'Wait,' I object, looking around as I turn. 'I must have that folder ...'

'Folder? What folder?'

'The papers that Lanky had on him.'

'Forget the papers. Run!'

'You don't understand! I have to know who they are, where that logo comes from...'

Mirna roughly grabs my arm and pulls me away from the building. 'You won't need any papers for that; I know who those snakes are. Now run!'

12

SHADOW OF EVIL, SHREDS OF SECRETS

We run harder than I've ever run before in my life. Mirna is running ahead of us, zigzagging between the trees and jumping over the jutting rocks, as if her feet don't touch the ground. She seems to find paths and turns that aren't visible to us. And during all this time I have no idea whether we're being followed.

After what seems like an eternity, it feels like my heart is going to burst. Black spots flash before my eyes. I stand, gasping for breath, my hands on my knees.

There's no sign of the three men behind us, just the sound of birds startled by our presence. I look around me. I've lost all sense of direction. Was the cell in the woods this side where the trees bend towards each other? Mirna has made us climb and crawl so much I don't know which way is up and down anymore.

'What are you doing? We're not out of the woods yet.' Mirna has also slowed her pace and looks at me disapprovingly with her dark eyes. 'We can't afford to stop.'

'I have to, otherwise I'll collapse.' I groan as I pull my tight plimsolls off my feet and chuck them into the rucksack.

'I don't hear anyone,' pants Arthur. 'I think we've shaken them off.'

The girl looks around suspiciously, but Arthur's right: apart from the three of us the forest seems to be completely abandoned.

'Good,' she says finally. 'It'll be dark soon. If you two don't want to keep going, we need to find a good place to take shelter. It can get icy cold at this time of year.'

'How about there?' says Arthur, pointing at the dark shape of a fallen tree a few meters in front of us, half-hidden by the undergrowth. 'That looks sturdy. We can build a hut out of branches up against it.'

The prospect of such a meagre shelter doesn't seem to please Mirna very much. I'm not exactly thrilled by the idea either, but I know it beats spending a night out in the open. Mirna puckers her lips but still follows Arthur to inspect the tree.

I stand there for a moment, breathing deeply. As I straighten my back and turn around, to my astonishment I find myself face-to-face with the elongated figure of a man, bright as the moon and translucent as mist.

I freeze. The hairs on the back of my neck stand on end.

All of a sudden the spectre disappears, as if it was nothing but a beam of light. Cast by what, though? I glance up into the treetops, where the last glints of sunlight are vanishing.

Am I hallucinating? As if on cue I touch my forehead. Of course my skin feels cool. If I'd suffered from a raging fever, surely I'd have noticed by now. My heart is beating restlessly.

I take a step forward towards the place where the figure was just standing. No – it can't have been a dream or an illusion. The figure had a remarkably recognisable appearance: two arms, two legs, a head, and a torso... if he hadn't been so pale I'd have thought we were being followed by an ordinary man.

I get to where he'd been watching me, next to a steep rockface covered by shrubs of the forest growing against it. In front of me is a young rowan tree, full of small berries. The instant that I reach for it with my hand, the wind sweeps the branches to one side, as if it were an invisible sign. My eyes catch sight of a narrow opening, no more than a crack in the rock against which the slender tree grows.

'Nimue!'

I start. Arthur and Mirna stand by the fallen tree. Arthur beckons me over.

'Look,' I say, hoarsely. I clear my throat and try again: 'There's a cave here behind the rowan. Come look, I think we'll fit.'

We inspect the opening, which is just wide enough for us to go through.

Mirna is the first to poke her head inside the cave; she sniffs around and lets out a short, sharp shriek. I nearly jump out of my skin but Mirna emerges again with a satisfied look on her face.

'No bears,' she explains. 'It's almost impossible with an opening the size of this one, but you can't be sure enough. Who's going first?'

'Go ahead,' I mutter. I've had my fair share of adventure over the last few hours.

Mirna straightens her back and disappears into the dark hole, her footsteps making shuffling noises. After a brief silence her voice drifts out to us: 'Come in, it gets wider once you get past the entrance.'

I look at Arthur. 'You go first. I'll be right behind you.'

Arthur nods and disappears into the hole in a flash. I look at how the branches of the rowan seem to immediately fall back over the entrance, removing any suggestion of there ever having been a cave. If one of those men did follow our trail and come by this place, they'll have no idea where we've gone.

I take one last look at the forest. Immediately I spot the heron. It's flying low over the ground and disappears within seconds behind the trees. As if in a trance I keep looking at where it's gone, until Arthur calls my name from inside.

I make myself as flat as possible and squeeze into the cave last. By the time this day is over I'll probably have bruises everywhere.

To my relief, the inside of the cave is indeed roomier, allowing me to breathe deeply and take a step forward. Someone seizes my arm, and moments later I hear Arthur's voice close to me as he mumbles directions to me. The ground slopes down slightly and my feet occasionally knock into loose stones, which roll away making a low, echoing sound.

Arthur lets go of me. I try to estimate how large the cave actually is, but in this darkness that's as impossible as breathing underwater. I'm just thinking about how oppressive it'd be to spend a whole night in the darkness of this cave, when my thoughts are interrupted by a hissing noise. A moment later, Arthur's face appears in a reddish glow and the stone walls of the cave seem to rise around us.

Arthur has lit a match.

My brother slowly turns around and the light from the flame reveals a low, round-shaped room. It's just big enough for the three of us.

'Wow,' I whisper, my breath causing the flame to flicker.

'It's cold here,' says Arthur.

'Less cold than outside, once the sun sets,' says Mirna. 'And it sets quicker here, what with those trees.'

'Can't we make a fire in here?'

'Inside? And where would the smoke go? They'd be able to find us immediately.' Mirna sits down against the wall and bends her legs so her knees are supporting her chin.

I follow her example, thankful for the lined hood of my anorak, which helps blocking the chill running down my neck. 'Can you tell us why those men were taking you? You're not some kind of escaped murderer, are you?' I say, letting out a nervous laugh.

'Me? They're the ones who are murderers.' She sounds bitter. 'Those people you saw are from Detection. By no means the worst threat if I'm being honest, but you should always watch your step so they won't sink their claws into you. They swarm over this land like a plague of locusts.'

Arthur's match goes out, leaving us in complete darkness.

'So what's the biggest threat out there?' he asks quietly.

'The people they work for.'

In the silence that follows I can hear all of us breathing. Arthur and I wait. I think we both feel it's better to keep quiet and wait for Mirna to clarify. After a few minutes our patience is rewarded when Mirna pipes up with: 'The Asclepius Congregation. We call them snakes.' You can hear the disgust in her voice. 'God and all his angels help you if you get caught by the snakes.'

Again we fall into stunned silence as I try to process the information. Rona's words from the diary hit me like a wave. When I finally regain control of my voice, I say: 'What does this Asclepius Congregation do, exactly?'

'They take you away to their huge institutions in the middle of Central Europe and there they... do things to you. I only know a handful of children who have ever returned.'

'Good Gwenhael,' I mutter as I feel all power drain from my body. I close my eyes and lean my head against the wall, slowly breathing until the feeling of nausea is gone. The sentences in the diary come to me once more, now clearer than ever. It's as if I can hear Mum's own voice as I bring to mind the bit where Benji tells Rona about his progress: *So far none of his patients have survived the experiments, but that seems to worry him less than the failure of his research. He is hopeful that he will soon develop a method that will allow victims of the Black Influenza to survive his cruel healing process ...*

'Nim? Are you alright?'

'Arthur,' I groan. 'This Asclepius Congregation... Benji ... don't you understand?'

'What do you mean?' asks Mirna confused. 'Who's Benji?'

I try to swallow but my mouth is suddenly very dry. I can't tell her anything about our mad uncle, not so long as we don't know whether he's still alive, where he is to be found and if he is still part of that terrible organisation. 'How do you know so much about it, Mirna?' I ask instead, trying to make my voice sound somewhat normal. 'Am I right in assuming this wasn't the first time they tried to get you?'

'They didn't just try, they got me. I was once one of the children that they have locked up in their institution.'

'You?' asks Arthur open-mouthed. 'So you must have ...'

'Escaped? Yes, but it wasn't easy and I had to wait painfully long for the right moment,' Mirna responds. 'I was eleven when they took me to the 'Institute', as they call it. I can still remember the walls ... yellow walls everywhere. They locked me up in a cramped room without any heating, food or water. There was barely any light. I thought they were going to let me die while they were watching me with a camera in the corner of the room.'

Mirna falls silent again, as if to gather her thoughts. I wrap my arms around myself and try to quell the rising tide of hysteria within me.

'It only lasted two days but felt like an eternity. Then, when people finally came for me, I was probed and tested. Measurements of my heartbeat, saliva and urine, they put tubes in me and took my temperature. Then I was alone again. Three days... maybe more. I can't remember anything else from that time. It must have been some sort of quarantine, but I don't understand why they thought I'd be some sort of danger and no one told me anything.'

'When I was taken out I was dehydrated. They let me eat and drink and they gave me an injection. I can't remember what happened after that, only that when I woke up, I was in a capsule with no clothes on. I could only move my head and the lid was so low that I thought I'd suffocate. There were... all these people who'd come to observe me and make notes. Every now and then they'd open the capsule and change the suction cups on my head, which were connected to the device with wires.'

'In the end I fainted again, but when it was over they put me in a normal room with a bed, new clothes and meals every day... they said everything was okay, that I didn't need to be scared anymore. I tried to believe them. I *wanted* to believe them; otherwise I'd have gone mad with fear.'

Only our breathing is audible in the silence that ensues. Arthur lights another match. 'How long were you there for?'

'Five years,' Mirna responds. 'I lived there for five long years. Every day I had to undergo experiments. Every day they took blood from me and injected me w-with...*poison*. Things that made me sleepy, nauseous and violently ill. But never too ill; they always made sure that I was well again within a few days. The truly dangerous stuff they kept for the others. I had to stay in my room, but I picked up information when they came to get me, or when they thought I couldn't hear them over the brain scanners and capsules. They thought I was a stupid, scared child. But I put it all away safely. In here.' She points to her forehead. 'Every day I swore to myself I'd get out and that they wouldn't break me. The older I got, the more I understood. There were reports of patients who'd reacted badly to the administered fluids... they called them *patients*.'

Mirna sounds terribly bitter. She stares wide-eyed into the cave. 'Stolen children, just like me, without family to protect them. They always took young children.... they were looking for... nobody knew.'

'A cure for the Black Influenza.' I realise my voice sounds like two stones scraping against each other.

'Flu?' Mirna looks at me anxiously.

'A plague.' I say, shaking. 'It ravaged Central Europe years ago. It turned out there was one person who knew how to cure the patients.' But it seems Benji hasn't given up on his crusade just yet.

Something seems to be bothering Mirna. She keeps quiet for a while and then enquires: 'How do you know all this?'

'They wanted me too,' I answer after a brief pause, in which the darkness of the cave swallows us once again and I debate how much I should risk revealing. 'I didn't know it at the time, but... my mother sacrificed everything in order to protect me from them. It worked, or else they'd have found me by now.'

'We're worried that the Asclepius Congregation has taken her prisoner,' says Arthur when I don't continue.

'I've never heard of anything like that,' mutters Mirna. 'A full-grown woman? That's not their style.'

But Rona is different, isn't she? Rona is Benji's sister. 'Where will you go now, Mirna?' I ask, hoping to steer the conversation away from my mother. There are too many new things that I'll need to think over first – things I need to process. 'Do you live in Brevalaer?'

'For someone like me it's too dangerous to live in the city, or even in a village. Arthur, light another one of those matches, please. This dark is scaring me.'

There is a flash – a new flame lighting up our faces.

'There is one place where we'll be safe.' Mirna looks from Arthur to me. 'You have to come with me, if what you say about the Asclepius Congregation is true. Seeking them out is about the stupidest thing you can do, even if they might hold your mother prisoner.'

I exchange a look with Arthur. We both know that nothing will deter us from our search, even Benji's organisation, but shelter and the chance to learn more about the Asclepius Congregation are two opportunities we can't pass up.

'And another thing.' The sharpness in Mirna's voice makes sure I take heed of her warning. 'Whatever you decide, don't travel any further than Brevalaer. I don't know what's happening there, but they've built a tall border post by the city. Something's stirring in Central Europe and I've got a bad feeling about it. Will is growing restless. He...' She seems to hesitate, shaking her head. 'You speak of an epidemic. I wouldn't be at all surprised.'

'There were rumours of overcrowded hospitals in Brevalaer,' recalls Arthur. 'Perhaps it has already reached the city.'

'If that's the case, they've done a good job keeping it out of sight. I've never heard anything about it, so don't worry for the time being. Sleep now. This night's cold and unpleasant enough without your scary stories.' Yet she doesn't sound overly satisfied with her words. In any case, I've got enough to mull over during the long night.

13

—·—

WILL'S ARK

Mirna leads us through the streets of Brevalaer in the same fashion she's led us through the forest: hastily, confidently and with a watchful gaze that never seems to fade from her eyes. I do my best to keep up with her, but I'm tired from walking so much and I soon fall behind. What's more, these new surroundings are piquing my curiosity; the shops with shiny glass windows, the flats, the cars that are parked out in the streets. We are still in Breizh, but it seems a million miles away from Gwennec.

'Keep walking, I don't like being in town,' says Mirna, when she notices me and Arthur have stopped to look at the small castle rising up in the centre of town. 'Those thugs from Detection might still be nearby.'

'Where is this place of yours exactly?' I ask cautiously. Brevalaer seems to be endless.

Mirna hesitates for a moment. 'In the marshes. Not too far from town but well hidden away.'

'In a swamp?'

'It's safe there, Nimue. There's not much to look for there and local superstitions keep even the guys from Detection away. We'll be fine there.'

'Who else lives there?' asks Arthur. 'How come they haven't seen your houses?'

'We don't have houses...' answers Mirna with a glint in her eye. '...as for inhabitants...there's Will, our leader, my friends, and a lot of children.' She

131

shrugs her shoulders. 'It may seem like an unorganised mess, but Will has strict rules. All of us also have one thing in common.'

'What's that?'

'No one has family to protect them, and no one has a home to go back to.'

'That's sad, Mirna, especially for the children,' I say quietly. Nobody should have to grow up without a family, I think to myself with a pang in my heart.

'We all get on together fine. They certainly have it better with us than with the Asclepius Congregation, that's for sure.' And with that, the topic is shut down by Mirna. She turns around and beckons us to follow her.

We stick to the hidden safety of shadowy alleys and narrow streets, as if Mirna's scared of getting pounced upon if we're in broad daylight. After about half an hour, we pass what I assume is the city centre. It is a huge four-sided square, ringed by tall houses which stand like stone trees around this urban clearing. Today there are no market stalls to be found, but on other days I imagine this place must be thronging with activity, just like Gwennec – even more so than Gwennec in fact. Brevalaer is larger and richer than any other place I have ever seen: even in Saint-Thonan there are no cars parked outside the houses, as if it were normal for people to have their own vehicle in the first place. I suddenly become painfully aware of my limited knowledge of the outside world. A fisherman's daughter from an unknown village, that's all I am. I might feel like I'm destined for bigger things than going into fishing, but what do I actually know about the world beyond the coast? The only one who could have told us anything about it has left long ago. Besides, Mum absolutely hated the big city.

In the middle of the square is a huge fountain, which inevitably catches my eye. We could all easily take a bath in it. I marvel at the large stone trough. The statue in the middle is adorned with scowling gargoyles; misshapen devils and nightmarish faces which could easily come straight out of one of Jodoc's stories.

Have I seen this before? Even though I can't place it, I stand staring at it with a sense of familiarity.

A few seconds later we walk past it and soon another building blocks my view of the square, so I shake off the feeling.

We slip out of Brevalaer just as unnoticed as we entered it.

Mirna takes us through a maze of backstreets and alleyways until we reach a meadow, where deciduous trees with bare branches form the entryway to the marshes. There is a strange smell in the air, a smell that gets stronger as we go beyond the natural tree gate and our feet begin sinking a few centimetres into the green goo. It smells of rotting wood and wet foliage, and also something that I can't quite put my finger on.

'Peat,' says Mirna, when she notices my pained expression. 'You get used to it eventually. Watch where you're going... pay attention to my footprints. The trails can be quite treacherous and you don't want to get stuck in the peat, believe me.'

Oh, I believe her alright. These marshes are even more impenetrable than the forest, and much more putrid to boot. No wonder Mirna and her companions feel safe here: no one in their right mind would believe that a group a children could survive in this place! Even I wouldn't believe it if Mirna weren't walking in front of me with such a serious expression on her face, her footsteps falling in precisely the right places. I step where she steps, with Arthur close behind me.

'There it is,' Mirna says as she points.

'Where?' I look around me. There seems to be no change in the landscape, apart from a few extra fallen trees before us, next to which a large, grey rock sticks out, blocking the road. 'I can't see anything.'

'That's the point,' says Mirna, grinning. She walks towards the fallen trees and stands there with a meaningful look.

Arthur and I follow her with a sigh, but then I suddenly see what she means. What I thought to be a rock is, in fact, a section of wall sticking out of the ground. It's manmade: a vertical piece of concrete, as thick as my waist.

'But what is it for?' I ask. 'Is it an entrance, or a sort of secret...?'

'I don't think it's for anything,' says Arthur before Mirna can answer. 'Look at everything growing over it.'

The wall was most likely once part of an old building. Now it looks like a strange part of the marshes themselves, covered with fungi and plants. Arthur scratches some of the moss away. 'There's something written here.'

I move closer to see. The blue paint is faded and almost illegible. '...*rk* 117?' And then it hits me what it means. 'Not *rk* ... Ark! You have an Ark!'

The idea of an abandoned underground bunker in the middle of a swamp is both simple and brilliant. I can't believe I hadn't thought of it before. 'Was there really a whole Ark near here? Is it still around? How dark is it inside? Are there still any signs of ...?'

Dozens of questions. I shut my mouth at once when I see Mirna smiling.

'Come see for yourself.'

We walk around the wall. The muddy, difficult path turns into a smooth surface, and as I look at my feet I can see we've entered a square. The tiles are half overgrown with ferns and grass, but underneath there are signs of another life and time visible. I begin to wonder if the Ark was purposely built in the marshes or whether the bog developed around it later.

On the other side of the square is a kind of concrete box, which is in much better condition than the wall, with a heavy iron door in the middle. 'Is that the entrance to the Ark?'

'It's the door that leads below. We can push those bolts shut, so when we're inside we're safe as foxes in a den. Nothing can get through that door.'

Mirna knocks on the metal with her fist. A moment later, the door opens very slightly. Not inwards or outwards, but from the side via a small rail, so that it disappears into the wall.

'It's okay, it's me!'

'Mirna!' From out of the dark hole appears a tall, pale boy who throws his arms around Mirna, nearly pushing her over, followed by a gaggle of children who swarm about us. I see a boy with a long scar on his face, a girl with sunken cheeks and a dripping nose and another child leaning on a stick and hobbling forward...

'I almost tore my hair out with worry, Mirna! You should have been back days ago, what ...'

'Conn, I'm okay.' Mirna pushes the boy away from him. 'I was in trouble, but...'

'Trouble? Did they get you? I told you...I told Will to... Goddammit, I'll kill him!'

'Hush,' snarls Mirna. 'It was my mistake, my responsibility. Yeah, they got me, but Nimue and Arthur here helped me. Those snakes had no chance to do anything to me.'

'What's that, Mirna? Your brother wants to kill me?'

I turn around to see the source of the unfamiliar voice. At the entrance of the Ark is another guy. He must be a few years older than me and must have silently crept out of the Ark, like a fox. He wears a hole-ridden pair of jeans, solid brown boots, and a grey fleece, its hood pulled up over his head. From his lips dangles a cigarette, the smell of smoke and wet leaves wafting over to me as he moves off the wall and smoothly walks over to us.

'He thinks you can't take care of yourself, Mirna... is that right?'

Mirna shrugs her shoulders and pulls a slightly uncomfortable face. 'I've done smarter things.'

'Haven't we all?' The young man takes the cigarette from his mouth with long fingers and blows a puff of smoke into the air. He then smiles, a small gesture that seems to transform his gloomy face as if a lamp has lit up inside it. He turns to me and takes my hand.

'Nimue, wasn't it? And Arthur? On behalf of the entire Ark I must thank the two of you. Mirna is our beating heart. Without her, we might as well just lie down on the floor and die. I'm Will.'

His eyes are as dark as ink, like a moonless night.

'I'm glad she's safe,' I mutter back.

'Will you be staying?'

'Yes, if we can. Please.'

'Are you in danger?'

'No...well, I don't know.'

His dark eyes scan me from top to bottom. There's a fiery sense of intelligence in his eyes, which makes me feel I can tell him no word of a lie. 'The two of you are alone. They can smell it.' He curls his upper lip – I'm not sure whether he is smiling or growling. 'Like dogs, you know?'

'You mean the Asclepius Congregation?'

A murmur rises from the group of children that still surround us.

Will smiles a crooked smile. 'Well, I see that you two aren't so scared. Best not to speak that name here, Nimue.'

I think about what Mirna told me. All these children are terrified of my uncle's organisation, and rightly so. I feel somewhat ashamed. 'I'm sorry.'

'Not to worry. Come in, or rather, come down. Have you two ever seen an Ark? When did you eat last?'

'We have some food in our rucksack,' answers Arthur.

'Good, you can share it with us. Where did you say you'd come from?'

We hadn't said anything about it yet. 'Gwennec. By the sea,' I say.

'Gwennec.' He fixes his gaze on me for a moment. 'Arthur and Nimue of the sea. You've had a long journey. Mirna, get Yuna and take the children inside, would you? Make sure they can rest. I want to hear everything about your little... misadventure.'

Mirna grabs the girl with the stick by the hand. I'm shocked to see she is missing a leg. The left leg of her trousers flaps unused on the ground. As Arthur and I walk behind Mirna, I can't take my eyes off it. Will stays behind. Without turning round I feel his gaze burning into my back.

'It's warmer down below,' says Mirna, who sees me shudder and misinterprets it. 'The earth keeps in the warmth, so even in winter we're well protected.'

At the entrance of the Ark, where the metal door slides into the concrete, it strikes me that there are hundreds of deep scratches etched into the concrete, criss-crossing over each other as if thousands of tiny creatures have scratched it with their claws.

'Old scars from the first poisonous rains,' says Mirna, letting her hand glide over the concrete. 'In the years following the Impact every raindrop was pure poison. It could burn your eyes out if you looked up to the sky without protective clothing. Fertile ground, trees, stones... nothing was safe. That's what they said at least. In any case the bunkers were built so deep underground that most of the rooms remained safe.' She smiles. 'Welcome to the Ark.'

I have never been underground. Now that we are standing at the doorway, my excitement soon begins to fade. Behind the heavy door a staircase leads downstairs. The last steps are smothered in darkness. Everything looks old, as if at any moment the whole structure could collapse in on itself in one fell swoop. I shake my head, determined to not get scared. The Arks were the safest places on Earth, built to protect people from the unpredictable elements of the outside world. They are the fortresses of our time. Here, there are no floods and no storms to threaten us.

'Aren't you scared of falling?' asks Arthur.

Mirna grins. 'You get used to it. Will has banned the use of any light in the hall, and sometimes we don't even have power to switch it on. Every Ark has a CORE, but this is one of the older models. The last time it went out we had to spend the whole day in complete darkness.'

A whole day underground in darkness? It seems like an image from a nightmare. I watch how the one-legged girl limps downstairs from step to step. She leans alternately on her stick and against the wall, although I can't quite see what she's holding onto. Just like the entrance to the bunker, the wall is made of solid, smooth concrete. I feel for every step with my foot before I dare step on it. Despite my attempts to reassure myself, I can't help but feel my anguish increasing with every step. The surrounding darkness closes in on me, as if it's sucking out the oxygen and doubling the force of gravity.

Mirna leads us through the hall and warns us of a sharp corner that I can't see. Half-blinded, I let her voice and hands lead me, keenly aware that without her guidance we'd be hopelessly lost. The bunker is a network of empty corridors, a frightening labyrinth, some wide and others so narrow that we have to walk through it in single file. Here and there, neon light flickers from fluorescent tubes that stick to the walls, giving me brief moments to let out a sigh of relief and take a look around me. Not that there's much to see; everything is drab and bare. I exchange glances with Arthur and know we are thinking the same thing. This is no place to live, let alone a place for children to grow up. No one should be forced to live here, where the damp has left traces on the walls and sunlight has no chance to penetrate inside.

At last, Mirna grabs my shoulder. 'We're nearly there, it'll get better. Look.'

Ahead of us a bright light looms, and before I know it we're in a large, rectangular room. It is certainly a lot more pleasant, since the room is furnished with a range of tables and chairs and there are seating areas where large cushions are arranged on the floor. Spread across the room are about a dozen or so boys and girls, some on the floor with blankets wrapped around them, while others sit at the table dressed in thick jumpers and frayed scarves. None of them look older than Mirna.

Mirna lets go of my shoulder and looks us up and down. 'Sit down where you want, there's plenty of room. Is that all you have? Don't you have a sleeping bag in your pack?'

'We don't, sorry.' After everything that's happened to me I've forgotten about our meagre belongings in the rucksack. 'We still have some food left, which we're happy to share with you. I'm afraid we don't have anything else, not even clean clothes.'

Mirna waves her hand. 'I didn't expect there to be much stuff in that small bag anyway. Not to worry, here we're used to making do. Anna!' she calls out to the other side of the room. 'Isn't there a spare sleeping bag over in the corner?'

A chubby girl with a thick mop of dark hair brings forth a thin sleeping bag. She's holding her right arm uncomfortably at her side. As she gets closer, I can see the fingers on her hand are stiff and bent, as if she were making a claw-like fist.

'There are sleeping quarters with bunk beds where you can sleep, if you want,' says Mirna. 'But it can get bitterly cold in there if the CORE cuts out, so most people sleep here at night.'

I nod, but I don't manage to avert my gaze from the other girl. When she sees me looking, she quickly turns away from me. I finally avert my gaze, ashamed that I've been staring.

My eyes wander across the faces of the Ark-dwellers, their curious yet cautious eyes surveying me and Arthur. Most of them are no older than ten, I reckon.

Yuna has crept over to a brown-haired boy and wraps her arms around him.

'Is that her brother?' I ask.

Mirna shakes her head. Something in her eyes tells me there is another sad story behind this. 'Broc lived with his older sister. That was until...'

'Until she was taken?' I bleakly suggest.

Mirna nods. 'Will and I tried to stop it, but they were too fast with their jeeps. Poor Broc hasn't uttered a single word ever since.'

'I'm so sorry,' I whisper, so softly that I don't think Mirna hears me.

Mirna's brother enters the room, followed by another boy. I immediately notice he's not a child anymore either and must be about the same age as Arthur. He is tall and thin, with a patch of wild red hair and a face covered in freckles.

Mirna makes a brief, sweeping motion with her hand. 'Cor! These are Nimue and Arthur. They saved me today. Nimue and Arthur, this is Corentin.'

'Will told me already.' He doesn't smile, simply giving us a small nod after an uncomfortable silence. 'Thank you. Mirna should have known better.'

'I … but … it wasn't her fault,' I mumble, slightly embarrassed. 'They attacked her on the train and there were three of them …'

'That's what they do. Stalk you like wolves until they've got you cornered.'

'That's what I've heard.' I zip open the sleeping bag and wrap it around my shoulders. Arthur grabs part of it and wraps it around himself. 'Mirna says that it gets cold at night,' I say, changing the subject. I want to hear no more about the Asclepius Congregation.

Corentin seems to relax a little and shakes his head. Now that the frown is gone from his face, he looks a great deal friendlier. 'Not as long as the CORE is on.'

'Mirna was just talking about the CORE. What is that, exactly?'

'Nuclear energy. When the bunkers were built they didn't know how long people would have to stay underground, so in each one they built a CORE that could last two hundred years. The Ark has light, heat, air-con, the lot. Unless it cuts out.' He shrugs his shoulders. 'It always turns back on, though.'

'For now it does,' says Mirna. 'But don't worry, Cor and Conn know their way through all the tunnels even in the dark, but the young ones don't, so don't let them wander off, okay?'

I can well imagine how terrible it must be for someone to get lost in those tunnels. 'What if we need to get out and the lights fail?'

'Feel the walls,' says Conn. 'The wall of the tunnel that leads aboveground has a groove in it.'

'And Will?' I can't seem to shake the feel of his eyes on me. He seems nice, but he makes me nervous, somehow. 'Does he know the tunnels too?'

Mirna shows me a crooked smile. 'He knows every step of every tunnel and every path through the marshes.'

I look around me. The children seem to have lost interest in us and are playing a sort of game with two white pebbles. 'I don't see him.'

'Oh, you won't see him until tonight, if you're not asleep by then,' Corentin replies. 'He always stays out until it gets dark.'

Anna comes back with a pan wrapped in a cloth, which she clumsily holds on to with her one good hand. With her crooked arm, she tries to keep it balanced with great difficulty. The children immediately drop their pebbles and run towards her like starving stray dogs. She sets the pan down on a round table and uses her good arm to give a scrawny young boy a clip on the wrists. 'Hands off, Josse, guests first! Here you go,' she says to Arthur and me, 'if you want to eat, you'll have to serve yourselves. I can't do it.'

I scramble to my feet to help her with the bowls and spoons. The soup consists of a thick slurry that lets off a huge amount of steam as I lift the lid. What it's made from I can't determine.

'It doesn't taste as bad as it looks,' whispers Anna next to me. She still doesn't look at me directly, as if she's embarrassed by me.

'Believe me, right now I could scoff down anything,' I say, grinning. 'Give me your bowl as well.' I take it from her hand and spoon some soup into it for her. 'I didn't mean to be rude.'

She awkwardly shrugs just her left shoulder. 'I've gotten used to people not looking at me funny here. They know who I am. But I understand why you do ... I know what I look like.'

'What do you think you look like?'

'Broken. Crooked.'

'Did... *they* do this to you?'

Anna nods. Her good hand moves over to her poor, deformed arm and pulls the sleeve further down so I can no longer see her twisted fingers and hardened knuckles.

'Perhaps I can help you,' I say gently. 'I know a bit about healing. Perhaps I can ...' *try to heal you, like I healed that man with the terrible wound*. I can't say it. I lick my lips. 'Let me take a look at it.'

Anna lifts her face up and looks directly at me for the first time. She makes a sad smile. 'I don't think there's much that can be done for me. The actual injury has long since disappeared, you see? This is how I've ended up. It's not pretty, I know… but the pain is also gone.'

'If you're sure …'

'You know what I want? To turn back time. If I could keep myself from being caught … if I could have done something to protect myself … I sometimes make countless plans to save myself.' She shrugs her shoulders helplessly and weakly smiles. 'Ultimately there's no point dreaming. I just live with it. I'm normally quite content, I suppose.'

I nod, my mouth dry. What do you say to someone disfigured by your own uncle? What would Anna say if she knew? I turn around before my face can betray my thoughts, and go to sit next to Mirna at one of the tables, the children taking my place next to Anna.

The soup tastes of sweet turnips and carrots. Every mouthful gives me a warm, glowing feeling inside. Perhaps Anna is right and her arm is beyond saving, but if she could just let me take a quick look at it… I put my spoon down in the bowl and briefly stare down at my hands. Did Mum always know what she could do? Why had she never told me anything about it?

Arthur's voice echoes through and I look up as he asks: 'How long have you lived here, then?'

'Some only a year,' says Mirna. 'Most so long that they no longer remember any other life. Especially the younger ones.'

'Like Broc and Yuna?' I'm afraid to ask the next question, scared of the answer that I can already feel in my bones. Nonetheless I whisper: 'Mirna, what happened to Yuna's leg?'

The neon light begins to flicker rapidly and I can't see anything. I freeze up. Moments later, the lights turn back on.

Mirna's face is tense. She mutters something I don't catch, but after a while she lets out a sigh and focuses her attention back on me. The lights stay on, yet I get the impression that Mirna's face has grown darker.

'You know what happened to her, Nimue,' she says quietly. 'You know who did it.'

'But why? What in the world compelled them to cut off someone's leg?'

Mirna stares at the ground. 'They didn't need it. That wasn't their intention. They made a mistake, that's all.'

'A *mistake*?'

'Forget it, Nimue. I don't want to talk about it, not with the little ones here.'

I almost don't believe her. What kind of mistake could Benji's doctors have made that it would lead to such disastrous consequences? Was Anna's arm an accident too?

Yuna has gathered up the pebbles and is now playing a kind of game of marbles with Josse. She doesn't seem at all shocked by the brief power outage. Her one leg is bent and with the blanket draped across her lap it's hardly visible that her other leg is just a stump.

Arthur has stopped eating. Perhaps it's due to the neon lights, but it looks as if all the blood is gone from his face. I swallow a few times, but the ball that suddenly appears in my throat just won't go away. My eyes are stinging. Perhaps it is the dry air inside the Ark produced by the CORE.

I ger up and shake my head as Arthur looks at me quizzically. 'I just need some air,' I mumble. 'I'll be right back.'

I find the groove in the wall that Mirna was talking about and follow the bends and corners upwards. Perhaps it's stupid to walk so recklessly through the Ark on my own, without even a lantern to light the way, but my thoughts are blurred. The only thing I know for certain is that those infernal snakes of the Asclepius Congregation are dancing before my eyes and I need the cold air of the outside in order to chase them away.

As I reach the main door I push it open and step outside, take a deep breath and breathe slowly. I can smell the cold in the air. A thin sliver of moon shines in the sky, as if someone has shaved the edge off a coin and hung it in the sky.

'Nimue.'

The voice startles me. Will stands like a shadow on the edge of the square, where the marshland trees form a wide border. Company is the last thing I need, but now that he's seen me I can't really ignore the tall guy who seems to oversee the entire Ark. Besides, I have to admit I also feel a tingle of curiosity about him.

He has pulled the hood on his sweatshirt up over his head once more, so that he looks like a dark figure from some sort of superstitious story even from up close. Smoke from a cigarette spirals upwards into the night sky and I can smell the tobacco on him, as I did earlier.

'You look scared,' says Will. 'Is it the Ark?'

I nod. 'I've never been so deep underground before. It makes me slightly anxious.'

'I was the same when I first arrived. You get used to it.'

'I guess.' I plunge my hands deep into my pockets. 'Why are you outside?'

'I'm waiting.'

'Oh.' I can't imagine what for. Other than the marshland birds I can hear in the distance, there's nothing else here at all. 'It's freezing here. Don't you have a jacket?'

'I used to. I gave it away years ago.' Will pulls back his hood and smiles at me. His dark hair falls over his forehead. My gaze is drawn to one straw-blond curl in particular, a braid that hangs down over his shoulder.

'Whose is that?'

'What? Oh, this.' He delicately runs his fingertips over the lock of hair. 'It's my sister's.'

I wait for him to say something more but Will falls silent.

'Is she here?' I enquire, trying to break the oppressive silence.

When he finally answers he does so in an abrupt tone of voice. 'I promised that I'd wait for her.'

'Here?' Mirna hadn't mentioned any sister of Will's when she talked about the Ark. I look around me, confused. 'Is she in the swamp?'

'The Asclepius Congregation took her. Years ago.'

'Oh God, Will. I'm sorry.'

Will swallows. I hear it clearly in the silence that hangs between us. If he's out here every night...waiting every single night...could it be because he's waiting for her?

I wrestle with my choice of words. 'If the Asclepius Congregation has taken her, how would she get back, Will?'

'Don't get me wrong.' He rummages around in his bag and lights another cigarette. For a moment I think I can see his hands trembling in the flame of the lighter, but it must be my imagination. 'I'm not insane, I know she won't be coming back, but I promised it to her. I promised Finola that I'd never give up on her.' He clamps the cigarette between his thin lips. 'So I won't.'

'You feel you have to find her again. I understand, Will. Believe me, I understand.'

'Oh, really? How would you possibly know what it's like?'

It's as if he's given me a slap in the face. I automatically step back. 'I just do. The Asclepius Congregation took my mother from me. I'd do anything to find her.'

'Then you know full well how difficult it is to just sit around and wait. Sometimes I dream that they're doing terrible things to her. That they're hurting her.' Will's gaze bores into mine. I wonder if I should take his hand. 'It's late,' he says, before I can reach out for him. 'You better get some sleep.'

'You're not alone in this, Will,' I tell his dark figure.

He breathes the smoke out slowly. 'Goodnight, Nimue.'

14

THE HOUSE WITH THE RED GABLE

There is no early morning light to shine on my face when I wake up, only the artificial light of the CORE.

I groan and try to block it out, but even with my eyes closed, the light gives me a headache, so I let out a sigh and scramble up. The children are already awake. I briefly watch them as they play with their pebbles. They seem unfazed by the constantly flickering light: they continue to laugh and play as if they're outside on the beach. Yuna startles me by catching Josse and scooping up the white stone from the ground in front of him. She raises her fist triumphantly and cackles.

I smile. The Asclepius Congregation has taken her leg, but not her life.

Arthur turns around and pulls the sleeping bag over his head. I give him a prod. 'Wake up, little brother.'

His head disappears deeper under the covers.

'Arthur, get up. It's morning.'

'Just five more minutes,' I hear him mumble.

'Fine, but don't start complaining if you miss breakfast.' I slide out of my sleeping bag. My stomach rumbles discontentedly. I wonder if there is actually any breakfast in the Ark.

Mirna is nowhere to be seen, and neither is Will. I wonder if he's come in at all. After last night's conversation, I don't quite know what I should say to him.

I look for the groove in the wall that will lead me outside. This bunker unnerves me. The light from the CORE makes it impossible to tell what time it is, and even the processed air from the air-conditioning smells stale. I need to see the sky.

As soon as I open the door, I can see that the skies are clear. The smell of the swamp is everywhere, and has even worked its way into my borrowed jumper. It is a mixture of plants, both fresh and rotting, water and muddy earth.

Mirna is seated on the ground with her legs crossed. Will is sitting next to her. He has taken his hood off and he's smoking once again. Where is he getting all those cigarettes from? Conn is whittling a piece of wood with a large knife. If he wants to make something from it, he'd be better off with another piece, as the stick in his hands is clearly rotten.

'Is your brother not up yet?' he asks.

'Sleeping Beauty says he needs five more minutes.'

Conn chuckles. It strikes me that Will keeps staring out straight ahead. Finola probably hasn't returned during the night. He's an odd one.

My stomach grumbles again. 'Could I have something to eat?'

'Berries and mushrooms.' answers Mirna. 'The real food is all gone. This afternoon, supplies will be replenished.'

'By whom?' I ask, curiously.

She smiles. 'By us.'

'Just give me some berries then. Don't the children get impatient without food?'

'They get used to it.' Mirna hands me a fistful of berries. They're fat and juicy, but do more to quench my thirst than to relieve my hunger. 'More than anything, they know this is better than aimlessly wandering around.'

'Arthur and I could go fishing,' I say after wiping my mouth. 'If there's a river or stream nearby, we could set a net or a trap.'

'The swamp gets deeper the further you go up north,' Will says unexpectedly. He gets up. Finola's braid slides in front of his face and he pushes it away. 'A labyrinth of branches, roots and quicksand that'll suck you in, so it's best not to go charging off into the forest on your own. There is a path, but you need to know your way around in order to find it. If you want to go fishing, we'll need to show you the way to the stream first.'

'I'll remember that,' I reply. 'Why haven't the marshes been drained?'

'They wanted to, but they couldn't. It's said to be haunted.'

'What do you mean?' I ask, feeling a chill run through me.

''They sent out teams to cut down the trees, but every time they either disappeared or drowned. So in the end they gave up. Now they just hurry through it by train.'

'Have you ever seen them?' I ask, my heart pounding loudly. 'The ghosts, I mean?'

'Never.' Will shrugs and puts out his cigarette. 'The swamp is a dangerous place, and it's easier for them to say it's haunted than to admit they have no control over it.'

'When you say *them*, do you mean the Asclepius Congregation?' I can't tell him that Benji must have believed spirits were real, just like his sister did. Did he pass down this fear of the Other World to the rest of his team when he set up the Institute? 'Don't you think that there could be something else between heaven and earth, Will?' I ask quietly. 'Something deep down in the sea, or amongst the trees of the marshland?'

He looks at me for a while, his dark eyes unreadable. 'Finola believed in such things. She believed that they were everywhere. In the trees, in the water, in the air.'

'And?'

He briefly shrugs and his gaze dwells away from me. 'I believe what's in front of me. An Ark full of hungry children. The cold that must be kept out every winter. People that have been maimed, both inside and out... If there are ghosts here, they can have the marshes. It doesn't bother me, as long as we can live, eat and scrape out a living here together. But perhaps you think I'm too simple, Nimue.' He grins, but his crooked smile does nothing to chase the shadows from his eyes.

Anything but simple, I think to myself. 'And how do you feed them? How do we survive the winter?'

'A freight train from Brevalaer is headed for the periphery today. There's a good chance that there'll be food and medicine on board. They're easy targets, with little security.'

'So you rob trains?' I ask, unsure if I've heard him right.

'We set up a blockade on the tracks and take what we can. That's all.'

'That's all, is it? Those goods are meant for other people.'

He makes a derisive sound. 'Do you really think the people in Rome care if any cargo arrives in that godforsaken place?'

'That godforsaken place was our home.' I think about my village, about the devastation, and about Yannick attending to the injured in St Gwenhael's with dark rings under her eyes. 'People's lives depend on those goods, Will.'

'Well, this is our home. Our life. As soon as they realize what's happened, they'll send another train. In the meantime, we can survive for weeks. Are you hungry or not?'

I can't say much to that, so I leave them and wander restlessly around the bunker, until I finally take Rona's diary from the backpack and nestle myself into a small gap between the trees that circle the square. The cold doesn't bother me; it keeps my head nice and clear.

I lean back against a frozen tree trunk and leaf aimlessly through the pages, casting my gaze over the now familiar words as I try to picture Mum during her long journey. If only there was a way we could let her know we're looking for her...

I turn the page to one of the many small drawings. For a second, I forget to breathe in. All of a sudden, I know where I've seen that stone fountain in Brevalaer before: right here, in Mum's diary!

Next to the drawing of a small, detached building, which seems to be in a slight state of disrepair, I recognise the gargoyles that had drawn my attention as we headed towards the Ark. The fountain...the apple tree...the house *Avalon*.

I shoot up and run down the stairs of the bunker and into the room where Arthur is still wrapped up in his sleeping bag. My patience is gone and I shake him roughly, just long enough for him to draw himself up. Impatiently, I thrust the open diary onto his lap.

'Look! Mum was in Brevalaer... the red house must be near the fountain. Get up, Arthur! We need to go there.'

'Now?' he croaks as he rubs his hand over his eyes. 'But what about breakfast?'

'There will be no breakfast until Will robs another train, and I frankly don't want to be there for that.'

'Will's doing what? Nim, hold on a second, I just need to get my anorak!'

I pace up and down as I wait for him to wrap his anorak around himself and slide his boots on. Then I grab him by the hand and pull him onto his feet. Will and the others have disappeared, slunk off to cook up more of their schemes, perhaps.

I look around. 'Brevalaer is that way.'

'Are you sure this is a good idea?' Arthur asks. I pace across the square and he follows me at a trot. 'Will says that those men can sniff us out like dogs.'

'In that case, we can ask them where they have stored Mum away,' I grunt through clenched teeth, not breaking step.

'Wait! Do you think this is a joke?'

'Do you see me laughing?' I turn around, almost causing him to bump into me. We look at each other, our breath coming out as vapour in the cold. 'You're right, there's nothing funny about any of his. The whole trip, the cold, the unresolved questions... We're doing all of it to find Mum, aren't we? Well, we've found another piece of the puzzle, Arthur. And I won't be held back by those snakes! I'm not afraid of them.'

For a while, Arthur just stares at me. 'If you're not scared, you're even dumber than Will and his train robbery.' I can tell he is trying to be calm. 'Benji's insane, remember? Even Mum was scared of him.'

I press my lips together and walk off in silence, my footsteps making loud noises on the frozen ground. A little while later, I can tell that Arthur is following me, despite his objections.

I'm not afraid of them, I defiantly tell myself again, but I know I'm lying. The thought of that slithering snake makes me choke up, as if he were actually choking me. When I think of Benji, I imagine a pale man with cold, piercing eyes, his hair blazing like fire. I know full well that we could get burnt if we get too close, and I know the Asclepius Congregation will never let us out of their grasp if they find out who we are.

'But perhaps they would stop their wild goose chase if they got hold of me,' I mumble. 'If Benji had his second Rona.'

'Nim!' Arthur sounds deeply shocked. 'You don't mean that.'

'Think about it. Benji couldn't access Sela's gift, that's why he needed Rona, and when she could no longer help him, he turned his attention to me.' Just saying this out loud causes a chill to creep up my spine. I try to ignore it. 'You heard what Mirna said and you've seen Yuna and Broc, haven't you? The Asclepius Congregation exists solely because Benji is looking for a cure.'

'But what he does is sick!'

'Not much sicker than the Black Influenza itself.' I wrap my arms around my own waist. 'Hundreds, perhaps even thousands of people have died because of this plague. What if you lost me to it? What if you knew that it was possible to save others? Wouldn't you do everything in your power to make that happen?'

'He would use you until you succumbed to it,' Arthur says quietly. All the blood has drained from his face. 'I care a lot less about people I've never met, Nim. You don't actually want to…?'

I slow down my pace so he can walk beside me and I give him an apologetic smile. 'I'm not going to walk straight into their arms, Arthur. Don't look so scared.'

'Promise me you won't do anything stupid,' he begs me.

'Of course. I'll never abandon you. You know that, don't you? Everything we do, we do together, or not at all.'

He nods, even though his worried frown doesn't quite leave his face. We walk next to each other in silence along the narrow path. I keep hesitating, unsure where we can safely tread. Eventually, we see the town sprawling out before us.

As discretely as possible, we walk down the same streets and alleys, until we reach the square with the dried-up fountain in the middle.

I randomly accost one of the passers-by; a slender woman wearing a thick winter coat, her face hidden behind the coat's huge fur collar. 'Excuse me, do you happen to know a red house?' I ask. 'An old house. It should be around here somewhere.'

She stares at me from behind the fur collar. 'The oldest houses are in the Western Quarter. You won't have much luck, that area is almost completely abandoned. What are you looking for?'

I pretend not to have heard her last question. 'Where is the Western Quarter?'

'Follow the alley behind the shops right down to the end. You can recognise the area by the old church tower.' Her eyes continue to peer into mine, as if she is inspecting me like a piece of meat. I force a smile and turn on my heels, dragging Arthur with me.

We go down a deserted cobbled street, closed in on both sides by the exposed walls of the shops. At the end of the alley, a slightly leaning tower looms over us, like a huge, lonely finger pointing to the sky, the church around it long since gone. The houses have faded gables and loose roof tiles. Many of the windows must have had shutters at one point, but now they are nothing but dark, open holes. Weeds cover the pavement everywhere.

I'm startled by something moving out of the corner of my eye, but it's just a cat tearing off around the corner.

'Spooky place,' Arthur says uncomfortably. 'Why has everybody left?'

'The Black Influenza?' I quietly venture. There's something about the oppressive silence that makes me whisper. 'Benji brought the sick to Avalon, to cure them...'

'Do you think it went... wrong?'

I shrug. 'There are many pages missing from the diary about that time. Hey look, over there! A red house!'

We halt in front of a detached building, tall and narrow like a storage house. The gable is still clearly red, even though the paint is peeling off on all sides. The roof is leaning so far to the right that it looks as if it could crash to the ground at any moment.

'Are sure this is the right place?' Arthur asks hesitantly.

'Just look.' Next to the house stands a solemn tree, the only one growing in the area. The branches are gnarled and bare, the trunk bent as if by some invisible weight. 'An apple tree. This has got to be the house.'

I press against the door, which immediately gives way and swings open. It's gloomy inside, and I am momentarily taken by the musty smell. This house was already old when Mum, Benji and Esoldi took up residence here. I don't think the house will collapse, but I'm still nervous when I cross the threshold and take in the empty room before me. Someone has taken the liberty to remove all the furniture. Once my eyes have adjusted to the dim light, I'm shocked by something else: the wooden beams are black and charred, the floor stained with the dark ashes from an ancient fire.

Arthur follows after me. We're both quiet. I don't even dare walk around, afraid that I might break something. Only after a while do I look back at my brother. 'Mum's diary...do you think this was the same fire?'

'It must have been.' His shoulders droop. 'There's nothing left inside.'

'How sad. I think Mum loved this house, even if it was only for a little while.' As I turn around, something catches my eye in one of the corners of the room. At first glance, it just looks like a place where dust and debris have gathered, but as I get closer, I spot three pebbles, roughly the same size, stacked on top of each other. They couldn't possibly have ended up like that by themselves. Someone must have carefully placed the stones on top of each other, keeping them in perfect balance. I squat down on the floor and gently blow away the old ashes. 'I think we were wrong, Arthur. There is something left here.'

The stones form a small shrine, reminding me of the stone slabs on the beach that our people from Gwennec would build sometimes, to beg favours of St Gwenhael. I can't imagine Benji or Esoldi having left this symbol of love here.

Arthur crouches down next to me as I tenderly touch the stones. I am sure this was Mum's doing. Rona, the one who so obviously carried the Other World with her, even when she was forced to leave her island home.

'After the fire, she went with Dad to Breizh, didn't she?' Arthur asks.

I nod. 'And then we were born. And for a while, we were happy.' I don't know where the tears suddenly come from, but they're there and I can't fight them. My hand finds the seal pendant under my clothes, and I clamp my fist around it, as if that can save me from drowning. Is this the last sign of Rona's life we will find, kneeling in the dust of a crumbling house?

We sit next to each other on the hard floor, without speaking. I try not to think, because if I do allow myself to think about Rona's stay in this house, I will irrevocably end up thinking about Benji, and about Mirna's bloodcurdling story – and finally, I'll worry we will never see Mum again.

Eventually, Arthur moves. Through the fog of my tears I can tell he's doing something odd, grabbing his head. For a moment, I think he is in pain – that the dust and ashes have made him unwell somehow – but as I blink the tears away,

I find he has cut off a lock of his hair with the hunting knife that Correntin lent to him. The lock of flaxen hair falls between the four stones.

'Why did you do that?' I ask.

'An altar needs offerings.' He shoves the knife my way. I cut off a handful of my hair, not caring what it might look like, and place it next to Arthur's. Whether it counts as an offering or not I'm not sure, but I think I see what Arthur is going for: for the first in years, we've united with Mum in a very small way.

'As true as the North star and as constant as the tides,' I say. Rona's last words.

'Nimue? We can't get around Benji, can we?'

I close my eyes. 'No, I don't think so.'

'Then we need to find out as much as we can about the Asclepius Congregation. The Ark is the only place where we can do that.'

'I know.'

'Should we tell Will who we are?'

I get up and slowly wipe the black dust off my clothes. 'Not yet.'

'Why not? He might be able to help us.' Arthur rises as well.

'He hates everything connected to the Asclepius Congregation,' I say. 'I don't want to find out if his hatred will include us.'

The moment I step out, I am grabbed from behind by a bony hand.

I scream, then quickly turn and blindly push against the person standing in front of me.

Their grip weakens, but does not disappear. 'Don't move!'

I freeze and give myself a moment to get a good look at my attacker. It is the woman with the fur collar. She stares at me intently.

I look back, my heart hammering loudly against my chest. Arthur appears in the doorway, bewildered, not seeming to know whether to fight or run. For a moment, no one seems to know what to do.

Then the woman removes her hand from me and pushes the fur collar down so I can see her face. She has a waxy complexion and hollow eye sockets. Her eyes, like two shiny beads, pierce into me.

'Why are you following us?' I ask.

'Why have you come here? You shouldn't be snooping around.'

'We aren't...'

'Hush! There is nothing good in that house. You two would do best to not dig too deep into the debris.'

Is that a warning or a threat? What does she know about the red house? Despite my clammy palms and pounding heart, I look directly at her. 'Why? Is there something we're not supposed to find?'

The woman gives me a look that makes it clear she doesn't think much of me. She steps away and gestures towards the house, its sagging door and its broken windows. 'They say a dark man lived here once. He brought something terrible with him and people started dying in droves. Even now, children still disappear if they come too close to the Western Quarter.'

I keep my mouth shut and swallow the sharp remark I have ready on my lips. A dark man, yes, but no matter how twisted he is or what things he has done, the Black Influenza was not of his own making. We can't blame Benji for everything, I think bitterly, as convenient as that would be. I look once again at the woman, at her pale face and the deep lines running along her mouth. 'Have you lost someone?'

She looks at me, puzzled for a brief moment, then the fire in her eyes dies out. 'My child. My daughter. She was as old as your brother must be now. Six years have passed since I last saw her.' The woman turns away from me and stares helplessly at the red gable. 'She used to come here to play, and then one day, she was just gone. No one has ever seen her again.'

'I'm sorry,' I whisper. *You have no idea how much that pains me.*

I want to tell her that it isn't because of the house, that it is nothing more than a deserted ruin, and that the real enemy is not hidden among the charred beams and peeling walls. But I can't tell her that, because at that very moment, Arthur pulls me out of the sunlight and back into the shadows of the alley. The look in his eyes tells me right away that something is wrong.

I stare past him. Yes, I see them now: the vans that drive past the church tower in a neat line. They have window blinds and thick off-road tyres. On the dark green paint of the vehicles shimmers the silver symbol of the Asclepius Congregation.

I shrink even further backwards. They haven't seen us, and even if they had, there's no way for them to know who we are. We're just some random children and a woman. Yet my knees feel weak as I press myself against the exposed brickwork of the wall and follow the small procession with my eyes until they're gone.

They are heading for the square. Is this a victory lap? Have they managed to pluck a few sorry wretches off the streets? Are they heading back to their headquarters right now and if so, where would that be?

'There,' I utter after a long silence. 'They're the ones you should be afraid of. They are the ones who took your daughter.'

The woman stares at us. 'What do you mean? The doctors?'

'Nim, let's go.' Arthur sounds impatient. The wail of a siren flares up in the distance, followed by unintelligible shouting. 'What if they...?'

He doesn't need to finish his sentence. A fresh fear suddenly fills my heart: what if they found the Ark? I imagine the children being thrown into the trucks, Mirna and Will not strong enough to save anyone...

'I'm sorry,' I tell the woman. 'If you want to do something useful, keep the children of Brevalaer away from those vehicles.'

'Wait!' she cries. She holds out her arms, as if she wants to grab me again. I have already jumped away. 'If you know anything about my daughter, please tell me! I've been looking for so long!'

My heart bleeds for her as we beat a hasty retreat from the town.

15

— · —

Black Influenza

In the area surrounding the Ark there are no signs of kidnappers. The square and ground nearby haven't been touched and there are no jeep tracks. The lower branches of the trees still seem intact. Besides, how would those great big tin cans manage to drive across the peat bogs? They'd sink hopelessly.

And yet, I only begin to calm down once we enter the room and find the children unscathed. Not everyone's there, but Mirna assures us that no one has raised the alarm – an alarm that will shrilly ring through the entire Ark if someone spots a Snake anywhere in the marshes. If they do manage to make it through the swamps and their wheels haven't got caught in one of Cor's bear traps, they'd never be able to penetrate the thick, armoured doors of the Ark, which will remain firmly closed in case Will goes ahead with a lockdown.

'This is the safest place in Breizh,' Mirna assures us.

'It isn't so safe on the streets of Brevalaer,' I say as I slump down on a chair. 'Get Will, Mirna. I think he needs to hear this.'

As soon as we tell Will the news, he wastes no time. He asks how many Asclepius Congregation vehicles we have seen and then he leaves with Mirna, Conn and Corentin in tow. He leaves us behind to watch the little ones. I force myself to sit down quietly and get used to the underground room. The wait gives me plenty of time to think about the thin woman's words. Perhaps I'd given away too much when I warned her. But if Will warned everyone in town about the doctors wearing the silver snake emblem, wouldn't the children be far

156

better protected? Or would Benji simply resort to other methods of finding his test subjects?

All these thoughts immediately disappear into the background when a small commotion kicks off at the entrance to the Ark. In the artificial light of the CORE, a battered Will appears. He's carrying something in his arms, which for a moment I think is a bundle of clothes. Mirna and Conn spread blankets on the floor – a rather strange thing to do for a pile of cloth, I think – until Will kneels down and gently lays his load down. Limbs are sticking out of the bundle of fluttering clothes: two spindly arms, legs, and a round head with a mess of blonde locks that seem to stick up in all places, like unruly gossamer.

'Katell?' I stand up in shock. It is her! I recognise her immediately, but how could this be? Katell belongs to the Saint Gwenhael, where Yannick should be caring for her. What's she doing here, deathly pale and sleeping on the floor of the Ark?

'She was on her way to the headquarters of the Snake,' explains Will, as if he can read my thoughts.

A thousand frightening visions tumble through my mind. If Katell was in one of those wagons, then the Asclepius Congregation must have been in Gwennec. Panic begins to boil inside me and I dig my fingernails into my hands. 'Where are the others?'

'We didn't have much time,' says Mirna. 'Three of the four trucks drove through. Hers was the only one that we managed to intercept.'

'But I need to know!' The shrill tone of my alarmed voice scares even me. Arthur puts a soothing hand on my arm, but I shake him off. 'My friends live there! Have they ransacked the church? How many children were orphaned by the water? Are they all ...?'

'You can ask her as soon as she wakes up,' Will curtly cuts me off.

'I need to know now!'

'No, Nimue, you don't. You must let her sleep and give her a chance to recover from the *Pax*. She's full of the stuff.'

'*Pax?*' I repeat, confused.

'A substance they use to keep the children quiet during transport. It drugs them.'

I sink down on the floor next to the sleeping Katell, fighting the urge to shake her awake right this minute. I silently watch how Mirna kneels down next to the girl and rolls her gently onto her back, so she's in a slightly more comfortable position. Yuna sits down beside her and frowns. 'Did she get beaten?'

'I think so.' Mirna brushes the hair from the side of Katell's face, revealing a swollen bruise underneath her eye, as if someone has indeed punched her.

'She has them on her arms too.'

'Be careful, Yuna. She's bleeding.' Mirna dabs Katell's face with her sleeve.

I try to concentrate, which isn't easy, what with the stormy feeling inside me. The girl from Gwennec is pale, almost grey. The ugly bruises on her skin stand out from the pallor, as does the trickle of blood from the corner of her mouth. There's something frighteningly familiar about this whole scene...

'Mirna! Don't touch her!' Arthur grabs Mirna's wrist and pushes Yuna away with his other arm. 'Stay away from her,' he warns again, while everyone stares at him as if he's lost his mind. 'She's dangerous! Nim?'

The moment he glances at me and I get up to take a clear look at Katell's face, I know Katell hasn't been beaten up by members of the Asclepius Congregation.

It's like a lightning bolt in my head. That grey skin, the boils, the coughed-up blood...*Saint Gwenhael, help us.* I know little of diseases, unlike Yannick, but I know with chilling certainty that Katell has been infected with the Black Influenza. I scuttle back, as if I've just caught a contaminated fish.

'Dangerous?' repeats Mirna. 'What's this madness? Nimue?'

'Mirna, do you remember what I said about that sickness?' I ask slowly, not taking my eyes off Katell. 'And the way the Asclepius Congregation was still searching for a treatment for it?'

'And the woman who could cure it?'

'That was our mother.'

'Stop,' says Will. He comes up to me and I finally look away from the sleeping girl to meet his gaze. 'Your mother was a doctor?'

'No...well, I don't know exactly. She was the only one who could cure the Black Influenza.'

'Why didn't you tell me this? And how would you know, if she disappeared like you claim?'

'You have to believe us,' says Arthur.

'We don't know you *that* well.'

'We have her diary,' I say reluctantly. 'Believe me; everything we've said is true.'

'A diary? Can I see it?'

'It's private.'

His eyes seem to grow even darker but his voice remains soft. 'Fair enough. So your diary details how to cure this sickness?'

'Not exactly.' I breathe slowly in and out. 'It's not influenza – not really. My mother called it a plague.' I fall silent, letting the residents of the Ark take in my words. Will and Mirna give me a blank look, but Corentin's face grows darker.

'Like the bubonic plague?'

'I think so.'

'What causes it?' asks Mirna. 'Is is because of all the poisons?'

'I don't know,' I admit helplessly. 'The disease was decimating the population when our mother came to this part of Central Europe. It was everywhere.'

'I know this sickness,' says Anna unexpectedly. All eyes turn to her. She stands with her arms folded across her chest, hiding her disfigured hand with the other. Anna licks her lips nervously. 'I didn't escape Pontorson to run from the Snake. They grabbed me when I was on the road on my own. It was this illness that took my family from me. Everyone was scared. It was …' She seems to be searching for the right words. 'It was hell. The district officials kept us all in quarantine. No one was allowed out and we were surrounded by electric fences. After my parents died, I managed to get myself smuggled out in a supply truck.'

'Will … the border post,' says Mirna quietly. Her gaze moves to Arthur. 'You said something before about an epidemic.'

'That was the story,' Arthur replies. 'In Brevalaer the hospitals were full. People were being transferred…' He turns very pale. 'The disease must have reached Gwennec by now.'

Will nods, but his attention remains focused on me. His dark eyes dart over my face, searching, probing, as if he's still trying to catch out any lies I might be telling. 'You said the Snake had taken your mother.'

'Possibly. All we know is they were looking for her.'

'So she could be with the Snake right now... she could be busy trying to eradicate this thing.'

I look down. What he says is a thought that has often crossed my mind already. 'It's possible. We don't know.'

In the oppressive silence that follows, I get the impression that everyone is holding their breath.

It is Corentin who breaks the silence. 'All this guessing will get us nowhere. What do we do now? Will, we can't leave that child in the marsh to die.'

'It makes no sense to give her shelter if we're all going to perish in the end,' says Will curtly. He turns to Katell with folded arms and lets his eyes run over her fragile figure. 'Mirna needs to wash herself. We all do.'

'Immediately,' says Mirna shuddering. 'Everyone needs to wash and scrub themselves.'

'Nimue,' says Will sharply. 'This plague is contagious for everyone, right?'

I nod.

'Is it blood-borne? Airborne? How quickly does it spread?'

'I ...' I feel stupid and useless when I can't give him a real answer. 'I don't remember exactly.'

'It's airborne,' says Arthur. 'At least, that's what it seems to be. Mum didn't mention any other way.'

'And how quick is it?'

I tilt my head down. 'Very.'

Will doesn't respond, but he gives Katell a look that leaves nothing to the imagination. Mirna must have seen it too, because she says: 'We can't save a child just to throw her back out again, Will. If she dies, she dies.'

'And die she will.'

'But it won't be *my* knife that slits her throat!'

'It might be the only ways to protect us all,' says Will quietly, which sends a chill running down my spine. Kill one girl to save us all? That sounds suspiciously like Benji.

I try to stay calm. *I am Rona's daughter ... Mum was never infected. I have Sela's gift...* I repeat the words in my head, trying to draw power from it. 'There are plenty of rooms in the Ark that no one uses,' I say, once I'm sure I'll be able to talk in a calm tone of voice. 'Let's isolate her until we can come up with another solution. I'll... I'll carry her.'

Will looks at me appraisingly. 'And what other solution could there be?'

'Perhaps she'll get better by herself,' I mumble as I kneel next to Katell. I gently lift up her torso in my arms.

'You are the expert in this matter,' says Will behind me, a slightly threatening tone in his voice. 'If you think she can get better by herself, then it'd better happen before we all catch it. What does your diary say about that?'

It depends, I think, not answering him. *On the power that comes out of my hands.* I lift Katell up. She's not heavy, but I'm still a little shaky as I try to keep my balance. Arthur races over to my aid and supports Katell's head.

'Don't,' I whisper. 'You don't have her gift...'

He looks at me somewhat worried, yet he sounds resolute when he says: 'I'm your brother. We'll do it together or not at all.'

'I know a room in the east wing which is safely reachable.' Mirna motions us to follow her. She looks uncomfortably at Katell, but when I see Will looking at us it seems as if she's avoiding his stubborn gaze.

The east wing is accessed via two staircases and a few corridors with tight corners which lead us to one of the higher levels of the Ark. In the room that Mirna shows us, there is a slight hint of plant smell. On one side there are empty greenhouses, and in the corner is an open cabinet with gardening tools.

'This was one of the four Green Rooms in the Ark, where food could be grown.' Mirna stays behind in the doorway as we walk in. 'The energy for the greenhouses was partly supplied by the CORE, but also through solar panels on the roof, just above us.'

'Why don't you use these rooms?' asks Arthur.

'We use the one on the north side. These greenhouses no longer work. The connection with the CORE must have broken somewhere along the line.'

We lay Katell down as carefully as possible. Mirna disappears for a moment, but comes back with a thin mattress and a pile of blankets. She doesn't touch Katell and returns to her position on the threshold as Arthur and I tuck Katell in as tightly as possible. 'Are you sure this is the Black Influenza?' she wants to know.

I cast my gaze over the dark lumps on Katell's skin. 'Pretty sure.'

'What do we do in that case, Nimue? Do you really think we can find a solution?'

I see the doubt flickering in her eyes. She may not be willing to leave an innocent child to die in the wilderness or – Gwenhael protect me – take a knife to her throat, but Mirna does understand the dangers of a deadly disease. This is her Ark, and just like Will she's fought hard to turn it into a safe haven. I can't blame her for her fear of Katell. Even now I can barely control my own trembling hands as I straighten the blankets. 'Don't let anyone else come in here. Get someone to guard this room if necessary.'

'She needs care and attention. Who will volunteer?'

I take a deep breath and put my hands in my pockets so as not to show Mirna I'm as nervous as she is. 'I'll do it.'

'Me too,' says Arthur.

I shake my head.

'Why?' asks Mirna. 'Why you two?'

'For so many reasons,' I say. 'But above all because Katell is one of our own, Mirna. We survived the great flood together.'

Mirna silently surveys my face. 'We have to trust you,' she concludes, not very enthusiastically. 'Or we have to get rid of her...which I'm not happy about.' With those words, she leaves us.

'You'd better go after her,' I tell Arthur.

He looks at me reproachfully. 'I don't want to leave you behind with her.'

'You wouldn't be leaving me behind; I'll just stay here on my own.'

'You're going to heal her.'

'I have to try, don't I?' I look uncomfortably at Katell. 'We can't just sit back and watch her infect everyone.'

'Nim, Mum felt weak whenever she cured someone of the Black Influenza.' He takes my hand. 'I'm scared something will happen to you.'

'But this is Katell,' I protest. 'You like her.'

'I know.' He looks sad. 'Just be careful. I'd rather see her die than lose you.'

'Arthur!' I pull myself away from him and look at him in shock. 'You won't lose me. Mum didn't die, did she? I'll be careful, I promise. I'm going to wait until she wakes up. According to Will, that Pax stuff will wear off soon.'

'Come down for a bit, then,' he insists, but I shake my head.

'I need time to think, to concentrate. You should get out of here, Arthur. If Benji was right, you aren't immune. Not like me and Rona.'

'Benji,' Arthur scoffs and kicks the door as he leaves the room. 'To the bottom of the sea with him. He can shove his arguments up his arse.'

Arthur is swearing, I realise as I look for the easiest spot to sit down, lean my back against the wall and slowly begin to bend and stretch my fingers. I didn't even know he could spell the word 'arse', let alone use it in a curse. He's grown up without me even noticing. Much like myself, perhaps.

I cross my legs. It's up to me now. Katell's life is in my hands ... I decide to take Mum's diary out of the front pocket of my jumper – in order to draw strength from it for what lies ahead. I read the last pages once more before I also turn these and stare at the final, blank pages.

Fresh. Unused.

Somewhere on the floor, against the edge of the greenhouses, is an old pencil. Perhaps dropped by accident when one of the residents came to rearrange the tomato plants, or by a bored artist who came to the Green Room to do some still-life drawings and dozed off to sleep. Whatever the case, I pick up the pencil and hold it between my fingers, rub the dirt off it and begin to scrawl a few tester lines in the margins of the paper.

Then I begin to write.

Dear Mum,

These are the last few pages of your old diary, and just like you, I have no idea where to begin.

We miss you, more than I can put into words, even if this letters reaches you one way or another.

The Ark is the strangest place I have ever seen – so very different from the world we know. I'm finding it difficult to get used to it ... just like you, I need the open sea. There are countless rooms. Rooms with beds where the children sleep when they're not in the big hall, rooms with chairs, incomplete crockery sets, bits of machinery I can't identify. All the rooms are full of cobwebs, and the light from the CORE sometimes flickers like a ghostly entity through the whole building.

Corentin has warned us of the bear traps he's set in the swamps. Devices with metal jaws and pointed teeth, which snap shut when they catch their prey. They lie hidden in the undergrowth, so he says we should never stray from the path.

Arthur is doing okay. He is almost taller than me now, and he's smart and brave. But I'm scared, Mum.

This journey and your own history – they're sometimes too similar to each other for my taste. I haven't told Arthur, but sometimes I lie awake at night and I wonder whether we should just give up – if we should just let you go. And yes, of course we could; we've lived all these years without you, so why not carry on like this? It was you who left us, after all... we never drove you away.

I'm sorry! I don't mean that.

I know why you had to leave. Who made you leave. But Mum, Dad died after you left and you never came back. The only conversation I can have with you is a dialogue written on this stupid piece of paper with some dusty pencil!

Of course I won't give up on you. I don't think I'd ever be able to forgive myself if I did. But right now, it's not about where you are or where we should go...I'm alone with Katell. I know very well what I have to do. I need to do what you would do – what you used to do, time after time, even though it drained you of so much energy. I just don't know if I'm as brave as you, Mum, because ultimately, what do I know about Sela's gift? I've never even known Sela, let alone known what her secret was because you never wrote about it.

In St Gwenhael's, I saved a man's life. Yes, I'm proud of that, but it felt awful. As if I'd been in a bath of icy water for an hour. And you left Benji and Avalon behind because you were scared I'd die! What if I'm about to die now? I can't just leave Katell here, and if Will has his way ...

I'm shocked to find I have reached the end of the page. I was so absorbed in my words that it comes as a surprise. Now nothing is left to me, just the grubby back cover. Not that it matters what else I entrust to these pages; my mother isn't there to answer me.

With a sigh, I put the book back into my pocket and let the pencil roll across the floor, back to the greenhouses. Perhaps someone will pick up the very same pencil in ten or fifteen years and write down their own worries.

If Will has his way, he'll cut this delicate girl's throat after she's told him everything she knows. I conclude that Arthur has come up with an expression of deep wisdom: Will can shove his way up his arse.

As I get up and lean over Katell, I see her eyes are open. For a moment, we just stare at each other while I wonder if she recognises me, or if she thinks she's still with the kidnappers.

And then she turns away from me and vomits.

16

—·—

FORGET US NOT

I stand with my feet on the narrow line that forms the edge of the cliff and keep my balance like a tightrope walker. Tall trees tower above me like giants – trees that rise higher than the pillars of St Corentin's, while beneath me, a piece of low-lying marshland stretches out: swampy, grey and stinking of peat, a smell that clings to my hair and clothing.

Cor is downhill, gesturing at me. He has chosen the safe route, crawling through a tangle of brambles and thistles, and looks as if he's crashed into an enormous hedgehog.

'You'll break your neck!'

The adrenaline rushes through my body, causing my hands and feet to tingle. My feet know exactly what they have to do; my toes curled, I balance on my heels, then take the next step. One wrong move and I'll fall. With the utmost concentration I shift my weight and move my feet forward, one after the other, until I finally reach the other side of the cliff, where a less steep slope leads down to the safety of the valley below. Once I get down there, the putrid smell of the swamp is much stronger.

Corentin stares at me as if I've just climbed down from the moon. I brush some entangled hair from my face and grin at him. 'You think that's high? You should see the cliffs along the coast then. Arthur and I used to do this kind of thing for fun.'

'At least if you fall off there, you have the water to catch you,' says Corentin, a hint of desperation in his voice. 'I can't help you if you fall off here.'

'If you fall there, you'll break your neck and drown immediately.' I don't tell him that my heart is still pounding in my chest, only sixty percent of which is down to a pleasant adrenaline rush and the rest being down to gut-wrenching fear.

'You're insane.'

'It's a game. Who can go the highest? Who can get closest to the edge?' I shrug my shoulders. 'The buzz from it makes you stronger.'

'So how many children die every day down your way?'

'There are too many ways to get killed in Gwennec, Cor, and falling off the steep cliffs is just one of them. Your boat might crash into an unseen rock and you drown. You might eat a contaminated fish by accident and you're dead within two days. Or when the oil platforms leak, the land and sea get covered in rancid sludge, you get ill and you have no money for the doctor....bam, dead. So sometimes you need to laugh in the face of danger and say "to the bottom of the sea with it!"!'

I take off the spare ropes wrapped around my waist, designed to tie rabbit traps, and set the wicker cage that I have been carrying on my back. We're halfway along Cor's route, a route which he calls the 'hunter's ring', where dozens of traps are hidden among the bracken and the trees, so that the Ark and its curious inhabitants are provided with fresh meat during the winter. We haven't had much success so far – only a very small young rabbit that now dangles from Corentin's shoulder by its hind legs, but Corentin seems unfazed.

He takes the ropes from me. 'It's no better than in Guer, my old town. My house had no solid roof like the Ark, just a few strips of corrugated iron that blew off every autumn, but at least it stood upright. Most of the houses were propped up against each other like those trees over there.' He nods to two trees blown over by the wind, the trunks of which are still leaning against each other. They look like they could crash to the forest floor at any moment.

'Do you think it's better in Rome?' I ask. 'No hunger, no winters and no storms?'

'No starvation if you're rich, perhaps, but I wouldn't say it's better. Take a deep breath. Go on.'

Puzzled, I deeply inhale the earthy aroma of the swamp. Something tickles my nose, something that doesn't quite belong among the scent of rotten leaves and murky water, and isn't caused by the treacherous peat bog either. 'I smell something odd.'

'It may not be pleasant, but at least it's not poisonous. In Rome and all the big cities you can't even go outside without an oxygen mask on, unless you have a death wish. The toxins linger in the air between the factories and the housing blocks. Such is the prosperity of Central Europe.'

I stare at Corentin in shock. 'How do you know all this?'

'I've been there before. Also, don't forget that Mirna was imprisoned for years in that Institute. Believe me, Nimue, this is possibly the best place on Earth.'

If this is the best place on Earth, I'm not sure I'll ever be able to feel at home anywhere in the world again. I quickly shake off the eerie feeling inside of me. 'Where's that stream that Will was going on about?'

'Just behind those three trees. You can hear it if you listen closely.'

There is a sound of water rushing past plants and stones at high speed. I nod.

'Animals come to the water to drink, so I'm going to put these traps along the banks of the river. You can go look for the best place to set a fish-trap. As long as you keep sight of the stream, you can't go wrong, and if you do just holler. That'll drive away any animals we might catch, but at least I'll be able to find you again.' He smirks at me. 'There's a crossing over there near the bend if you need me. Don't step in the bear traps, though, those things are vicious.'

'Take your own advice.' I grin and leave him alone with his traps and nets on the riverbank. Along the two witch-like trees that Corentin has pointed out, I see animal tracks. There is barely enough room here for me to put one foot next to the other. Where the tracks stop, the stream swings back towards the trees and makes its way through the valley. I let the fish-trap slide down into the water, the ice-cold water washing over my arms. I quickly tie the ropes that keep the trap in place to a large tree root, before my fingers get too numb for me to hold the trap – and Arthur and I might end up spending another couple of hours making a new one. I assure myself the knots are not too loose and dry my hands on my anorak. All we can do now is wait: a couple of worms are dangling from the improvised thorn hooks inside the cage, which has been woven like the shape of a funnel, so that the fish can easily swim in, but once inside they'll discover they can't find their way to swim back out again. I insert three sticks into the grounds as a marker and decide to take the same route back to the crossing.

After a few minutes I begin to suspect that I've taken a wrong turn somewhere. I don't recognise the hills at the end of the valley, while I really thought I came from the this side. Hesitantly I take a few more steps, the stream to my right, until I'm sure that I haven't walked any further from the spot where and Corentin and I parted company. From here, the two witch trees should be visible – the problem is that there's no trace of them anywhere. The stream also seems to have become deeper and flows more quickly, which rules out wading across as an option. I anxiously turn around and make my way through the brush in the other direction, not quite breaking into a run yet. There's nothing wrong, I tell myself. I'm a little out of the way and the marshes now seem to close in around me from all sides. This doesn't mean I'm lost; Corentin is somewhere close by, he's sure to hear me if only I called him.

Since I haven't quite reached the point where I'm willing to scream out for help like a little child, I start to climb the upward slope in order to have a look from there. It is a breathtakingly beautiful sight. The marshland extends in all directions; there's nothing but trees as far as I can see – a greenish haze of leaves and roots sticking out of the ground, interspersed with pools of dark, stagnant water.

Will's words echo in my ears: every time the government of Breizh tries to drain the marshes, people drown and disappear. The marshes must be the largest uninhabited area of the western half of the Periphery, in which small towns like Brevalaer are like islands in the sea. And just like the sea has its own laws, the marshes have their own way of holding reign.

I turn to the other side, where a wall has been put up hidden behind the rugged hills. This is because of the quarantine, according to Mirna. Beyond that wall are the cities and factories that had made Rona feel so trapped, and where nobody can safely breathe outside, if what Cor claims is true.

The unmistakable sound of running water distracts me from my thoughts. Surprised, I tear my gaze away from the horizon and look around me. The stream runs far below me, so that couldn't possibly be the source. What's more, this sound is not as loud: it's irregular and dripping, like melting ice, and it seems to be close by. Groping along the tangle of tree roots and plants, I move towards it.

There! My fingers get wet. Between some stones a trickle of water flows down the hillside. As I creep further along the hill, I discover its source: a small, crescent-shaped pool, surrounded by a thick treeline and embedded with stones. A remarkable shape, as if someone has intentionally arranged the stones this way. There's a strange feeling in the air – other than the dripping of the water, steadily flowing down below, everything is very still, as if the marshes are holding their breath in anticipation. The trees that grow around the pool have twisted trunks and high roots that protrude from the earth like toes, as if they're about to wander off at any moment. I look up to the tops of the trees, which grow so tall around me that I feel dwarfed by them. My attention is caught by a movement, a slight figure slipping through the trees and out of sight before I can completely turn around.

'Cor?' I ask hopefully, although I know I'd have heard him approach if it was him. Was it just my imagination? My heart begins to pound loudly and my hands grow clammy. I thought I'd seen a similar figure in the hills between Daouloc and Saint-Thonan, a creature made of mist that had disappeared just as quickly into thin air. And what about the apparition near the entrance to the rowan cave – hadn't that clearly been a man with white, translucent limbs?

Again, something stirs; this time it's a glint in the water that doesn't seem to have been caused by anything. Is there someone, or some*thing*, following me? I want to call out to Corentin, but my mouth is dry and my throat seems to be shut tight. I cautiously move closer, ready to flee if necessary, and for a moment I forget to breathe.

The crescent pool looks like a mirror. I see my own reflection and I see the trees, but the picture changes in an instant. I blink, and when I look back down, the trees no longer stand like silent sentinels around me – a row of dark fir trees and a tangle of ferns and thorny shrubs have replaced them. And in the middle of this chaos of plants is someone staring at me. It's not my own freckled face, but a white face with two moon-like eyes that bore into mine.

I can't tell exactly how ancient this being is; to me he seems utterly ageless. Yet I get the feeling that he's tired, maybe even ill, although that may just be because of the pale skin that seems to cover him from top to bottom. As he bends down, he makes the surface of the water ripple, as if he has uttered a deep sigh above the surface on his side.

'At last you see me.' His voice is like a gust of wind, his lips barely moving. 'I have tried to call out to you, Nimue, daughter of Rona.'

I try to say something, struggling to form the words in my head. 'What's happening?' I finally sputter out. 'Is this real? Are you...a ghost?'

The Pale Man smiles. This is the first time I see his mouth move, and it causes his face to light up like the silvery light of the moon. 'Every day my strength grows weaker,' he whispers. 'I must speak with you in a place where I am stronger than here.'

'Who are you? Why are you following me? How do you know my name and why did you mention my Mum's..?'

'It is important for you to know this,' his ghostly voice interrupts me, causing goose bumps to erupt across my whole skin. 'Forget us not.'

'I ... I don't understand...'

'Nimue!' Corentin's calls penetrate the ring of trees and break the silence. A moment later he ducks down next to me, a broken bear trap slung over his shoulder. 'There you are. I was wandering around looking for you; I half thought you'd already made your way home.'

I stand up, goose bumps still covering my arms. The pond is now an ordinary pool of water again, which just reflects my shocked face back to me. 'I'm sorry, Cor. I was planning on going to the crossing and I ended up here...I must have strayed further than I realised.'

'Well, the marshes do have that effect on people, at times.' Corentin scans me from top to bottom and frowns. 'You look really upset. Don't worry – you'll learn your way around before you know it, even in your dreams. All set to go?'

I nod as I scramble to my feet, and together we descend the hill. Before the strange place disappears from sight I catch one last glance of it over my shoulder. There's nothing remarkable about the pool of water or the trees that surround it. Corentin doesn't seem to notice anything strange about the place either. He talks about the traps he's set and about the coming winter, when Brevalaer will be closed off from the rest of the world for weeks on end because of snow blocking the rails. I hardly listen to him and my thoughts keep going back to the words of the Pale Man; *forget us not*. What did he mean? I've never met him, let alone forgotten him. The only thing mentioning him is that vague bit of story in my mother's diary. Because one thing seems as clear to me as the very eyes that were staring at me: the Pale Man is of that other kind – the beings of Jodoc's stories. The inhabitants of Mum's beloved Other World.

We reach the end of the valley and the wind is coming at us hard. I bow my head and shove my hands deep into the pockets of my anorak, but I can do nothing to stop my ears and nose from feeling dry within seconds. Then I come to a sudden stop and stand there as if petrified. The wind carries with it the same smell from before, and any thought of what has just happened to me is quickly pushed from my mind.

'Iron,' I say out loud, causing Corentin to stop in his tracks and look back.

'What's up?'

'Can't you smell it?' I hold my hand up, as if I can somehow point at the ominous odour. 'This is what hung in the air before the storm broke over Gwennec.'

Corentin sniffs a few times and shrugs his shoulders. 'I smell peat and water. Are you sure you aren't imagining things?'

'You know how blood tastes of metal? This is the same thing, like blood in the air. The weather's going to turn.'

'I doubt it, Nimue. Winter will be here, but that's still a few weeks away, and storms are a rarity down here. This is the strongest the wind will get. Now don't give that disapproving look and keep going. I'm starving.'

Corentin may not have believed me but my prediction comes true. That very night, the wind whips up into a hurricane that brings the trees surrounding the square crashing to the ground, nearly bursting their trunks. In the higher passageways we can hear the wind howling outside. Even as a pale dawn finally breaks the next day, nobody dares venture beyond the main door, which we bolt shut after a few more hours. During the course of the next few days we sit locked inside the Ark, with nothing else to do other than adjust and repair items of clothing. Anna spends hours rummaging around in her medicine cabinets, where she dries bunches of herbs and keeps some stolen first-aid kits. Will loiters in passageways and rooms where nobody normally goes. When he's in the main room he sits there with a gloomy face, staring out into space and speaking to no one. I wonder if he feels just as trapped as I do.

With the storm winter falls over the land. Just as Jodoc has warned us, the cold sinks its teeth into the area with the jaws of a vicious predator. Heavy snow flurries prevent us from seeing where we're going, so Will keeps us cooped up inside even longer. Daily squabbles erupt among the children, whom Mirna tries to placate with increasing desperation.

And I try to placate myself. In this season it's clearly impossible for us to continue our journey, but I can't get that brief encounter with the ghostly apparition out of my mind. His words prey on my heart. Who is he? *What* is he? I can't come up with a single satisfactory answer, and sometimes I wonder if I have just imagined the whole thing. But he must be real; I've seen him too many times now to doubt that. Arthur is shocked when I tell him about it. He tries not to let it show, but I can see the fear in his eyes. After all, it is a rather frightening idea that Arthur and I are being followed by this strange being, even if he doesn't seem malicious. He also seems to know something about Rona. The thought gives me new energy, and it is that very thought that I cling to if I ever feel trapped or useless. This winter won't last forever. As soon as the weather permits, Arthur and I will go looking for answers.

In the beginning I have to force myself to attend to Katell every day, terrified that I will pass the disease on to the rest of the Ark-dwellers, even though I am the only one who is immune to it. After three days, however, I find myself using the Green Room as a place to escape the hustle and bustle of the main room. Mirna and Will have made it very clear that no one except me is supposed to enter the isolated room, so the passage leading to it is always deserted. The children seek out other nooks and crannies of the Ark to explore, and the few rooms where things are stored are temporarily abandoned to their fate.

Katell herself is nobly holding out. The Pax has worn off long since, but even without a sedative she spends a lot of time sleeping or napping. Sometimes I'm able to exchange a few words with her. Questions to which I get whispered answers back. That way I find out that many houses are being temporarily rebuilt in Gwennec by using straw, mud and canvas, until the bricks arrive from

Brevalaer to build new walls which can better withstand the impact of the water. I am relieved that they haven't torn down St Gwenhael's, even though it would have provided an immediate source of material. It was somewhere in the chaos of reconstruction that the trucks with the silver snakes came to the village; doctors and surgeons who finally offered the sick and injured the help they so desperately needed. As for Katell herself, the last time she saw her family was just before the water came pounding down on their house, just as the storm now rages outside the bolted main door. The doctors took her away in their trucks, together with three other newly orphaned children. Katell was too scared and too weak to resist, but Taran, Marci and Judikael, all a few years older than her, put up stiff resistance until Katell saw them plunge needles into their necks. She was also put to sleep not much later.

Not once do I dare try again to cure her in one fell swoop. Instead, I develop a new strategy: every day I use a little of my power on her in exchange for the shadowy nature of the Black Influenza. Never too much at any one time, though, so I won't get trapped in that nightmarish feeling again. It isn't Rona's method, but it seems to work anyway. Katell is still alive, she isn't getting any sicker, and although the constant tug of war between me and the disease means she can't leave the Green Room any time soon, she gradually seems to be improving, so that after a few days she's able to sit upright and take a few sips of the steaming cup of tea I give her. This exchange unfortunately has a less than invigorating effect on me. I often feel exhausted and cold, and on the edge of my dreams lurks a shadowy, evil being, as if it's spying on me. During the day I largely forget about this being, though. When I do think about it, I believe that my dreams are generated by the dark corruption that I'm absorbing from Katell. Perhaps this is the way my body cleanses itself. It seems an altogether reasonable deal, though I don't feel particularly animated as a result.

After two weeks, the storm finally begins to weaken, the sky is clearing, and a period of freezing cold temperatures follows. When we emerge from the Ark, dazed like hedgehogs after hibernation, we see the devastation the storm has wreaked: the square has disappeared under a blanket of snow and everywhere fallen trees and branches ripped from their trunks scatter the ground. We break our backs clearing the snow in an effort to create a navigable path.

Conn and Corentin bravely venture out into the snow, and upon their return they bring the news that the stream has completely frozen over, the traps stuck underneath the ice. Corentin finds two thin, frozen-stiff hares in his traps, the rest having become inaccessible underneath the snow. All the children are suffering from sore throats and coughs, and Anna and I do our best to minimize the number of runny noses.

I can hardly think of anything else than the Pale Man and his words about my mother. At the same time the Ark seems to sap my energy more and more every day. Only late in the evenings, when I invariably collapse onto my mattress, exhausted, and pull the sleeping bag over my head like a tent, will I allow the whirling mass of questions to wash over me – questions that follow one another without ever being truly answered. And as soon as I fall asleep, these questions dissolve into the strange dreams in which I always feel watched.

17

— · —

THREADS IN THE TAPESTRY

I wake up because of a loud commotion. As I run outside, it's as if a small battle has taken place on the square, which seems to be more or less free of snow. My jaw drops and I stare confused at the group of children running around and beating up each other with sticks and fists. Has an argument broken out? Corentin stands in the midst of the chaos, his arms behind his back like a captain calmly steering his ship and seeing his crew are doing his bidding.

I stagger towards him. A club narrowly misses me and I duck down, my arms protecting my head. 'What on earth is going on here? Are they fighting ghosts?'

'I'm teaching them how to defend themselves,' Corentin states. 'No one from the Ark must ever fall into the wrong hands again.'

'Do you think you can take on the Asclepius Congregation just with sticks?'

'It's not just about them. There are plenty of other dangers around here, things we need to be prepared for out here in the wild. There are soldiers at the depot in Brevalaer, there are guarded freight trains ... hell, there are even people who might try to steal away orphaned children for other reasons.' He shrugs his shoulders. 'It's a harsh world, Nimue.'

'But they're just children.' I look again at the groups fighting and find Broc and Josse rolling and wriggling over the ground in a big, tangled mess. I wince at the thought of all the bruises and aching bones that will follow. 'Even Yuna's joining in! I don't believe my eyes.'

'They won't stay children forever,' Corentin points out. 'What's learnt in the cradle lasts 'till the tomb. Will and I agree.'

176

'So you're creating an army?' I mutter, unsure what to think about all of it. 'An army of outlaws.'

'Everyone has something to defend... here.' He suddenly has two sticks in his hands and is handing one to me. 'Don't knock it until you've tried it yourself. From what I remember, you're not easily scared, are you, ravine girl?' He grins at me.

'Oh, it's like that is it?' I tighten my grip on the stick. 'Fine, I'm not scared of your hits.'

'Don't get too big for your boots just yet,' grins Corentin. 'Do as I do.'

I relax my hands and mimick Corentin's slow movements. He shows me how I should attack, how to quickly block his stick using mine, and also how to safely spin away like a whirlwind as fast as possible. He dances around me and makes my bones tremble as he hits me hard with his stick. My fingers get numb and I can only try my best to not drop my weapon. He comes charging towards me. I shrink back, but nimbly glide over the tiles, which are cleared of snow but still contain a smooth layer of ice. Corentin shoves in the shoulder and I fall backwards. Spots dance before my eyes.

'That's cheating,' I moan. 'If that's how we're going to play it...'

'Use your surroundings. Don't let anything get by you that you might need to win a fight if cornered. Are you okay?' He pulls me up.

'I've had worse.'

Over the next half hour, I lose myself in circles and hits from my stick. Most of them don't do much damage and whenever I do hit, Corentin seems to block me effortlessly, so I end up with more bruises than victory points. I finally have to drop the stick. 'Mercy! I'm black and blue.'

'You didn't do so badly,' he says, as he drops his stick on to the ground.

'Yeah, right.' I rub my back. It feels as if he's made a direct hit to my tailbone. 'If you need me I'll be in the sickroom, licking my wounds before your little brats use up all my salves.'

'If you're interested in plants and herblore, you should have a peak inside the library – flip through one of those compendia of medicinal herbs.' He spreads out his arms to show how many books there are.

'There's a library in the Ark?'

'Didn't you know? When people were preparing for the Impact, they took a fair amount of their valuable written documents with them down below. Most likely they were afraid it would get destroyed otherwise. It's a locked room and everything is very well preserved.'

'And nobody uses it?'

'We use it sometimes. Want to see?'

'I've always wanted to be a Medical Caretaker ... So knowing about herbs does come in handy.'

'Just like your mother?' It's as if he's reading my mind.

'Yeah,' I mumble. 'Just like Mum.'

Corentin leads me through a maze of bends and narrow passageways – a deep part of the Ark that I have never visited during my explorations of the tunnels – to a room that is sealed with the same type of sliding metal door as the entrance. And just like at the entrance, there's a small box on the wall with buttons. Corentin keys in a sequence.

'It took us a while to figure out the code so Will was able to change it,' he tells me as he waits for the computer screen to turn green, and then he presses the button that says *OK*. 'We use the same code for lockdown, so don't forget it in case you lock yourself out. It's *FINOLA*.'

'Finola? As in Will's sister?'

'Exactly.'

'I thought that the Ark was always open.'

'We can retreat into the Ark like a snail retreats into its shell. An impenetrable, concrete shell, that is. There we go.' The computer screen shows the code has been accepted and Corentin slides the heavy door to one side. I follow him inside, this being the second time that day that my mind is blown by a surprise. As the door slides away, it reveals a large hall, much bigger than the main living quarters, where well-stocked bookcases in long rows fill the room. The ground is also littered with precarious towers of books stacked one on top of the other. The smell of dust and old paper gets my senses tingling. I slowly walk between the rows of bookcases and let my hand glide over the dusty covers. I feel the bumps of the paper that have got wet and then dried again and read the letters printed on the spines and covers of the books; names and titles I've never heard of before. I randomly pick out a brown, leather-bound book from one of the stacks and cough from the cloud of dust arising from its yellowed pages. The letters are small and printed close together. I struggle to read the name on the front cover; it isn't easy to get my tongue around the long string of letters. 'Dos... Dostoyevsky?' The book has the simple title of *Works*.

'I think he was drunk when he wrote that. It's a very strange story,' says Corentin, looking over my shoulder. 'You have to see this one.' He places another large book in my hands, on top of the Dostoyevsky. *The Lord of the Rings* by J.R.R. Tolkien. That name is easier to pronounce. 'What is that language?' I ask. 'I can't read it.'

'It's in English,' explains Corentin. 'Will has read from it for us. It's about heroes and an eye in a tower and a magic ring that must be destroyed.'

I don't understand much and stare in amazement at the book. I myself only know a few words of English. *Computer. Are you going to Scarborough Fair*, part of a song that Grandma used to sing, the rest of which she had long since forgotten. On the inside of my anorak are the words *made in USA*. It's an acronym for *the United States of America*, a huge continent on the other side of the great ocean. It had once been the mightiest empire on Earth, but that was before the Impact. Nobody knows what happened to it after the meteor showed up and caused mighty waves to roll across the world's oceans for many years after.

I nestle onto the floor, surrounded by towers of books, and leaf through everything I can lay my hands on, sometimes reading slow and carefully, and at other times fast and uninterested. Corentin gives me a book with pictures of knights. It is called a *codex*, a collection of sheets of paper with descriptions in handwriting that looks like a spider fell into the inkpot before walking all over the page. The drawings are amazingly bright, as if the dust of centuries of confinement has had no effect on them. I feel the hairs on my arms stand on end as I let my fingers caress them; pages and pages of information about a time I could hardly have dreamed of. An ancient world, full of stories, that has almost been pushed to the brink of oblivion. With the book open on my lap, that world seems to get a little bit closer, as if the turning of every page causes it to awake from its slumber.

'Are there any more of these?' I ask.

'Not as old as that one,' says Corentin. 'But there are story books and fairy tales and sagas, some of which have drawings.' He shows me another book, in which most of the pages are covered with colourful drawings of knights with long lances clasped in their gauntlet-clad hands and girls with long hair and even longer dresses. 'Most of them are in English,' he adds disappointedly.

'This one isn't,' I say, looking through one of the fairy tale collections. 'Peronnik and the Grail.'

Corentin moves a pile of books and sits down next to me with crossed legs. I begin to read aloud the story of a poor shepherd boy who wandered through rocky hills and past fast-flowing streams in order to find a golden cup that would bring him eternal life. As I read I can see him before me: a thin boy with a mess of curly hair and bright blue eyes, like Arthur. 'He placed his lance before the feet of his king and held the chalice aloft,' I say, arriving at the end. 'They lived for a century, and when their time came Peronnik and the king and his court boarded a long procession of royal ships and they disappeared off into the sunset. What a strange story,' I add. 'A cup that brought eternal life?'

'No stranger than other stories,' says Corentin. He draws figures in the dust on the ground. 'I will have to ask Will to translate the English stories for us.'

'Why do you care so much?'

He looks at me with a sidelong glance. 'Stories are what weave our lives together. Don't you know?'

'Maybe.' I think of Rona's story, which wouldn't have been the same without Sela's sad history, and then my thoughts shift to Benji, who may never have become such a bitter man had the Black Influenza not taken Esoldi and Finn from him. And what about me an Arthur – would we have ever made this journey if Dad hadn't died? 'Then everything is a story, really.'

'Everything,' Corentin emphasises with a sweeping gesture around himself. 'This room, the dust, the hands that brought these books here, the Ark, you, me, and the marshes. We are all threads in the great tapestry.'

'So what is your place within it?'

He takes the time to ponder his answer. 'Maybe we only find that out when we die, but I know where my place is now. Here in the Ark, at Will's side.'

'He must miss his sister terribly, given that the door code is Finola.'

'What would you do if the only remaining member of your family was taken by the Snake? Finola was a friend of mine too, and if I miss her this much, I can't begin to imagine what Will must be feeling.' He gets up and seems to shake something off before he speaks again. 'The botany section is over there. I have to get back to the training session, before it turns into a riot.'

I spend the remainder of the afternoon tucked away in the library, browsing bookcase after bookcase, setting apart every book that I want to read into a distinct pile. After a few hours, the pile has transformed into a dangerously high tower and I have to be careful to not let it topple over.

I make unsightly dog-ears on the pages, and if I really can't resist, I tear a page with an illustration out of an already neglected book so I can take it to Anna's sickroom. Like a sponge, I absorb every modicum of information that I find: information about new salves for bruising, a better method for extracting the oils from plant stems and leaves, and I also learn about new plants that don't grow along the coast. As soon as the weather gets warmer outside, I want to see if the marshes are more bountiful than the hills around Gwennec.

When I finally leave the library, tired and hungry, I don't take the trouble of locking the door behind me with the code that Cor gave me. I decide to go back the next day, or the day after that, or possibly all the days that this winter is going to last. I can't wait to tell Arthur about it. I think he will want to read the story books in particular, or perhaps the codex...

My head still swirling with thoughts, I turn down a new corridor, when I suddenly come to a stop. To my right is the room with the red cordon. It is deserted, the cordon ordering me not to become too curious. No entry, for anyone except Will and Corentin ...

What in Gwenhael's name could those boys be hiding in this huge underground complex? I glance around me. Further along I hear the sounds of children's voices, but they're not coming this way.

We tell each other the truth in the Ark. Yeah, right, and yet there's a forbidden room? My curiosity is too strong to contain, so I crouch down, slip underneath the cordon and push against the door. It's shut tight. My eyes catch sight of the lock, which has a small keypad indicating that this door, too, has a code. My fingers slowly punch in: F I N O L A. Will it work? Corentin said the whole Ark uses the same code.

For a moment nothing happens, then a green light flashes above the door handle. I grin contentedly, but the smile is soon wiped from my face as I enter the room and finally discover what Will has kept hidden.

I have entered a war zone. On my left is a large metal gun rack stocked with firearms. There are long hunting rifles, like the hunters in Gwennec use, but also small, heavy revolvers that could fit perfectly into my hand. In front of me there are bows and arrows with steel heads, clubs made of thick tree branches, wooden staffs like the children were using on the square... then, as I look to the back, my heart sinks in fear and I can't breathe. Behind a metal fence with a padlock are things that I'm almost certain are explosives.

My head is spinning. I lean against the door so as not to fall over. Is Will insane? Is there a madman hiding beneath that charming exterior? Who would allow so many weapons to be stored barely a hundred metres from a place where little children are running and playing on a daily basis?

My gaze is drawn to a small, locked cabinet to my right. I swallow a lump in my throat, not entirely certain I want to find out what's inside. After a brief moment of hesitation, I move away from the door and open the cabinet.

What a relief: it only contains books.

They are lined up next to each other in neat rows. No dust coats these pages, and these spines aren't torn or bent. I remove one from the cabinet. The front cover betrays little about its contents. I open it onto a random page and feel all relief washing out of me like water flowing out of a pipe.

Will has no storybooks or beautiful illustrations here. This is an old manual for soldiers in hostile territory. The next book I select explains how to load and reload a gun, and another outlines in chilling detail where to hit a person and how hard your hit should be so as to seriously injure your enemy without killing.

Chilled to the bone, I put the books back into the cabinet. Just as I close the door I become aware of a presence behind me. I am no longer alone.

I slowly turn around. Will is looking at me, his eyes like two black holes. His mouth betrays nothing and his eyebrows are only slightly furrowed. For a second I wonder if I can slip past him, but his body blocks my way out.

The hairs on the back of my neck stand on end as he takes a step forward.

'You must really like secrets.' Another step towards me; I can smell his familiar scent. He raises his hand and lightly touches the trimmed lock of hair dangling close to my cheek. 'You keep so much concealed, and yet you can't let others keep a few secrets of their own.'

'Will, it wasn't my intention...'

'Don't lie to me!'

I shrink backwards against the cabinet. 'Okay, sure, it *was* my intention, but I honestly didn't know that you kept this...this...' I helplessly search for the right words. 'I mean, what *is* all this? What are you up to down here, Will?'

He looks like he wants to lash out at me. With his half-raised hands he could easily give me a slap that would leave me reeling on the floor. Our gazes collide and seem to stick. Or at least I am unable to look away. My heart beats with a fast panic.

'You know what I'm up to.' To my relief he lowers his hands, but the tone of his voice doesn't get any nicer as he continues. 'I don't have to tell you anything, do I? About secrets. About never quite telling the truth. You just waltz in here, into the Ark with your brother in tow, you have this whole story about that fantastic mother of yours, you disappear for hours into the Green Room and God knows what you're up to with that stupid girl.'

'That's different. I'm trying to help Katell. I've told you everything I know ...'

'Yeah, sure, everything you "know".' He doesn't seem impressed. 'Who are you, Nimue of the sea? Who is this mother of yours that you keep going on about? What secrets do you keep? I can't quite put my finger on it, but...' He is standing so close that he pins me against the cabinet and moves his face right up in mine, his nose in my hair. 'You smell like a Snake.'

I try to hide my apprehension as he continues to stand over me. I slowly let my gaze trail upwards so that we're looking at each other again. 'And you smell of war.'

He remains motionless for a moment before he smiles and takes a step back. I move away from the cabinet and do my best not to show how relieved I am. 'What are you going to do, Will? Lead your own children's crusade into Central

Europe? Blow up Snake HQ with your grenades and blow their heads off with your shotguns?'

'If necessary.'

'They're just children!'

'For now they are.'

'It's not worth their lives ...'

'Don't say that!' He suddenly lunges himself at me again and shoves me roughly against the cabinet. Will is about a foot taller than me, but now he leans in so close that I'm able to count the lashes around his eyes. 'Say something like that again and you're out of the Ark!' he snarls. 'What do you think freedom is worth, Nimue? Huh? If it was your brother, or mother...or even yourself?'

'Stop,' I gasp. 'I understand! Believe me, I understand that you're angry.'

'Now listen here and listen well,' says Will. 'Secrets, weapons, wars... people like us cannot just sit idly by while our loved ones are stolen from us. We fight back. We bite down on the truth, like a wolf. Don't we, Nimue?'

I nod slowly.

He smiles. It isn't a pretty sight and once again I feel a chill running down my back. 'And what would you do to free your mother from the grip of the Snake?'

'I...I don't know.'

'Oh, but I think you do know. We're not so different, you and I.'

'Does Mirna know? Or Conn, or Anna..? Do they know what you and Cor are planning?'

'If the price of freedom must be paid in blood and lead – at least have the guts to look at me, Nimue! You know I speak the truth – would you let Arthur pull the trigger?'

For a long moment we are both silent, until I give him the honest answer: 'I wouldn't want him to have anything to do with it.'

'Now you understand.' He leans forward and trails a single finger down my hair. He lingers for a moment before he moves over to the door. There, he gives me one last, piercing look. 'Silence is golden.'

He turns around and leaves me alone. For a while I stand motionless, wrestling with my feelings. I think about Benji, as well as about the Asclepius Congregation, his little creation. The Institute that strikes such fear into the hearts of all the Ark-dwellers had come to be because of my uncle's compassion for the sick. Was that his mistake? And even when his compassion turned into obsession, he was still driven by love; he couldn't accept the deaths of Esoldi and Finn, and I can't blame him. Maybe, I posited, it was a kind of love that's fatal, and perhaps it was something that no one in our family could escape. Rona's own actions hadn't been so radically different from Benji's, after all. Her desperate flight to God-knows-where in order to protect me and Arthur has brought us into just as much danger in the end. How can I blame Will for doing what he does? He's already lost Finola. How could he allow someone or something to threaten his Ark?

And me? I'd take a life for Rona, maybe two, maybe even three, but to me she is still a stranger. A distant memory. Some sentences written in a book. What really terrifies me is the question what I'd do if someone ever took Arthur away from me.

I return to the main hall long after Katell has drifted off into in a deep sleep. I actually didn't want to leave her side. I want to hold her until her eyes shine again and the colour returns to her cheeks. I want to see her run and play and laugh, but the chilling fatigue that Sela's gift brings with it and the draught in the Green Room drive me back to the rest of the Ark.

I plop myself down on a pillow in the corner near Arthur, who is sitting next to Will and Anna. Yuna comes running in and inelegantly sits down on the floor between us. She has a sheet of paper with her, which she begins to colour. I wonder where she's got the crayons from.

'Where have you been?' Arthur wants to know.

'With Katell, you know that.'

'I haven't seen you all day.'

I look over at Will. He doesn't turn to face me but I know he's looking back at me from the corner of his eye. 'Corentin showed me the library. I forgot about the time.'

'Since when are you such a bookworm?'

'Since when are you such a little brat?'

Arthur grins. 'Anyway, you've missed dinner.'

As if my day hasn't been bad enough. I'm absolutely famished.

'He's just teasing you,' says Anna. 'I set aside some leftovers.' She hands me a bowl of soup, which consists primarily of stock with some chopped turnips and a few bits of carrot.

I take the bowl and spoon, and wolf down its contents within a few minutes. That's no problem, since the soup's nearly cold anyway. After I finish the soup I smack Arthur on the head with the spoon. 'You could have been a good brother and saved me a bowl of that, you know.'

'What? I just make sure I'm on time!'

'Yeah, and I'm your sister.'

'My untraceable sister.'

'I'll think twice about letting you see the knight's codex then.'

'Knight's what...?'

Too late!' I grin. 'Ask me again tomorrow. Say, Yuna, what are you drawing there? A dog?' I say as I lean over the drawing. The girl shoots me an unreadable look and shakes her head. Her piece of paper now features a whole forest of trees, and hidden between the trees is a creature with a rough coat and piercing, yellow eyes. 'A wolf, maybe?' I guess.

'It's the White Prophet,' she says, her tone suggesting that should be enough explanation. The others smile.

'Who's the White Prophet? ' I ask.

'You mean you've never heard the story?' Mirna looks rather surprised.

'Nimue and Arthur are from the coast.' Will also smiles, but I'm still unable to look at him directly without feeling awkward. 'They've grown up with other stories.'

'The White Prophet is no story,' says Yuna. She stops drawing. 'He really exists.'

'It's just a legend, dear,' says Mirna.

'Cor says all legends are true.'

'Corentin says people live on Mars. He's a big fat liar.' Mirna grins.

'And Mirna is such a pragmatist it'll make even cows go cross-eyed,' says Will with a wink at Yuna. 'Cor's right. Some legends are true. Others are half-true, and other stories... what's less than half, Yuna?'

Yuna pulls a confused face.

'Draw a circle for me.'

On the back of the piece of paper Yuna draws a circle. Will divides it into three with a crayon. 'And this is ...?'

'A third?'

'Exactly, only one-third part of truth.' His gaze shoots up towards mine. 'You're wondering who the White Prophet is. No one is exactly sure. He may be a vengeful spirit from the wilderness who wants to destroy our towns and cities. If you pay attention, you'll find him in many fairy tales. It's tempting to conclude that he has no stories of his own. He often slips into other stories where you might least expect him. He's like a shadow.'

'A shadow,' I repeat. I think of the apparition that I've now seen three times: the first time along the road, the second time at the hidden cave, and finally again, in the water of the pool.

Arthur and Will say something; I didn't hear it properly. '... and then I'll tell you the tale of the fisherman and the selkie bride,' says Arthur. 'I bet Yuna doesn't know that one.'

Will smiles. 'Very well. Just like all good stories this one begins with "once upon a time"... See, Yuna? If it wasn't true it'd start with *never upon a time...*' He begins to talk more quietly. 'But if you really believe the White Prophet has no stories of his own, think again. While he may be a shadow, this is his origin story. The oldest story of them all. And you'll see he's more than just a shadow...'

18

The White Prophet

“In the first days of the world, man was made from clay and fire. They were man and woman, and they lived on top of a mountain which looked over the whole continent.

During those first years they lived in peace with the wilderness, which provided them with wood to make fire, clean water to drink, and enough food so that they might survive summers and winters. Nonetheless conditions were harsh, and soon the wind had whipped their skin to leather.

In those first years they had a son, who they named Wind. His parents loved him very much and watched him grow for three years. But what an unfortunate name they had chosen for him! For when after three years Wind went outside to play, a storm from the heavens reached down its chilling hands towards him. He began to cough and soon caught a high fever. No matter what his distraught parents did, the young boy quickly slipped away. His father and mother buried him under the rocks of the mountain.

The woman was blessed with child again and in the spring gave birth to a daughter, who from the very first moment was healthy and glowing. They named her Blossom, and they were so happy with her that they sometimes forgot the loss of Wind. Blossom's parents made sure that the wind could never make her ill. Many springs passed until she had grown into a young woman. One day she went down the mountain to go pick berries in the valley below. When night fell, her parents began to worry when she hadn't returned. The father took a torch and looked under all the berry bushes in the valley as he thought Blossom may have got lost. But deep in the wood, among the tall trees, he found his daughter. Her face was pale as the moon shining above. A bear had found her and ripped her apart.

Broken, the man returned. So devastated were the parents that it was years before the woman became pregnant again. But one midsummer night, she gave birth again, and this time the clay and fire couple were blessed with twins. One had red skin and a shock of curly locks which hung over his eyes. They called him Flame. The other child was not as strong: he was sickly and pale, but his bright eyes were like clear pools of starlight. The mother did not see the baby's strange and mysterious eyes as he looked out onto the world. All she saw was his short stature and his white, almost translucent skin.

'He surely will not survive,' she said to her husband. 'It is best if we leave him outside and pretended that he never existed. Flame will become a brave, strong boy, but I do not want to lose another child to illness or accident.'

The father then took his pale infant to the foot of the mountain, where the valley stretched out before him. The child looked up at him with his starry eyes as his father laid him down between the trees, and the father had to avert his gaze out of shame as he went back up the mountain.

There he built a house with stone walls, where no wind and no bear could find them. They cut down the trees around the house and used them in the fire that kept burning all year round. The mountain was soon bare.

'At least this way we know the trees will never fall on our son if the wind blows,' the parents told each other.

The man also built a dam on the river so they could choose when the water would flow.

'This way we can be sure our son will not be killed by a flood,' said the parents. They hunted more and more beasts to turn them into thick blankets and coats, should the winter cover their mountain in snow and ice.

'This way he won't get cold and die from a fever,' said the parents with a sense of relief.

The man and the woman took good care of their son. Flame grew like a strong, young tree until he was old and wise enough to look after himself. The parents then said: 'It is a blessing that we have sheltered him from all the bad things in the wilderness which took our other children from us.' They no longer thought of the sick child that they had left in the valley to die.

Yet against all odds the weak child had not died. Although he had been cold and had suffered from illness, he had for a long time laid in his reed basket and stared at the heavens above him. It was strewn with stars and had kept watch over him. Near the end of the night, a snow-white she-wolf had emerged from the shadows of the trees. She had carefully walked around the basket and then taken its handle between her jaws to take the child back to her den. Not long ago she had lost her own pups to a bear and her teats were bursting with milk.

The baby soon became a child who frequently roamed the forests alone. It had never occurred to the mother wolf that a little human baby would be vulnerable out there in the wild! As a result the child would sometimes go to the mountain. He was shy and never let himself be seen, but watched from the bushes how the boy Flame walked on two legs.

The wild boy recognised his own face in that of the other boy, not knowing that he was his brother. He learned to walk upright by watching Flame, and as the years went by he learned to speak by listening to him. The boy eventually became man, and he saw that the people living on the mountain had cut down the trees so the forest was wounded. He observed his family as they came down the mountain and turned the valley into farmland, and he saw how they eventually exhausted the land so that nothing could grow there anymore.

His wolf-mother was afraid of them. 'They destroy everything in their path, like a forest fire,' she warned her son.

'I am like them,' he reminded her. As he said those words he looked down at his hands: as much as he turned his fists up or down, they never looked like wolf paws.

'You are my son,' answered the she-wolf. 'Your hands might look like those who live on the mountain but they are not like you. You belong with the creatures of the forest.'

Despite his mother's words, one day the young man plucked up the courage to climb up the mountain. When the woman saw him she began to cry. There was little left of his sickly figure, but because he was still as white as milk she recognised him immediately. The father was speechless and embraced his lost son. The brother was out working the land. When he returned he did not know what to say, for his parents had never told him he was part of a twin.

The nameless young man implored his family to stop ravaging the valley in their hunger for produce. But when Flame realised that this was the main reason why he had come to them, he became angry with his long-lost brother and convinced his parents to send him away. Three nights later he came back, again begging them to stop exhausting the land, but again they sent him away. 'If you want to come back to us, you have to do as we humans do,' they said.

The young man knew that he could not abandon the forest and his wolf-mother: he loved her and the forest was his beloved home. Thus when he was turned away for the third time he built a shield around his heart. One misty day he went to the mountain, the white she-wolf at his side. He ran his hands down the walls of the house and wherever he touched the stone, branches with leaves began to sprout from the cracks. The family immediately emerged from the house. Under their feet the earth began to shake and the house slowly collapsed. Finally, with a great groan, the mountain itself split in two.

On one half, the family was left furious. On the other half stood a lone man with his wolf, and while night fell around him, he looked like a silver spirit, bathed in moonlight.

'That is no son of ours!' the parents cried. 'That being is no longer even human!' Flame then swore that he would kill his brother, should he ever see him again.

And so it came to be that the people who lived on one half of the mountain built houses and worked the land, and on the other half the forest grew once more in the places stripped bare by man. The man and his wolf-mother continued to live in that thick forest, although he would sometimes still look mournfully across the gorge to the other side. Perhaps his parents were right about his humanity. The white wolf's son had irreversibly split the world in two, and it seemed that it would never be restored. This cast off youth, this lonely prince, thus became the first White Prophet."

19

FINOLA

In the silence that follows, the light of the CORE flickers two, three times, as if it can't decide whether to stay on or not. I look around at the tall walls of the underground room. When will these collapse like those of the house in the story? No building stands forever. It may take a hundred years, or even a thousand, but eventually, the wilderness will reclaim the Ark once more too. Or will Central Europe have triumphed by then, and will people on the coast have to wear oxygen masks too?

'Who was right?' Mirna's question breaks the silence.

'The White Prophet,' says Yuna.

'Flame had a point,' Corentin says. 'His family needed a place to live in a way they wanted.'

'But they took everything,' says Anna.

'The wolf-boy wanted to protect his world,' says Will gently. I have the feeling he's looking at me.

I say: 'The family on the mountain wanted to do that as well.'

If anyone notices the tension between us, no one is saying a word about it. Anna and Mirna lean towards each other to discuss the supply of carrots and turnips, as well as the snow that makes hunting outside virtually impossible.

I am only half-listening, until I'm startled by the smell of cigarette smoke. Will moves towards me and leans in so close that our shoulders are almost touching. He conjures up a plastic bottle, which he holds up to me.

'Nimue, Nimue,' he mumbles, my name gliding off his lips as if it were the first line of a poem. 'You and I have got off on the wrong foot, don't you think? We need to set things straight. Why don't we start afresh?'

He unscrews the cap and I immediately pick up the unmistakable smell of alcohol. He slides a cup towards me and pours me some drink. A small nip, that's all. I see the others drinking too and frown slightly as I see Arthur bring his cups to his lips. Will doesn't let me leave the cup on the ground. He pushes it into my hands and leans back contentedly. An unlit cigarette dangles from the corner of his mouth. 'Cheers,' he says. 'To friendly relations.'

'How do you come by all these things?'

'The weapons were already here when we arrived. I pinched the whisky.' He looks at me as if to challenge me to take him on. When I say nothing, he smiles. 'You're not drinking?'

'Cheers.' I lift up the cup and gulp down the drink. It burns as it travels down my throat. I change colour and hold in a cough. Will doesn't need to know that I've never drunk anything this strong before. The elderflower wine in Gwennec is much weaker. Perhaps cheaper too. 'Arthur's a bit young for this.'

Will cocks his head like an inquisitive bird and looks at Arthur from behind his own glass. 'I think he behaves like a proper man.'

I follow his gaze and see how bony Arthur's hands seem as he brandishes the cup of whisky. How large they are. He is now as tall as I am, and very soon he'll be even taller. 'You're right,' I admit. 'He's not a child anymore.'

Will pours himself a second glass. 'You have hair like fire but eyes like water.'

Yes, like Benji. Like Fergus. Not features to be proud of, exactly. I uncomfortably brush my hair out of my face. 'You're right, let's start over. Tell me about yourself. I imagine you haven't always lived in the Ark.'

He laughs, and this time it's a real laugh. 'Of course not.'

'Where did you live before?' I ask, pleased that the awkwardness has passed.

He looks at me inquiringly, then averts his gaze. For a while he seems to be looking at absolutely nothing.

'Will?'

'Lum Urbo.' He turns his head back to me and I see his dark eyes glistening mockingly. 'A few kilometres north of Rome. They call it "The City of Light".'

My surprise must be evident from the look on my face, because he runs a hand through his brown hair. 'I don't look Central European enough for you?'

He doesn't look anything like the few people from Central Europe I've seen during my lifetime. His hair is too dark, his eyes too black. 'And you speak Breizhonic...'

'You asked me where I lived before Finola and I found the Ark. My family came from Wales. That was before...you know.'

I swallow and nod. The islands off the coast of Breizh have largely disappeared, swallowed up by the unruly sea, long after the meteorite had struck the Earth.

'Our languages are similar,' says Will finally. I can now hear his lilting accent, how musical his words sound and how he rolls his Rs. I realise that we have something in common: both of our birthplaces have been flooded – swept away forever by the greedy sea.

'The Asclepius Congregation,' I say after a moment. 'What do you know about it?'

He looks at me. 'Aren't you our new expert? You and your brother?'

'Our trail ran cold in Brevalaer,' I say honestly. The red house is the last sign of Rona we came across. My gaze moves across the chamber. On the other side of the room is Broc, engrossed in a game of marbles with the other children. Yuna has walked over to him. Her crutch lies idly beside her on the ground and I see the stump she has for a left leg sticking out. 'What do the children know about it?'

'They don't need to know more than they already do.' He casts a menacing look into his glass before downing what remains of his drink.

'You say everyone here has had a run-in with the Ascl... the Snake.'

'That doesn't mean everyone knows why they're after them. The less they know, the easier they sleep at night. When they get older they'll ask about it, and I'll be honest with them.'

His glass now empty, he takes out another cigarette and plucks a few strands of tobacco off the tip. I wonder how many cigarettes he gets from the raids and how many of them he actually smokes. His fingers are as restless as his eyes whenever he isn't fiddling with a cigarette.

'They seek out the orphans,' he finally says. His voice doesn't go beyond my ear, as he leans in close to me while he speaks. His breath is warm against my cheek. 'If they catch siblings, they separate them in order to get the best results... the same happened to Mirna and Conn.' He points in their direction with a nod of his head. 'Conn managed to escape. Mirna wasn't so lucky.'

'And then they conduct their experiments.'

Will doesn't answer. It's as if he wants to say: just take a look at Yuna; look at Broc. Look at Mirna, who still has scars that run across her arm like a spider's web. Look at this barely organised, ragtag band of children and you'll see the hidden mutilations left on them by the Asclepius Congregation.

I fight in vain against a rising tide of nausea. 'And they drive through the city streets like a predator searching for its prey.'

He is quiet for a while, taking so long to reply that I'm beginning to think he doesn't want to answer. But then I see him staring at Broc and the other children. This time I follow his gaze. Red-haired Josse throws a white, round stone with great precision against a pile of grey pebbles, the top one rebounding off the wall and falling into a hole on the floor. The other children stand around him in a small circle, except for Broc, who stays seated on the ground and points with his finger at the others like he's counting them. He's singing a kind of counting-out rhyme as he is doing it:

'White stone, white stone,

Sea salt, gravel, earth and bone.

The prophet he is coming.

His enemy is running.

White stone, white stone,

Sea salt, gravel, earth and bone.'

Next to me Will is gesturing wildly with his arm. Startled, I recoil from him. He's turned paler, his lips tightly gripping the butt of his cigarette in a grim line.

'That was her game. Finola's.' Will swallows, his Adam's apple moving up and down. 'Her rhyme. She always made up little songs.'

'Will ...'

'There's one thing I know for certain,' Will carries on brusquely, as if he hasn't heard me. 'Before the Snakes took her away, my sister was the smartest person I knew. "Gifted", they used to call her. That's why they wanted her, and not me. They took her away in those cursed jeeps.'

'Did you try to …?'

'Of course. I had the whole thing planned out in my head, but I needed a few weeks to catch up with them, and when I got there…' Will shakes his head. 'I never thought they'd be able to break her so quickly. I didn't understand it at first, but she had changed.' Again, he swallows. He seems to struggle to speak up enough. 'By the time I found her, she was terribly confused. I thought she was in shock and I tried to calm her down, but she was distant, almost as if she couldn't see me. Anxious, always worried and always upset. The things she said…they didn't make sense anymore, Nimue. It seemed like the babble of a young child, but I did understand from her words that they'd hurt her somehow. Sometimes there were clear moments, when she'd look at me and she knew who she was – who *I* was. But I couldn't protect her. They found us. Finola was like a ragdoll. She didn't fight at all, but I did and I managed to get away. I haven't seen her since….' His voice trails off.

My mouth fills with the bitter taste of disgust. This could well have happened to me. 'I'm so sorry,' I finally manage to croak. 'Oh, Will…'

'I'll get her back.' He clenches his hands into fists on his lap. 'I will do anything to get her back, one way or another. And if she turns out to be dead, I swear my wrath will hit them like the meteor once crashing into the Earth. I'm like the White Prophet, Nimue. I won't settle for exile in the wilderness. So don't ask me why I keep weapons in the Ark. Don't ask me why we teach the children to fight. Don't ask yourself if it's fair or if it's worth it. You *know* why. And you know it's true.'

I look at his thin face, into his dark, wild eyes and at his broad fists, and I nod.

'What's going on?' Mirna is suddenly standing there. Her eyes dart over me and the fire that seems to be smouldering within them startles me.

'Nothing, I was just asking Will about…'

'We were talking about the Snake.' Will holds up his cigarette. Mirna sits next to him and lights his cigarette. The tip begins to smoulder, much like her glowing face.

'You're upset.'

Will's mouth twists into a stiff smile. 'You worry too much.'

'I know what you're like.'

This time he smiles for real. His arm wraps around her waist and he draws her near. 'No one knows me like you, Mirna.'

I feel a pang in my chest – am I jealous? I quickly shake the thought from my head. I don't even really like Will, let alone wanting to feel his arm wrapped around my waist, or to feel his lips brushing mine, as he's now doing to Mirna... I gulp.

Mirna seems reassured. When she looks at me again her eyes are friendly. 'Your brother's getting along well with Cor.'

'True.' I turn to look at Arthur so I don't have to witness Mirna nuzzling up to Will. 'He certainly seems to be enjoying himself with whatever's in that flask.'

The light flickers again, then turns into a soft glow. The Ark is telling us it's time to go to sleep. I get up to lie down on my mattress and pull the blanket over me. Why am I thinking about Will? I have other people to think about, like Katell. Like Mum.

I feel the mattress shift when Arthur lies down next to me. He smells of whisky. And I reel from it. The drink makes my head warm and fuzzy, as if I'm sinking into a sandbank made of dreams. Soon I forget the Ark around me, and the sounds of the children quickly fade away, as well as Mirna's voice who sternly orders them off to bed.

20

THE PALE MAN

The man stands a little way away from me, tall and translucent white, as if made of mist. He is waiting for me between the menhirs, which stand in a semicircle by the edge of the stream. I recognise this place, but I know I must be dreaming as there is no ice on the ponds and the grass is too long for it to be winter. I cautiously enter the stone circle, my footsteps making no sound.

The Pale Man turns towards me and I can see his narrow face. His features are strangely stretched, his skin covered in faded tattoos: spirals, circles and waves, which gives me the feeling that every cell in his body is flowing and that he might dissolve at any moment. He looks at me and I stare up at him. He towers over me like the stones that surround us.

'Why do I keep seeing you?' I whisper.

He stretches out a long arm towards me and touches the middle of my forehead with the tip of his index finger. I feel warm, then cold, and finally my skin begins to tingle.

'Go,' he says, although I don't see his pale lips move for even a moment. His voice laps against me like a wave. 'Go.'

I awake with a start in the darkness of the Ark and listen in confusion to the heavy breathing of the sleeping children around me. I put my hand to my forehead, which is still tingling.

Now that I'm awake, I can feel the cold of the sleeping quarters around me. With the blanket draped over my shoulders I sit up. The CORE must have gone out – even at night, there's usually a soft glow from the fluorescent tubes, which have been set on a twenty-four-hour delay. Will calls it the 'nightlight'. As it is I can hardly see my own hands, let alone the dark outlines of the others.

As if a little door in my mind has been opened to a crack during my sleep, I suddenly realise where I know that pale, white figure from. Not from my own, fleeting visions, but from Rona's written memories. On that dark night at sea, she'd dreamed of a white man. *He said: 'Be brave and strong, Rona, daughter of Sela...'*

Now that voice echoes through my head: *Go.*

Go now?

Why not... I'm awake now anyway, and if both Rona and me are being visited by the same figure, it isn't just a dream that has awoken me. By now, I've familiarised myself with the Ark's surroundings. The place that I saw isn't far from where Arthur and I have recently cut a hole in the ice on the stream to set a fish-trap. I could walk there and back within an hour.

I cautiously grope around me looking for my boots. I wrap the blanket around my shoulders like a cloak and creep away from my bed as quietly as possible. A couple of times I bump into someone, but to my relief no one wakes up. I eventually find the door to the hallway and grope along the wall until I feel the groove etched into the stone.

I hesitate for a moment. Even during the day, the marshes are a dangerous and unpredictable place. You can never be sure if the path you followed yesterday will still be there today. Perhaps I should go back and wake up Arthur? I shake my head. I have no desire to crawl back. What's more, I remember it's a full moon tonight, so once I'm outside there should be enough light for me to see where I'm going.

I find the way out by slowly following the groove in the wall, step by step. With great concentration I recall the route. Three steps forward. Left here, then turn right... ouch. Damned CORE. Back again. Yep, there's the turn.

After a few long minutes of shuffling forward in the darkness, I finally reach the doors and push them open with a great sense of relief. The moonlight streams in. I breathe in the cold night air and look up to the sky. My breath rises up like steam towards the stars, which seem to be closer than ever. I pull the blanket tighter around me and walk towards the line of trees as my feet make crunching noises on the frozen grass, the moon occasionally disappearing behind the branches of the trees. The larches and pines are dark outlines full of prickly needles. Mistletoe is growing on the bare oak trees.

I reach the stream and follow its course, along the bend where the water flows over a rock sticking out. I pass the trap, and for a moment I'm tempted to stop to see how many fish have already been snared, but I'm not here for that. Further along there are three flat stones, which serve as a crossing. In the darkness I miss a step. My boots fill with bitterly cold water. I gasp and scramble onto the bank on the other side.

The trees move to one side and let the moonlight through. In the white light, I can clearly see the stones standing there like tall, silent humans. My heart begins to beat faster as I suddenly become nervous. Was it a good idea to come here all by myself, especially at night? I have a vision of men in green uniform sneaking past the trees and grabbing me before I can scream out. No one would hear me.

Chin up, Nimue, you are completely alone here. I shake off my fear.

As I get nearer, the stones begin to tower over me. As soon as I am within the stone circle, I feel safely enclosed – protected from the rest of the marshes. It is as if this place has nothing to do with the ordinary world. I feel it without being able to explain why, much like how I could sense the sea back home without being able to see it. It's *different*.

For a while I stand erect, ramrod straight, the blanket wrapped around me against the nightly chill. I'd more or less expected the man from my dream to be waiting here for me, and even now I still expect him to hover out from behind one of the stones at any given moment, like a corporeal patch of fog. There is no movement however – not even a rustle of branches from the trees.

This was a mistake. My gaze darts in all directions, searching amongst the menhirs and the trees, but to no avail. Perhaps it had only been a dream after all, brought on by the story of the White Prophet, or perhaps the Hunter on the edge of my sleeping mind was replaced by the Pale Man. That would be a relief. Whatever the case may be, here I am, standing alone in the cold like some idiot!

My whole body is cold, my wet right leg in particular. If my dream was indeed a sign, why did the Pale Man not say more to me? What did he mean by "Go"?

'Here I am!' I shout, my voice sounding surprisingly loud in the quiet of the dark marshland. I stamp my feet in order to keep warm. What a sight, I think to myself. I could be back in my sleeping bag before the others wake up if I went back now.

I'm about to turn back when suddenly, a memory comes to me. It's an old one, from long ago, when Dad was still alive. Arthur was a toddler and I wasn't much older myself. But still our father had taken us out on his sloop, because a fisherman's child couldn't get used to the sea quickly enough. He showed me how he would cast and pull in a net, cast and pull, over and over again. Then he let me try. I cast the net and waited until he gave me the sign to pull it back in. It took so terribly long and I really wanted to see all the wriggling fishes that I'd caught. I took the line in my small hands and I began to pull. My father wrapped his long fingers over my hands. 'Not yet, seal pup,' he said, smiling. 'Wait just a little bit longer.'

I breathe slowly and take a decision. The ground is hard and cold as I sit down with crossed legs; even with the blanket spread under me I can't prevent the cold from seeping into me. I see how the moonlight slowly moves from one stone to the next, as if the people who built this circle wanted to dance with the moon itself. After a while I can't feel the cold or my own body. Instead of waiting for the Pale Man, I slip away into my memories. I think about our house, how it sat on the hill as if it were fused to the Earth, as if no storm could ever move it from its place. I think of the *Ragdoll* and the nets, which would leave our hands rough and calloused, as well as the shimmering scales of the fish we'd catch on good days. With my eyes closed I can see the jagged cliffs and the impressive rock formations along the coast before me, the foaming waves crashing into them. And in the summer, the sea looked like a pane of glass and lukewarm water lapped against your legs, while the seagulls cried and seals lay on the sandbanks like black dots ...

It dawns on me that it may be a long time before I see another summer in Gwennec.

After that, I remember nothing for a while. When I wake up from my brief sleep, there's a large bird standing in front of me. I can see every feather on its body, as well as its dagger-like beak and the penetrating stare of its little, yellow eyes, as if it has woken me up with just his stare.

It's another heron.

I dare not move, scared of frightening him off. At the same time, the hairs on my arms stand on end and my legs are cramped, so I eventually pull them gently from under me. The heron stands there, undisturbed, slowly moves one leg up, and begins picking at a frozen blade of grass.

'The fish are in the stream further along.' Despite having numb lips, I smile.

He looks up at me at once and again it strikes me how sharp his beak is; he could easily peck me until I bled, if he wanted to. It's strange for him to be sitting here so calmly. Could he be injured? I can't see any blood on his feathers.

Everything about him it long and elongated, while his black feathers create a dark pattern on his body.

'Have you come for me?' I ask. Should I risk reaching out with my hand? 'I dreamed that I should come here.'

The heron stares at me and I'm touched by his clear gaze. It's as if he's thinking. As if he can *understand* me...

Then I hear his voice. It is a scratchy, wild, inhuman sound, piercing right through my bones: 'Know me, recognise me, hear me, answer me. Nimue!'

I just about stop myself from letting out a shriek. His voice falls silent in my head, but the creature keeps looking at me, as if urgently waiting for my reaction.

I gulp. 'I can hear you.'

This time, I crawl cautiously forward and touch his feathers with trembling fingers. I expect the stabbing pain of his long beak in the palm of my hand, but the bird just shivers and remains motionless.

'I recognise you,' I whisper. 'But I don't know you.'

'We are the forest and the trees and the stream and the waves. You are Nimue of the sea, sister of Arthur who shall soon come, child of Rona who knew us, granddaughter of Sela who had long been lost...'

'Where are they?' I ask, trembling. 'What happened to Sela? Where's Rona?'

'She has crossed over. You must no longer search for her, she has gone far away.'

'Of course we have to search for her! Tell me what's going on! If Mum is in danger, we have to...'

'Rona did not stop it. Listen, Nimue of the sea, before my powers fade. Search no more for the child of the lost one. She has strayed too far herself. Search for me, the Fisher King. Find me on the other side. Hurry, before the boundary fades away forever and my world is torn asunder. My strength is disappearing like a shrinking moon ...'

'Wait,' I say as I find myself gasping for breath in order to process his words. 'No so fast! I don't understand! Before, in the pond, you told me you were looking for me ...'

'The child of the sea and the coming king. Blood from the line that turns the cogs and puts all in motion. Bone of the limb that is tempted to do evil or do good. Yes, I am searching for you, children that walk the boundary.'

'What do you want from us?' I can barely talk any more. Only with difficulty do I get the words out. 'What can Arthur and I do?'

'Once we were breathtaking and wild, and I was king. Once, we were free and interwove our world with that of the world of men, until they forgot to live by the fabric of world in world – that is when our names disappeared. One by one, we fell prey to the living darkness, which distorted and twisted us until we were no longer what we had once been.'

'You know the disease too?'

'No disease, but something broken, an absence of connection. Whosoever should fall prey to it is lost. Listen, Nimue of the sea. The poisonous gasses in your land have displaced the last of us who remain there. Soon we will pass into oblivion. The world will be torn asunder and you shall find the air sucked out of the sky and the blood halted in your veins. Where we pass away, you too shall pass.'

'If you are the king, why won't you do something?'

'I cannot leave. I remain hidden in my castle. I was looking for you, I followed you and now my strength is depleted. Soon I shall no longer be able to travel. I will fade like mist in the morning light. Listen, Nimue of the sea. That cannot happen.'

'But what can be done? What can I do? All I want to do is find my mother!'

'Free the Fisher King from his castle. Save me, children that walk the boundary, I beg you. Save us from corruption. Stop the illness, cure the sick, and heal the poisoned land.'

'The poisoned land,' I repeat, confused. I remember what Corentin told me about cities where people have to wear masks to protect themselves. 'The industry in Central Europe that once started with the Phoenix Group, where Benji worked.' I wait but the heron – the Fisher King, the Pale Man – has no answer. He trembles in the cold wind that blows through us. 'I don't have enough power to heal,' I say, ashamed. 'I can't even cure Katell. All I can do is keep the illness in check a little.'

'Close your eyes and breathe.'

'What? I ...'

'Close your eyes and breathe. Trust the Fisher King.'

I do what he says and feel a breeze on my face that's nothing like the cold air of the night.

'All of your strength is sleeping within you, daughter of Rona, granddaughter of Sela. Feel it flow through your veins. Feel it in your lungs. Feel it in your skin and in your bones and in your muscles.'

Something touches my forehead. It is cool at first, then burning hot. I scream and shoot back, but seconds later the pain disappears.

'It is like breathing. Draw the strength in. Force it through you. Then push it back out.'

I open my eyes and stare at the heron. My heart is beating wildly. All feeling of sleep is gone, along with my fear. Even my sense of dismay and astonishment has faded into the background through the immense power that I have felt flowing through my body. Like a river, like a surge. Why did I think it was difficult to access – or that I was weaker than Rona? I can now cure Katell, I'm sure of it.

'Now that I have given you this, I can no longer appear to you.'

This snaps me back to the reality of the moment. 'Don't go,' I beg. 'I understand so little. How can I find you? How can I find Mum? You say she's gone, but I...'

'Yes, she is gone. I must go now also. And you. Both of you must also go.'

'G-go?' I wipe my face with an icy hand. 'But where to? Our trail has run cold.'

'Take heed of my warnings.' The heron grows restless. He pulls his other leg up and his feathers come forth like a frayed hood. 'I see winding serpents and fire. The young man is full of shadows. Go quickly.'

'Will? I didn't think he was really that evil ...'

'Go.'

The heron spreads his wings. I feel the air move as he takes off and flies over me.

'Wait!' I scramble up. 'My mother ... Please!'

But he is already gone, melted away into the night and into the trees.

A few branches snap behind me.

As I turn around I see Arthur standing there, surrounded by clouds of breath. His hands are tucked deep into the pockets of his padded anorak.

'What are you doing here?' I ask in dismay. I have no idea how long I've been here before the heron appeared. Is it nearly morning?

'You were gone,' he says, coming closer. 'I was worried.'

I get to my feet with great difficulty. All my muscles seem to be frozen and I have no feeling in my hands, even if I dig my nails into my palms. 'Did ... did you see what happened? Did you hear him too?'

'Did I hear who? What are you doing here, Nim?'

'I dreamed something,' I say as I stagger inelegantly. Arthur thrusts his arms out and holds me up. 'I dreamed that someone was calling me, and then there was this heron. But how did you know I was here?'

His blue eyes scan my face in confusion. 'I dreamed too. I saw you sitting by the stones. When I woke up, your sleeping bag was empty.'

For a moment I don't know what to say. Then I begin to violently shiver, as if my body is crying out for warmth. 'I'll freeze if I don't start walking.'

As we walk out of the stone circle I tell him about what I remember from Mum's diary, about the flashes of the Pale Man when he appeared to me, and the things he'd told me. Arthur's as speechless as I am.

We follow the winding path of the stream. As we reach the fish-trap, a streak of dawn light pierces through the trees. Arthur comes to a stop.

'What does *the coming king* mean?'

'Don't ask me. You're a lot of things, but certainly not a king.' Besides, there are no more kings, not since the old world was destroyed by the Impact.

'You're right.'

I look at him in surprise. 'I was only teasing you, you know.'

'I mean about what you just said. Our trail has run cold. We don't know where Mum is, or what happened to her. But we do know where Benji is.'

'Yes, at the Asclepius Congregation.' Which made him both very far away and yet dangerously close by at the same time.

Hesitantly Arthur suggests: 'We could visit *him*.'

We stare at each other, his face reflecting my own sense of fear.

'Or we listen to this Fisher King,' he adds.

'Or we carry on our search for Rona.' I swallow. We are at a crossroads. 'Whatever we choose we have to go see him,' I conclude. 'Benji, I mean. He's the centre of everything now.'

'Shark's blood,' sighs Arthur. 'There's a trip I'm not looking forward to making.'

I think about the Pale Man. Although I've seen him with my own eyes, I am finding it difficult to believe that all of this is really happening. Perhaps I'll wake up in my sleeping bag in a moment ... I look over to my brother. His ruddy cheeks, caused by the icy wind, seem very real to me. Besides, the cold that's penetrating my bones doesn't seem very dream-like either.

'Nim? Hello?'

Arthur's voice gets me back to the present. 'What?'

'I said let's take the fish-trap back. Or we'll be eating just water for soup in a few more days.'

I remember what Mirna and Anna said about supplies. Is it really that bad? I lean over the stream with Arthur. The hole we carved out has frozen over, but the fresh layer of ice is still thin. He stomps on it with his heel and it breaks into pieces.

My hands are already so cold that I can barely feel the icy water of the stream as it flows past them. 'We've caught five, maybe six,' I say. 'Oh well, that's good enough.'

When we get back to the Ark, Will is outside smoking a cigarette. His gaze moves over us, down to the trap and then back up, lingering on my face. He doesn't smile. 'The marshes are dangerous in the dark.'

I shrug my shoulders.

'Where were you?'

'Fetching breakfast.' Somehow, the way he looks at me makes me nervous.

He blows out some cigarette smoke and I watch it disappear in a spiral into the night sky. 'Fishing with a blanket, were you?' he asks.

'It's cold.'

'And you're wet.'

'I slipped in the water,' I reply. 'We have a good catch.'

'You're shivering,' he says. 'You'd better go inside to warm up.'

I quickly nod and gesture at Arthur to come inside. The CORE has been switched back on, as bright neon lights shine in the hall below. I wonder if Arthur's heart is racing as badly as mine. *The boy is full of shadows,* the heron said. It's true; when I look into Will's eyes, I can see the shadows moving in his pupils.

But he keeps us safe, I sternly remind myself. What's more, Will has reason enough to feel bitter. I leave Arthur busy with the catch and hurry to put on some dry trousers. They belonged to Mirna before, and the legs are a little too long for me. I don't wait until I'm well and truly warmed up, because the power that the Fisher King has summoned within me flows like a turbulent stream, sloshing against the inside of my skin. I have to put it to use right this instant. I have to see Katell.

On the way to the Green room I run into Mirna. Her arm shoot up and she stops me. 'We have a problem. Have you seen Will?'

'He was outside just now.'

'Damn, I hope he hasn't decided to take a walk.'

'He was having a smoke,' I say. I try to walk around Mirna's arm. The energy is pulling me automatically towards Katell, as if it knows what needs to be done.

'Where are you going? I said we have a problem.' Mirna blocks my path. 'Everyone in the main hall, now. I'll fetch Will.'

'Shark's blood, Mirna! I have things to do as well! What's happened?'

She looks at me angrily. 'The water treatment plant has broken down. There's not a single drop of uncontaminated water left.'

21

THE SHADOWS ON THE INSIDE

When Will enters the room, the others are already assembled there. He seems a little paler than before, although that may be down to the artificial light coming from the CORE. His eyes scan us all. I imagine his gaze lingers on me for a second longer, but before I can react he has already turned away from me.

'Mirna says the water purification plant has frozen over. Winter's forcing us to retreat into our burrow faster than we would like. If we can't get fresh water we won't last another month. If a new snow storm breaks out, less than a week.'

'Will – the children,' mumbles Anna.

'The little ones had best know what's going on,' says Will sternly. 'But this day has just begun. We have a few hours to act and prevent a disaster. The sky looks clear. I don't think we'll have a storm today. That gives us until nightfall for a group of us to go to Brevelaer. Mirna, you take the lead. Keep it short and sweet. Corentin, take Arthur and Anna with you to set new traps. On a clear day like today, animals will flock to the water and who knows, we might catch enough for the next few days.'

'You're staying with the little ones?' asks Mirna with a frown. 'That's not like you, Will.'

'Today it is. Is everything clear?'

'Clear as day.' Mirna beckons me and her brother as she picks up her army coat from the floor and zips it up to her chin. 'The guards won't have changed yet, but we'll have to risk it. Nimue, how good's your acting?'

'What in heaven's name are we going to do?' I ask.

'Put on your coat,' says Conn. He takes out a pair of fingerless gloves and dons them. 'We're going to District 15.'

'The castle,' clarifies Mirna. 'It's an army depot. The final destination or loading point for freight trains. We need bottled water, so we have to steal it.'

Fear immediately seizes me. 'I think I'd rather go with Cor...'

'You're coming with us. You're nimble and you're smart. Conn and I can't carry everything.'

'Okay, fine.' I grudgingly shrug on my anorak, doing up all the buttons in order to keep out the cold. 'At least tell me how scared I should be. Have you ever been caught?'

Mirna looks uncomfortable.

'Well?'

'Once,' says Conn, glancing over at his sister. 'After that one time we deemed it safer to go to a far-off post. Unfortunately, Mirna didn't pay enough attention when we were out there. If you hadn't rescued her, she would now be well and truly back in the Snake's nest.'

That's far from a comforting thought. I follow him in silence as Mirna, annoyed by Conn's choice of words, turns and leads us out of the Ark. I have a brief look around, and as I do so, I catch a glimpse of Arthur, who is next to Corentin and Anna and talking to little red-haired Josse. When he sees me he chuckles and gives me a wave. I wave back, feeling envious that all he seems to have to do is go into the swamp. The winter weather and the maze-like marshland are pretty dangerous, but a lot more predictable than what awaits me.

Brevalaer is different from the last time we were there. Gone is the lively, bustling city, the people strolling past the fountain, the carts and cars roaring and rattling through the streets. Those same streets now lie empty. Many houses are barricaded up, their windows boarded up with planks. The few people we do see hurry past without looking at us. I pause for a moment as we are about to cross the square. What happened here in those few weeks we've been trapped inside the Ark?

'Keep moving, Nimue.' Conn is pulling on my sleeve. His face is hidden behind a dark scarf that he used to cover his nose. Only his dark brown eyes, which clearly resemble Mirna's, are visible. They turn in all directions, nervously surveying the whole area.

I get moving again and follow the siblings to a street behind the square, which tapers off to little more than an alleyway, and eventually leads us near the castle. From here I can see part of the stone wall and the iron gate. 'Is this town always this animated?' I say mockingly.

'I've never seen it like this.' Mirna sounds somewhat anxious, but a moment later she seems to shrug off her worry. 'A lucky coincidence, I suppose. The fewer people see us, the better. Here – time to get changed.' She pulls out a few large bundles from her bag and hands one to me, Conn getting the other. I roll out the fabric and see they are clothes: a white jumper, a moss-green cap that covers my ears, and bright-orange overalls with a pair of sturdy, black boots.

'What's this for?'

'You can't look like an intruder.' Mirna stuffs her thick hair under the cap. Her face suddenly seems smaller and more boyish. I follow her example, the cap causing my head to itch.

The orange overalls are a little too large for me, the legs being too long, so I tuck them into my boots in order to conceal they're the wrong size. When we have all changed, Mirna looks me up and down with a probing look. 'Near perfect. Just take that look off your face.'

'What look?'

'The one that says you're afraid you might be swallowed up by a monster at any moment.'

'Oh, excuse me for still having a bit of common sense,' I snap back. I turn away from her and glance back at the gate. Someone's standing there, wearing the same uniform as we are. 'Is that a sentinel?'

'It is indeed. God, that guy must be bored out of his mind.' Mirna grins a crooked smile.

'How so?'

'District 15 is only a small depot. An outpost on the arse end of Central Europe,' says Conn. 'There's not much to guard here…unless a medical convoy is expected.'

'Let me guess – that's not today.'

Conn shakes his head. 'And we've only come for water, until Cor can fix the water facilities.'

'Well, now that we're here, we might as well take some other things,' protests Mirna. 'The taste of water just doesn't compare to the taste of a good, stocky soup, you know.'

Conn snorts. He looks from me to his sister. 'Ready?'

I can't say I feel ready, exactly, but Mirna nods without a hint of hesitation on her face. As they sneak off, all I can do is follow them.

The lane takes a turn and I briefly lose the District 15 post from sight. When the building appears again, we've ended up in front of the gate, hidden behind an entrance building that is jutting out. The guard is now in plain sight. As we get closer I can see he's just a young boy, not much older than myself. Mirna studies him with a look of relief that I can't quite place.

'If I don't know him, chances are he won't know us. Follow me.' She moves out of her corner and confidently sets off in his direction. 'A bit chilly for the time of year, isn't it?'

Conn and I follow her on foot. I feel the guard's eyes taking us in. 'I don't know you.'

'We're new here.' Mirna fumbles in her bag and hands him something small and flat. A pass of some kind? The guard tilts his head to one side. 'I didn't know they were taking on new ones. Strange,' he mumbles, more to himself than to us.

'Strange? How so?' Mirna's smile diminishes somewhat.

The boy shrugs his shoulders. 'That's just what they say.'

'Have you worked here long?'

'Only a month. That was before the quarantine.' His face turns gloomy. 'To be honest I think I'd been better off in a different job, but money is money, at the end of the day. Were you hired to monitor the quarantine?'

'That's right.' Mirna shifts her weight from one foot to the other.

The guy snorts. 'I wouldn't want to be in your shoes, I can tell you that.'

'Well, like you said: money is money. Are you going to let us in or what?'

He seems to remember the pass that Mirna gave to him and turns to a built-in computer next to the gate. I see it really is a pass, which he holds against the screen until I hear a bleeping sound. Mirna conjures up another smile. She holds out her hand.

'Hold up.' The guard frowns down at the pass, not giving it back. 'The date on this thing has expired.'

'The date?' For the first time, a crack shows in Mirna's mask of confidence.

'When was this pass last updated?' He sounds very firm now. I hold my breath, ready to run away at even the slightest indication he might turn against us. Conn balls his hands into fists beside me. What's he going to do, fight his way in?

'I don't know,' I hear Mirna mumble. 'This is how it was issued to me.'

The young guard looks from her to Conn and then from Conn to my pale face. I hope he hasn't noticed Conn's fists. After a silence that makes my heart skip like a frightened deer, he says contemptuously: 'You really don't know what the hell you're doing, huh? This quarantine is no joke, I assure you. There are new orders. Make sure your pass is always up-to-date, got it?' He inserts the pass into a slot next to the computer and keys in some sort of code. The screen flickers before he pulls the pass out and hands it back to Mirna without making more fuss.

'I'll remember it for next time,' she says quickly. 'Can we go inside now?'

The young man steps to one side. He makes a grand gesture with his arms, accompanied by a derisive bow. 'Feel free. Rather you than me.'

Mirna's radiant smile returns as she walks past him and pushes open the gate. 'Thank you!'

'Thank you,' I echo as I hastily follow them, not looking back. Only when Conn slams shut the heavy metal door behind us do I take a moment to look around the bare walls of the coldly-lit corridor. It is a bit like the Ark, except it has tall, arched windows. These must have been fitted with stained glass in the past, I think; now there is just frosted glass with iron bars. Above us hangs a huge sign full of names and arrows. I cast a curious look up at it.

Brev □ Gwen, et al.; platform 3
Brev □ Lum U. et al; platform 4
Brev □ St. Th. et al.; platform 5

They must be the loading and unloading areas for the freight trains, I realise. If Arthur ever becomes a train driver, he'll eventually find himself in stations like this.

'Come on, Nimue.' Mirna spurs me on impatiently. There's no one else in the corridor but I flinch because of her loud voice. Can't she at least *try* to be discreet? I soon catch up to her and Conn. They take me through various divisions and doors until we enter a room where the sheer cold hits me immediately. The door makes a hissing noise as it closes.

'What is this?'

'A storage room. It has to be kept cold, otherwise everything will spoil.'

I let my eyes wander to the sign that hangs above the door: *Gwen, et al.*

'That's my town,' I say. 'You want us to steal from my own town.'

'Come on, Nim, don't be such a downer.' Mirna opens a glass case that covers the whole wall and begins to take large plastic bottles to stuff them into her bag. 'Take the meat boxes. To your right.'

When I do nothing, Conn pushes me aside and starts filling his backpack with the heavy packages. Processed and dried meat – emergency supplies for Gwennec? Is it still as bad as just after the flood?

'We've left plenty for them,' he says, when he sees my face. 'Gwennec's by the sea, isn't it? Plenty of water there, right?'

'Wow, what a genius idea,' I say, annoyed at his words. 'Of course! Seawater! Why didn't we think of that ourselves?' I open my own bag and fill it with what seems to be the least necessary foodstuff for the inhabitants of Gwennec: strips of dried fish. Which bigwig in Rome has thought this up? This fish most likely originates from the region itself, was shipped to Central Europe at some point and is now being sent back home as part of an utterly clueless outreach programme.

'That's enough,' says Mirna, the necks of the bottles sticking out of the top of her bag. 'We can't carry any more without compromising our speed. Ready, Conn?'

'Ready. Nimue?'

'Alright, yeah.' I hold my bag up to show them I've actually done something. 'Can we go now?'

Mirna nods. She leads us once again through a maze of corridors and staircases, and again I'm reminded of the layout of the Ark. 'Why don't we just go back to the main entrance?'

She pats her bulging bag. 'Do you want to take a shot at explaining this?'

I don't. We come to a narrower corridor where there's hardly any light. I look up and notice that all the lights and bulbs are gone. 'This used to be the kitchen, before the castle became District 15. If we take this passage to the left there's a back door that I ... what in the world?'

Our path is blocked by a yellow-red ribbon, stretched across the width of the hallway. Behind it is a door, which once would have provided access to the kitchen. Now there's a sign in front of it in bold white lettering: No entry for unauthorised personnel.

'To hell with that,' says Mirna. She ducks under the rope and pushes the sign aside.

'Mirna, think about it!' I stand my ground. The hand clasped around my bag has turned unexpectedly clammy. 'You don't know what's behind it.'

'Of course I do. That's our exit.'

'And I'm pretty sure that they've converted it to the quarantine now.' I look at Conn, hoping for backup from him. To my relief he nods his head.

'Nimue's right, Mirn. This looks weird.'

'What do you suggest, then?' She pulls open the door, but it won't budge. 'Damnit, that one too. Where's that pass...' She reaches into her pocket and pulls out the pass, pressing it against a small screen next to the door that I only just notice now. For a moment nothing happens. I'm starting to think we ought to turn back around and, if need be, find a different way of smuggling our stolen goods out, when Mirna suddenly inhales sharply. 'Look at this!'

Conn ducks under the cordon, and despite my bad feelings about the whole situation I follow him, drawn in by my curiosity. On the screen a text has appeared:

Personnel of District 15, Brevalaer:

Do not enter without orders from AC or an authorized member of staff. Consider patients as extremely dangerous. Keep in quarantine at all times. Pick-up date: 3rd of February.

Sent by:

Dr. Cormack Cairn,

CEO Asclepius Congregation Medical Institute.

We stare at each other in the dim light. In their eyes I can see my own bewilderment. I want to bet Will knows nothing about this. Despite a growing pang in my stomach that's urging me to run as hard and as fast as possible, another part of my brain registers the name that has appeared on the screen: 'Cormack Cairn' ... why does that name seem so familiar?

'Mirna, what are you doing?' Conn's shrill tone shakes me from my contemplation. To my horror, Mirna has started walking down the long dark corridor that lies before us.

'We can't let a warning get in our way,' snarls Mirna over her shoulders. 'I want to know... I want to see what these bastards are hiding. Patients, Conn! You know what that means? Children! New pigs to the slaughter!' With every word she's saying she grows angrier. 'Don't stop me, Conn! Tonight the Ark is going to have a few new residents.'

Conn mumbles something, but I understand exactly what Mirna means. I push my fears down into a secluded spot in my chest and duck under the ribbon myself, pursuing Mirna. She has reached a door on the left-hand side and is fiddling with the lock.

'Mirna, come on.' I reach for her bag, which is still hanging from her arm, but she forcefully shoves me away.

'I told you: don't try to stop me!'

'I'm not going to stop you – I want to help you.' I take the bag off her, so both her hands are free. 'Swipe your pass through that slot. It's been updated with information about the quarantine, remember?'

'Damnit, you're right.' Mirna swipes the pass through the lock, and immediately a small beep resounds and a green light comes on, like before. I look at Mirna. Her hands are trembling as she pushes the door handle down. Is it from fear or anger?

With a jerk she pulls the door towards her. I jump to one side to stop my head from getting caught on it, but I'm still close enough to see a dark room is behind it. No daylight seems to penetrate into it. I cover my nose with my hand. The smell that hits us is unbearable. What are they keeping in here, excrement?

'Oh God,' Mirna whispers. She stands frozen beside me, her hand stuck to the door handle.

I peer into the room with squinted eyes and I suddenly realise what I'm seeing. People lying down, others sitting, and people who huddle together as soon as the small amount of light coming from the hallway falls on their dirty faces.

I fight the feeling of cold that passes through me like a gust of wind. These are no imprisoned children, no orphans that are driven to the Asclepius Congregation like cattle.

'What is ... Why are they ...?' Conn can't even string a sentence together. When I briefly look aside, I can see his face has turned pale, as if he were the Pale Man himself.

Somewhere in the room a few people are stirring. A man crawls towards us, causing us to reel back, as if his hideous stench is actually physically pushing us back. My hands are shaking. I stare at him as he lifts his face up towards me. His eyes are bloodshot and his skin is grey, except for spots where it bulges like overripe prunes. Black buboes. As he opens his mouth to say something, I see he is missing most of his teeth already. The hand he stretches out towards us is that of a skeleton. I can't make out what he's trying to say. Help us? Or perhaps 'get out of here'? All he makes is a rasping noise as he breathes, a noise I am eerily familiar with, as I have heard Katell breathing in much the same way.

Somehow in the back of my mind I realise that I should step forward now. That I should lay my hands on their disintegrating bodies. That is my task, my *responsibility*, exactly like Benji has always claimed. I swallow hard, woozy from the stench and fear.

'What's wrong with them?'

'Is it the plague?'

'Mirna, get away from there.'

The words of my companions shake me out of my trance. I feel overcome by an intense feeling of disgust, which pushes me further and further out of the room until I find myself pressed against the wall of the corridor. I don't know these people. They aren't from Gwennec, and I haven't held them in my arms like Katell, so feverish and sick, after the great flood... Mirna and Conn are also running a great risk. They have to go and I don't want to stay behind on my own...

I gruffly say: 'Run!'

They obey without question. We run down the hallway with our bags. Mirna regains her composure as she steers us towards another door. The exit perhaps? I hope so – I hope it with all my heart...

Behind us, the silence is shattered by a blaring alarm. It roars three, four, five times before being interrupted by a calm female voice: 'Warning: quarantine breached. Protocol C is now in force. I repeat: quarantine breached. Protocol C is now in force.'

My mouth is as dry as if I've eaten sand. I've left those people behind, people who needed my help...

Before I can finish my train of thought, we reach the rear exit. Mirna swipes her pass through the lock and throws all her weight against the door, causing it to fly open. We stumble into the winter cold. I take deep breaths, feeling my lungs being cleansed of the rancid air that hung in that room.

'I have to go back. I have to get back inside!'

'Are you crazy?' Mirna stares at me. She's just as pale as her brother.

'But I can help them! Gwenhael's grave, I've abandoned them.' I drop my bag on the floor and hide my face in my hands, overwhelmed with shame.

Conn yanks them away from my head. 'I don't know what you're thinking, but whatever it is, it's not true!" he growls.

'It *is* true! It's...'

'Shut up and run!' He picks up my bag and drags me along again. All I can do is follow him and try not to slip on the icy cobbles of the street.

At the Ark everything is quiet. Corentin, Arthur and Anna are gone and I don't expect them to return any time soon. Mirna drops her bag on the floor as soon as we enter the main room and looks around bewildered. 'Where's Will, for God's sake?'

I couldn't care less. I lean my back against the wall and hide my face again. Will can't do anything about the situation anyway – he can't lay his hands on those dying people and suck the disease out of them like marrow from a bone. It's not even a real disease, I think to myself, defeated, as I remember the words of the Pale Man. What did he say? A lack of connection? A sort of corruption? That certainly describes the hideous feeling that coursed through my body when I tried to help Katell. A living nightmare, an evil entity. Despite the warm air that the CORE pumps through the Ark, I'm freezing cold.

I have to go back. Of course I have to go back. Rona would be ashamed of me if she saw me just sitting here. Even Benji has done his bit in helping strangers to be rid of their strange affliction... And me? I ran away like a frightened cat.

I can't ask Mirna and Conn to take me back – that would be madness. What's more, they'd be exposed to a danger that I hope will never catch up with them. The only way to do this safely is to go alone. If I could just steal Mirna's pass and lie my way in again...

Although by now the young guard will have certainly rallied the other members of his team. They'll have found the opened room and forced the sick back inside, possibly with violence, and soon my uncle's snakes will come to collect them.

No, not my uncle's. Cormack Cairn's.

Cormack.

I suddenly sit up. I know where I've heard the name before: the first day she was here, Katell mentioned him; the man who has found a treatment for the Black Influenza.

Katell. In all the chaos I've almost forgotten her. I spring up and dash to the Green Room as fast as I can. If I can't do anything for those poor, lost souls in quarantine, I can at least make sure Katell doesn't suffer the same fate. Not now that the Fisher King has awoken me inside by pouring liquid sunlight into my soul.

As soon as I open the Green Room, I know something isn't right.

There's a deep silence that can't be here in the presence of a sleeping girl, no matter how quietly she breathes. My hand feels for the light switch. As the CORE sends its signal to the neon tubes in the ceiling and cold light begins to fill the room, my heart stops in my chest.

Impossible. She was too sick to have left the room herself. Who's taken her? There has to be a normal explanation for this.

I run back through every corridor until I arrive back in the main hall, puffing and out of breath. 'Will!' I shout. A few of the children look up, startled. Mirna open her mouth but I don't wait to listen. I run outside, put my hands to my mouth and shout: 'WILL!?'

Nothing moves within the marshes. No reply. I stand rooted to the spot, the icy winds messing up my hair. Mirna and Conn appear at the entrance. I see the confusion on their faces, as well as the fear that hasn't quite subsided yet.

'What the hell is the matter this time?' Mirna's words are harsh but her voice is shaky.

'Where is she?' I ask hoarsely. 'Where's Katell?'

'What do you mean? Nobody's taken Katell.'

'Will has taken her!' I'm suddenly sure of it, even though I have no way of proving it. I feel the cold gradually give way to heat and rage. I see Mirna and Conn give each other a look.

Conn takes a step towards me. 'Will has no reason to ...'

'Then where is he? He said he'd stay with the little ones! Why is he nowhere to be found?' I can't stop shouting, even though it does little good. I thrust my hands into my pockets so as to hide my trembling.

'Perhaps he decided to go with Corentin,' says Mirna reasonably. 'You're worrying about nothing, Nimue. Come inside, all three of us are still in shock. I think we should discuss what our discovery means.'

'I know what it means,' I growl. 'The Asclepius Congregation is trying to rid people of this disease. That's great! Just brilliant! Let them carry on with their noble task, so I don't have to ...'

'Nimue.'

'But if it's really such a great thing,' I plough on, not minding Mirna or Conn, 'why did it all look so incredibly *sick*?!'

'Nimue! Calm down!' Conn pulls at my arm to yank me back to the door. 'You've lost it.'

He's right; I'm shaking from top to bottom and can't control my voice. 'I have to do something! You have to understand, I can't just bum around here while people are perishing back in Brevalaer! And if I can't even help Katell … *Where the hell is she?!*'

'I don't know,' says Mirna softly. 'But you have to come inside with us. Come on, you're as cold as an icicle. No ifs, no buts,' she adds sharply when I try to start a new argument. 'Let's just wait until Will gets back and then we can figure it, okay?'

It's not okay. Nothing is okay. However, I don't know what else I can do, so I reluctantly let them bring me back inside. Mirna sits me down at a table in the corner, wraps a blanket around me and puts down a steaming cup of tea in front of me. I sit motionless, as she and her brother heave the bags of supplies down to the store room.

In my head a storm is raging. I can no longer distinguish one thought from the other. Maybe Mirna's right; maybe I'm too upset by what I've witnessed in District 15, and that's the reason why I can't think of a logical explanation for the absence of Will and Katell. Perhaps he's even mentioned something about it … Has he? I can't remember. All I can remember is the look he gave the girl when he found out she was ill.

It is hours before he appears on the edge of the square. He walks towards the Ark with his hands in his pockets. I'm waiting for him, shivering in my anorak once again. Mirna and Conn haven't tried to stop me this time.

As soon as he sees me, he stops in his tracks. Something in his eyes tells me he's startled by my presence. He looks back over his shoulder: is he hoping I'm staring at something else? No, there's nothing for it. He knows he'll have to come my way and there's no avoiding me.

'Are you cold, Nimue?'

'Where is she, Will?' I hiss. 'And don't lie to me.'

For a long time he just stares at me. I'm almost certain he is trembling himself, if only a little. 'You don't make the decisions in the Ark.'

'No, but I want to know where she is. Now.'

'She's safe.' He takes his hands out of his pockets and fumbles clumsily with a cigarette. 'I did what I had to do in order to help her. To help everyone.'

'What?' I don't have the strength left in me to start shouting again, even though I really should. 'Where? Will, for God's sake, where?'

'Shit!' He suddenly turns away from me.

'Don't walk away!' This time my voice is shriller. 'Look at me!'

But Will swears as he points toward the edge of the forest. I follow his gaze.

Out of the twilight emerges a human figure. He walks slowly, dragging his right leg as if it were a piece of dead wood. As he reaches the square, he staggers, nearly toppling over. For a moment I remain frozen. It is then I recognise the blond curls and the gaunt build.

'Arthur?' Before Will can rush over, I leap past him and catch my brother in my arms as he collapses. 'Arthur, what happened to you? Where's everyone? Will, help!'

'Cor,' sobs Arthur. He doesn't sound like himself. 'The snow fell. The bear trap ...' He doesn't seem able to say anything else and moans in pain. Only then do I see that his right leg is covered in blood.

Will kneels next to us. He takes Arthur's head between his hands and studies his rolling eyes. 'Where are they?'

'Will, he's bleeding!'

'Where's Corentin?' He grabs my brother and shakes him roughly. Arthur lets out a scream.

'Will!' I'm choking on my own anger and tears. 'Help me, you arsehole! Mirna! Mirna!'

'Shut your mouth,' snarls Will. He seizes Arthur even more violently. 'Tell me where they are!'

'Dead.' It's just a whisper. Arthur's lips tremble and I realise he's crying. 'All of them.'

22

Until the Light Returns

A cold feeling of disgust clings to me, just like the blood clings to Arthur's leg. He has lost a lot of blood, after freeing himself from the bear trap with his own hands and staggering the long, icy route back home.

Between his tears and cries of pain, Will has managed to get the story of what happened out of him, little by little. They were on the crest of the hill, setting new traps. Who fell first Arthur didn't know. He remembers their cries, then the force of someone falling against him and dragging him down. The cold and the panic of the snowfall that covered him and stole his breath away. Arthur was able to wriggle free and roll down the hill, but he got his calf caught in the bear trap that Corentin had set only minutes before. The pain was so great he was blinded, but he still remembers the blood: not just his own, but that of Corentin as well. By the time he was able to free himself, he was numb, cold, scared, and alone. No one answered his cries.

Will didn't hesitate. Lantern in hand, he went out to fight against the darkness and retrieve his friends. Mirna and Conn also went to help carry them back. I stayed behind, peeling the remains of Arthur's trousers from his leg, cleaning the wound with snow and antibiotics from Anna's first aid kit and then wrapping layers of bandage around it. He winces at every touch.

Now he's asleep, a rest induced by a white powder that I found, and the dead lay around us on blankets, brought in under the cover of an oppressive silence. Even the youngest of the children seem to sense it is best not to cry.

I know that I can't protect myself from it. I know at some point I will have to open my eyes and look at what is left of my friends after the accident – they deserve that, at the very least. But I'm scared. I prefer looking at Arthur, even though he isn't looking much better. At least he is still breathing, and I can feel his heart still beating as I place my hands on his chest.

Be brave, Nimue.

I cast my gaze upwards.

For the second time in my life, I am face to face with the dead. I stare silently at their beaten and broken bodies, covered in bruises and wounds caked in dried blood. Anna has a deep cut on her head and her dark hair is stuck together in bloody clumps. Perhaps she hit her head on a rock as she fell. Oh, good Gwenhael, I hope she lost consciousness soon. Her eyes are still open. They look like broken glass beads.

It's just like the flood again, I think. As if Corentin, Anna, Josse, and Alan have also drowned ... drowned in a tidal wave of snow.

The two boys lie side by side: impatient Alan and playful, mischievous Josse. It's almost as if they're sleeping, with the worst wounds being only cuts and bruises, like every young boy has. Only their unnaturally pale, almost blue skin betrays the truth, making their bodies seem as if made of wax.

Corentin – oh, God, Corentin. Just like Anna he has a deep wound on his head. The trail of blood runs from the top of his skull to his jaw. His nose is clearly broken and the skin around his eyes is black and swollen. His lips are blue, like Dad's were the day we pulled him from the water. I look at them and try to determine what I feel, other than an increasing feeling of nausea.

It is Mirna who snaps me out of my stupor as she quietly sits down next to me. Her cheeks are wet with tears.

'Do you think...it was quick?' I hear myself ask.

She nods, biting her quivering lip. It's obvious she's using all of her strength to stop herself from collapsing. 'In a flash...what with all that snow ...'

I nod. She doesn't need to explain further.

'We almost didn't find Cor,' whispers Mirna as she stares at his body. 'He lay buried under a metre of snow. He has...he must have ...'

'I don't want to hear it.'

Mirna falls silent.

Suddenly I feel Arthur's hand clasp mine. He is awake. He pulls himself up with difficulty. *That could have been him,* is the thought that keeps running through my mind. He could have been there next to the others; hideously maimed, with his blonde hair sticky with dark blood, and with dead eyes, like Anna's.

'Please don't ever die,' I whisper close to his ear. If he'd been one of those corpses, my life would have been over in an instant.

'Not without you,' Arthur promises weakly. 'We are a chain.'

Will looks around. His dark gaze skims the paltry band that still remain. In my head I count them: Arthur and I, Mirna and Conn, Broc, Yuna, and a handful of other children standing close together, and Will himself, of course. For an instant I forget how upset I was about Katell, and I look up at him. He doesn't look like a traitor. All I see is a tired, sad boy with sagging shoulders, crushed at the loss of his friends.

'I don't know what to say,' he says after a long, ashen silence, his voice cracking. 'I don't know what to do.'

Everyone stares back at him quietly. No one knows what to do. We don't even know where to start.

It's Mirna who breaks the silence. 'We can't leave them like this. They must be buried.'

'How? The ground is too hard and we can't build a funeral pyre here without drawing attention.'

'Then we'll give them over to the marsh. This place has protected them from the Snake in life. Now it'll do the same in....in sleep.' Mirna worries her lip.

'That seems like a good idea,' says Conn gently. I nod slowly, unable to utter a single word.

'Good.' For a moment Will seems to waver, but he quickly recovers. 'Tonight we hold a wake. When dawn breaks we'll give them over to the marsh.'

Nobody says much that evening. We all sit in a circle, like a ring of menhirs, around the dead. Will passes his whisky flask around and we drink. Even the young ones take a swig now and then, in order to stave off the cold. I try to get drunk. Being drunk seems a better option than the current, searing pain in my chest, or the feeling of being choked by a pair of cold hands.

I don't get drunk. I get dizzy and flushed, but the pain remains.

Arthur finds it difficult to stay awake. He sinks into my arms and I cradle him in my lap. He shivers every now and then. From the pain?

After a few hours, my eyes also begin to grow heavy. Helped by the drink, I begin to doze off occasionally, not long enough to actually fall asleep, but every time I drift off I'm overwhelmed by half-dreams, or strange thoughts that I can't recall when I wake up moments later.

I'm standing in a cave with a copper chalice in my hand. I am overcome by a feeling I lack time to complete a certain task, but I before I can remember what I ought to do, the image disappears.

I'm standing in a snow-covered forest. The trees around me are huge. Far away is the sound of an animal howling.

I'm swimming, deeper than anyone should dare swim. The light is smothered by a mass of seawater. Shadows dance around me. No, not shadows – seals. I want to join them, but a voice crying out stops me.

I'm standing on a beach. Behind me rises a wall of cliffs, before me roars the surf. I stand face-to-face with a woman. Her black hair falls loosely around her body, reaching down to her waist. She is soaking wet. I can tell she's sad, even though she doesn't utter a single word.

The long night finally comes to an end. In the breaking dawn we walk silently into the marshes. The frozen pools between the trees look like mirrors. Arthur wraps one of his arms around my neck, leaning on Mirna with the other. His pace is slow, his face twisted with pain, but he insists on coming with us. Behind us come the dead, on sleds made of tree branches, pulled along at the same slow speed and leaving deep tracks in the snow. Now and again, I look back over my shoulder at them, at Anna and the children, as they make their final, brief journey.

Will has chosen a small, round pool that lies enclosed by the trees. Further along I see the contours of the stone circle where the heron forewarned me of flames and darkness. Is this what he meant? I leave Arthur propped up against a tree and I help carve out a piece of ice. The dark waters of the marshes rise up and spill out over my shoes. *You won't get me*, I say in my mind. *I have escaped.*

Will asks if anyone wants to say a few words. I search for the words, for a clear thought in the grinding mass of cogs that is my head, but nothing. I come up with nothing.

The moment passes and Will sits slightly hunched over the first stretcher. Mirna rushes over to help him, supporting his trembling hands with hers. They carefully lower Josse down into the hole in the ice, kneel down, and let him slide into the water legs first. Before they let him go, Mirna runs her fingers over his face for the last time. I hold my breath as I see the water slowly swallow him up. The ripples spill over onto the ice. *Thus people slip away*, I think dejectedly. One minute they're here, the next minute they're out of reach, just like Gran.

Anna lies with her legs bent, clutching her crooked arm against her chest, as if instinctively protecting it from the snow when it fell. Mirna tries to close her stiff eyelids, but gives up after several attempts. I stand fixated, staring at her frozen blue eyes until she, too, disappears under the surface of the water.

Corentin is the last one left. Slowly, even more so than the others, he is lowered into the water by Will and Mirna. Arthur presses his face into my side. I ruffle his hair, not yet quite able to say anything comforting.

When Corentin has gone, we are left standing in the emptiness of the marshes. Empty as the hole in my heart that remains. A half-scattered circle of orphaned children now stands around the hole in the ice – a hole that reveals nothing about their friends, now drifting beneath the ice. I feel the biting cold again, more intensely than before.

'We must go back,' I hear Mirna tell Will. 'Supplies are still scarce and someone needs to repair the water plant. We can't put it off much longer.'

'You go ahead,' mumbles Will.

'But you are our leader.' I look up and see the sharp look Mirna is giving him. 'You're not going to abandon us because you're sad, are you, Will?'

'No. trust me, Mirna.'

I carefully push Arthur a few steps away from me. His eyes are swollen and red. I kiss him on the forehead. 'Go with Conn and Mirna, they'll help you walk,' I say softly. 'You must keep warm. I'll be there in a minute.'

'What are you going to do?' In his voice I can hear that he doesn't want me to leave him alone. 'You're cold too.'

'I ... I have to ask Will something.' I give Arthur over to Conn and wait until the others have gone back inside.

Daylight begins to seep through the branches of the trees ringing the marsh. I lift up my face to catch those few rays. It's not enough to comfort me. It is, however, just enough to give me some fresh courage. I slowly breathe in and out, and then focus my attention on Will.

23

— ◆ —

THE DEAD AND THE LIVING

Will stands with his back to me, a cigarette between his nervous fingers. As I position myself behind him, I remain quiet. My breath slides down his neck and I watch him shudder slightly.

'I keep expecting one of them to swim back up,' he says.

'They won't.'

He squeezes the cigarette between his fingers. Pieces of tobacco fall onto the ground, a few dropping into the water. 'You better go with the others. Leave me alone for a bit.'

'No.' I put my hands in my pockets and ball them into fists. 'I want to talk about Katell.'

His whole body tenses up. 'I have nothing to say.'

'Don't you dare,' I snap. 'Look at me!'

He finally turns towards me. His lips are pale and pursed together. His gaze roams all over my face, as if he's searching for some sort of uncertainty so he can call my bluff. But I have nothing to hide, nothing to conceal. Unblinking, I stare back.

'She was my responsibility,' he says finally.

'That isn't true.' I still have my fists clenched. 'She was from Gwennec. You know that. She had survived the wave just like we had, and she was my patient, I was taking care of her! Did you think I wouldn't figure it out? That no one would notice?'

'Nimue ...'

'Don't you "Nimue" me!' I yank my hands out my pockets and go for him. He avoids my punch by jumping onto the bank of the pool, and I slip on the ice.

'You sold her to them, didn't you?' In my anger I can't scramble to my feet. Sat on the frozen water, I stare back up at him. 'You handed her over to the Snake!'

'If you just let me explain ...'

'Explain? What is there to explain?' I shout.

'Nim... it's not what you think ...' He slowly moves towards me, his arm outstretched to help me up. 'She was ill. Very, very ill. How long was I supposed to let this go on? I have no idea what you did to her, but as far as I could see it had no effect, and you said it yourself – the Asclepius Congregation is looking for a cure. Yes, they are snakes, but apparently someone among them has found a cure for whatever it is she was suffering from... You said it yourself, didn't you? Some doctor...Cormack?'

'Stay away from me! You have no idea, do you, Will?' I gesture towards him to go away. 'Whatever this Cormack guy has come up with, it isn't the right way. I am the right way! I have the power: I have the skills to rid humans of this disease. My mother was able to do it, and now I'm stuck with this ability!' I hold my hands out to him, as if he can read something written in my palms. 'But you've sold an innocent child to torturers and murderers.'

'What?' Will turns pale, whiter than he already is. I see the fear in his eyes, as well as the disbelief. 'What are you trying to say?'

'My mother had a gift,' I say slowly. 'How she came by that gift I have no idea. Her mother - my grandmother - was a strange woman. She disappeared, just like Mum, and this ...' I hold my hands up once again, 'this is my inheritance.'

'If that's true, why didn't Katell get better?' He looks at me with an air of suspicion.

'Because I was scared. It's terrifying. It feels like a nightmare. But now I know I can. I' was finally ready, and then you went and took her away from me!'

'How was I supposed to know you were our fairy godmother?' snarls Will. 'You and your damned secrets.'

'Would you have believed me? Do you believe me now?!' I am about to explode with rage. 'You never should have done it, Will! How could you? How dare you! You, you who lost his sister to them! You know what they're going to do to her – good Gwenhael, no, you *really* don't have the faintest clue what they're going to do to her! All you have is hearsay about experiments, confinement and fear, but you won't be there to witness the pain they'll be submitted to, the loneliness, and the other sick things. You aren't going to be there for her, to hold her or to comfort her! Go rot with the fishes down below, you arsehole!'

'Stop!' He falters. 'I know it was a stupid idea, I know it was wrong. I was … I *am* desperate, Nimue. It was a stupid idea; I did it before I could think twice.'

Before he could think twice? Does he expect me to believe that? I finally get to my feet, my back straight, my chin up high. 'You're disgusting. You're a Snake yourself!'

'It's not forever, Nimue! I couldn't just leave her there. There is a plan…it's almost ready, but then this happened and…'

'Do the others know?' I ask. 'Does Mirna know about this?'

'Shh, not so loud!' He looks back, as if he's afraid of seeing Mirna there. The deluded bastard. He won't find her here. At least Mirna went back with the children to care for them, unlike Will. 'The others don't know. But you're different, aren't you? You know that running doesn't help, that we can't protect all children if we just hide… We have to fight the Asclepius Congregation, Nimue. We have to destroy them.'

I look at him, searching for any trace of lies or regret. He looks back beseechingly. *He's scared I might betray him,* I realise. Scared that he might lose his power. 'You're right. The Asclepius Congregation must be destroyed.' I take a deep breath to calm myself down. 'But that is not your task. It's mine. Mine and Arthur's. You've made a terrible mistake.'

His jaw draws tighter still. 'Whether you trust me or not, I have the knowledge, the means, and enough anger to feed me. I am the one who can destroy them.'

For a while we remain there, silently looking at each other. The morning sun lights up the frozen pool, making it shimmer like a mirror. Above us, an early bird breaks out in a dawn song, the sound lilting along the tree trunks.

'I can see your hate and your anger,' I finally say. 'Enough to fight a war. They'll follow you.'

'Follow?' He makes a dismissive gesture. 'I keep them here to protect them. I don't need followers, Nimue. I can fight this war on my own if necessary.'

'You think you can really protect them?'

He leans over to cup my face in his hands. His ice-cold fingers caress my cheeks and forehead. I taste the tobacco on his lips as they press against mine. 'I swear it, Nimue of the sea.'

'Stop.' I pull his hands off me and take a step backwards. 'You don't know what you're saying. The Asclepius Congregation is mine; this is my legacy. Do you understand? The head of the Snake is my uncle. The one who should have stopped them is my mother! That's why they had to flee, that's why she wanted to hide me. Now that my mother is gone, they want me. Don't you see, Will? It wasn't Katell who you should have sold. It was me.'

'You sound as if you're leaving.' Will forces a grin onto his face, but it disappears just as quickly again. 'You need me too, Nimue. Both you and your brother.'

'That's right. We can't go anywhere anytime soon. Arthur can barely walk.'

'Nimue.'

I turn away from Will towards the path that leads to the Ark. 'I have nothing more to say to you, Will.'

'Just wait a minute.' Will stops me after three long strides. Unless I run off into the marshes, I won't get a chance to shake him off.

'Undo this tragedy. Use your *gift*, or whatever it is – for God's sake, I don't care anymore. Bring them back!' He starts making wild gestures towards the pond. 'Corentin, Anna, and the children! If you want to create something good out of the mess I made, then help them!'

'Will.' I stop dead and look at him in amazement. 'They're *dead*! I can't do anything for them.'

'Can't you or won't you? Is this you taking revenge on me?'

'Oh God.' I shake my head. 'Don't make yourself out to be more important than you are.'

'Nimue! Nim! Please! I'm begging you... if you can, if you want to try...' His words shock me, but what I find worse is the crack in his voice – how lost he sounds. He's crying, his shadowy eyes spilling over with tears. 'Cor's my best friend.'

'My God,' I whisper again. I push my anger away, forget about my disgust for a moment, and take his cold face in my equally cold hands. 'The dead can't be brought back, Will. I'm sorry, I truly am.' I swallow. 'But there is still so much you can do for the living. For all the children who are at risk of being taken. For us, the children who already have been kidnapped... for the people in District 15.' I fall silent as the plan begins to crystallise itself in my mind. It's clear and bright, yet dangerous. 'I know how you can help. Smuggle me into the Asclepius Congregation. You obviously know how to, so do something good with that knowledge: help me get inside.'

'Are you insane?' He stares at me with widened pupils, his breath coming out in puffs and cascading down my face. 'Do you think you can destroy the Snake? On your own?'

'Maybe not, but I do know someone who could...perhaps. My mother, Rona. In order to find her, I have to pick up the trail, and there's only one place I can think of.'

'You really are crazy.'

I let go of his face and take a step backwards. Somehow, I've calmed down. There is a path forward and I know where to tread now. 'Look after Arthur while I'm gone. Make sure his wounds heal well.'

*

Mirna thrusts a piece of paper into my hands. Will stands in front of me with his hands on his hips. They have put me in a corner, out of the hearing range of the others.

'We won't let you go into that snake's nest without a plan,' Mirna says rather sharply. 'So we've decided to ...'

'So *Mirna* has decided,' Will interrupts her, frowning, but as he turns his gaze to me his tone softens. 'Listen, I'll give you one chance to get out. If you feel the need to escape from this uncle of yours, come to the meeting point after ten days. I'll be right there, waiting for you with a vehicle for one hour exactly.

If you're there, I'll drive you out of there like wildfire. If you aren't there, then I'll just assume you don't want to leave, or that you're in trouble.' He is silent for a moment. 'Either way, you're on your own.'

'These are places where I was able to hide when I escaped.' Mirna points to the sheet of paper. She has drawn a rough map. 'I don't know if they're still there. This is Will's meeting point.' She points to a circle that could be a town or village. 'The area on the south side is close to the hills, a few kilometres away from the Institute. There is a road, but not a very good one. Wide enough for one sturdy jeep, that's all.'

I look up. 'Thank you, Mirna.'

'Good,' says Will. 'Count the days from the moment you get there. You'll have ten. I'll expect you an hour before sunrise.'

24

TOGETHER OR NOT AT ALL

'Nimue. Wake up!'

I suddenly jolt up, as if I'm falling back into my body. I put my hand to my temple, where a throbbing headache is developing.

Mirna is bending over me. It takes a moment for me to realise what she's saying to me. 'It's time. Get up.'

I get up. My mouth is dry, my hands trembling. But all remnants of sleep are gone at once. Mirna hands me my anorak and a rucksack containing a few items: her hand-drawn map, the compass I got from Jodoc, an extra jumper, a warm shirt, and Mum's diary, which I take out of the bag and look at pensively. 'If this should fall into the hands of anyone from the Asclepius Congregation, I won't be able to hide who I really am.'

'Shall I give it to Arthur for you?'

I hesitate for a moment, then shake my head. It's too dear to me. Besides, there may be something in it that I'll need. I slip the old leather time into a hidden pocket inside my jumper, close to my heart. There it will be safe, and from the outside it looks like there's nothing in there.

'They won't let you keep those clothes,' warns Mirna. 'If you're really wild they might even frisk you.'

I sigh. I can think of no other place for the diary.

'Nimue, are you sure about this?' I can hear in her voice that she disapproves of the plan. The fear in her eyes is clearly visible. After losing Anna, Corentin and the children, she doesn't want to lose anyone else.

'Don't ask me that question. I'll lose courage like that.' And I can't lose courage. Now that Rona is no longer here, it's up to me to confront Benji, and if it's not really up to me according to the people around me, I beg to differ – I'm going to do this. Perhaps Mirna understands me while she runs her gaze over me, or maybe she sees I'm so pale I might collapse if she pursued the matter further. In any case, she nods and takes me by the arm as she accompanies me outside.

'Think about what I told you,' she says. 'The harder you fight, the harder you'll have it. If you want to stay unnoticed, you must be smart and quiet.'

'Like you were.'

'Yes.'

'I'll be fine,' I say, breathing slowly. 'As long as I get inside.'

'Getting in there isn't the problem,' says Mirna dryly. 'It's the getting-out-unscathed that poses the biggest challenge.'

She takes me across the square to the marsh, but soon deviates from the path. To stop myself from thinking about the task ahead of me, I ask: 'Where are we going?'

'Will has arranged a meeting point as far away from the Ark as possible. It's quite a walk.'

That isn't so bad. The walk gives me renewed energy and the fresh air helps to clear my head. After a while Mirna doesn't need to hold onto me anymore, and I'm able to walk by myself. My hands continue to shake, though – there's little I can do to prevent that.

It is still early and a thick layer of mist clings to the swampy woodland between the meres and bogs. Mirna insists on going first. She's probably afraid of me forgetting where I have to put my feet, and to be honest, I don't pay much attention to the zigzagging path that presents the only safe way through.

Finally the trees begin to clear. The ground is covered by a carpet of ferns. And among the ferns sits Arthur, his injured leg stretched out before him, Will kneeling next to him.

'What are you doing here?' I ask bluntly.

'I'm going with you.' My brother is trying to sound matter-of-fact, but his tense face tells me he is as nervous as I am.

'No. Absolutely not, out of the question.' I round on Will. 'What on Earth possessed you to bring my brother into this?'

'Nimue, calm down.'

Bewildered, I look from him to Arthur before my eyes begin to scour the surrounding area. How much longer will it before we're no longer alone? I have no time for this discussion. 'Arthur, this is madness...what with your leg...'

'You don't get it, Nim. This isn't a negotiation.' He says it with such conviction and seriousness that for a moment, I keep my mouth shut and don't know what to say. Arthur uses my silence to continue: 'Rona's my mother too, and we can't be separated. We belong together.'

'But Benji knows that! If the two of us go, we'll look far more suspicious.'

'I won't let you go into that snake's nest alone!' Now it's Arthur who loses his composure. 'We're a chain, remember? Or have you forgotten your promise? We'll do this together or not at all.'

That's what we have always said. But this is different, I remind myself. If my plan fails, we could end up like Mirna, who had to claw her way out and cut her arms in order to not lose her mind...or like Yuna, who only has one leg. I'm about to open my mouth to tell Arthur all this, when Will suddenly raises his arm and hisses.

'No time to reconsider.' He gets up and takes a few large steps away from us. Mirna shoots off into the bushes like a frightened hare, disappearing from sight. If something goes wrong, I may never see her again, it dawns on me. I suddenly feel weak and dizzy, as if I'm standing on the edge of a ravine.

Will points to Arthur. 'You were left injured. Nimue, you found him. I lured you here under false pretences and you're both shocked and angry.'

'Will ...' *I'm scared.*

'Pretend. Act as if your life depends on it.'

A twig snaps in the bushes behind me. I turn around, petrified, even though I know they're coming. A figure emerges from the low-hanging mist between the trees. He's wearing the colours of the marsh: green and brown. Behind him is someone else, and then another. A veritable little army, it seems.

Despite all my intentions I stumble back as Detection approaches. The world seems to be crumbling before my eyes before rearranging itself again.

Pretend. You have to pretend.

I turn to Will. 'Please,' I beg. My own voice seems to sound as if it's coming from afar. 'Will, please ...'

It's as if a hand is clamped around my throat. The men of Detection surround us in a tight circle. I can't look at them. I don't want to see their ugly faces. Will's face is cold and unreadable. 'Coward,' I snarl, with some genuine glee. This is no effort at all. 'You traitor!'

'I'm sorry, Nimue.'

His gaze bores into mine, darker than night. How could I have missed what he was planning to do with Katell? Why didn't I see it in his eyes? 'You lied!'

'There was no other way.'

'Filthy snake! I hope you never get Finola back! I hope she's already dead!'

Two men pull my arms back as I loudly start to curse. Steel handcuffs click around my wrists to secure them from behind. I make sure that I don't struggle too hard, but as they start to pull me backwards, I feel that adding a little extra drama to the whole show wouldn't be misplaced. I gather all the saliva in my mouth and spit it right into Will's face.

For a moment he seems ready to blow his cover. He takes a deep breath and wipes his face clean with trembling hands. 'Don't bring Finola into this.'

And with that, he turns away from me.

I look at his back as he walks away from me. The man who is holding me pushes my head down to one side. As he does so, I think I hear something snap and feel something fall out of my anorak. There is no time to realise what it is. Moments later I feel a sharp pain in my neck, followed by a feeling of melting ice, spreading through my shoulders first, then seeping into the rest of my body. The light fades, the trees disappear in a blur, and everything turns dark. Just like Will's eyes.